KILLSTRAIGHT RETURNS

A KILLSTRAIGHT STORY

KILLSTRAIGHT RETURNS

JOHNNY D. BOGGS

FIVE STAR
A part of Gale, a Cengage Company

GALE
A Cengage Company

GALE
A Cengage Company

LIBRARY OF CONGRESS CATALOGING-IN-PUBLICATION DATA

Names: Boggs, Johnny D, author.
Title: Killstraight returns / Johnny D. Boggs.
Description: First Edition. | Waterville, Maine : Five Star, a part
  of Gale, a Cengage Company, 2022. | Series: A Killstraight
  story |
Identifiers: LCCN 2022016110 | ISBN 9781432899912 (hardcover)
Subjects: BISAC: FICTION / Westerns | FICTION / Historical /
  General | LCGFT: Western stories. | Novels.
Classification: LCC PS3552.O4375 K553 2022 | DDC 813/.54--
  dc23
LC record available at https://lccn.loc.gov/2022016110

First Edition. First Printing: November 2022
Find us on Facebook—https://www.facebook.com/FiveStarCengage
Visit our website—http://www.gale.cengage.com/fivestar
Contact Five Star Publishing at FiveStar@cengage.com

Printed in Mexico
Print Number : 1   Print Year : 2023

In memory of my mother, Jackie McGee Boggs
(1929–2020)
whose ghost stories and tales of surviving malaria,
tough parents, and the Great Depression in the Deep
South inspired this novel. I apologize for the language,
Mama, but, please, don't blame it on Aunt Fay or Daddy.

CHAPTER ONE

August 1892

"Killstraight returns!"

Daniel Killstraight stood underneath the awning of the agency when he heard that loud voice anyone within four miles would recognize as coming from the mouth of Homer Blomstrom, civilian scout out of Fort Sill. Despite having the door closed and the building's one window cracked just enough to let in hot summer air, the new agent heard Blomstrom, too.

"Damn that sinner to hell." Athol McLeish's face knotted. "He's in his cups again, and it's not yet noon."

Daniel knew better. Homer Blomstrom had neither slurred his words, nor had he punctuated his brief sentence with three to five selections of profanity. He had to be as sober as any temperance leader wandering across the territory.

McLeish had much to learn, but the potbellied Scot was new to the agency, fresh from Rochester, New York. Over the years, Daniel had known many agents, Quakers and Baptists, good and corrupt, teetotalers and drunkards. He had yet to form an opinion on McLeish other than, unlike the previous agent, young, quiet, and naïve Joshua Biggers, this one was brusque, fiery, held a fine opinion of himself, and had firsthand experience about being *in his cups*.

Spurring his big dun, Blomstrom waved something colorful in his gloved left hand and loped the remaining thirty yards.

Scarf? No. Newspaper? Daniel had never seen a newspaper

that green and yellow. He turned his head when the scout pulled hard on the reins and did not look back until the dust had passed. By then, Blomstrom was tying his horse up close on the hitch rail and held the book—perhaps the thinnest one Daniel had ever seen—in a mouth hidden by a thick red beard and mustache.

It looks like a duck bill.

Blomstrom, stationed at Fort Sill for roughly three years now, ripped the thin book with the gaudy cover from his mouth and thrust it at Daniel.

"Killstraight returns!" the scout yelled again.

Maybe he has been drinking.

The door to the agency scraped open, and McLeish stepped outside. "What on earth are you yelling about, Mister Blomstrom? In a voice that might raise my damned grandfather from his grave—which happens to be in Mount Hope."

"Killstraight returns!" The scout's eyes sparkled with delight.

"I haven't left the reservation in a month," Daniel said.

Blomstrom thrust the thin book first toward the agent, then at Daniel. Blomstrom's saliva, teeth marks, and shaking hand made it hard to read. So did the wrinkles and tears in the cheap cover, and the miles the book must have traveled, but Daniel drew in a deep breath when the title finally registered.

KILLSTRAIGHT RETURNS;
Or, Captives of the California Trail

The author's name, in much smaller type and a font not quite as elaborate, was Major Titus Wheeler.

It must be another Killstraight. But when Daniel opened the flimsy book, Blomstrom said, "You don't show up till the third chapter."

Daniel flipped the pages, and, sure enough, found "Daniel Killstraight, Captain of the Indian Police," in black and white, with an illustration on the facing page of a tall, thin, muscular man brandishing saber and revolver—with a curled black mustache above a mischievous grin—shielding an "Indian maiden" while fending off a dozen "fiendish savages"—Pawnees, from the looks of them, charging at hero and heroine with tomahawks and lances.

"It doesn't look good for you, *Captain,*" McLeish said with a snort.

"Oh, he gets out of it just dandy," the scout said.

Daniel tried reading, but quit after three paragraphs, closing the book and turning to the agent.

"You look more white than red." McLeish laughed and fetched a pipe from his jacket pocket.

The painting on the cover and other sketches of that two-gunned hero certainly did not resemble Daniel. Short and pudgy, Daniel wore a mix of white man's clothes and traditional dress of The People: buffalo-hide moccasins and deerskin britches; an Army gun belt and holster holding a .44-caliber Remington from the long-ago War Between the States, though adapted to take modern cartridges; a collarless cotton shirt of blue with black vertical stripes; necklace of trade beads; dark blue jacket, patched with leather and canvas with the brass shield of a tribal policeman pinned over the breast pocket; the well-beaten hat of black felt, dented and dusty with more than a half dozen tears in crown and brim, but given new life with a wide white band of thin leather decorated with shells and small brass buttons.

Daniel opened his mouth, closed it, then tried again, but could not form any words, in English or in the language of Nermernuh. He was no captain, could not grow a mustache if he tried for fifty years, could not recall ever meeting anyone, major or unranked, named Titus Wheeler, and had never been on the California Trail. He didn't even know exactly where it was.

"This . . ." At least he got one word out. His Adam's apple bobbed, and he bit his bottom lip. "I had nothing to do with this." He sighed, relieved that, at least, he had defended himself.

The book was ripped from Daniel's hand, and Blomstrom, his face bright with delight, jabbed a finger at the title. "You be the only Dan'l Killstraight I know. Hell, you're the only Killstraight I know. And come to think on it, I ain't never met no more than six or seven Dan'ls. And see that." His finger ran underneath the words as he read, "Kill-straight *Re*-turns." He flipped the cover open and jabbed at a line in smaller type at the bottom of the page. "That means you been somewhere before. Like it says right here, 'By the author of *Killstraight, the Magnificent Comanche.*' "

"Magnificent?" McLeish almost spit out his pipe. "Christ a'mighty." The new agent, Daniel had learned, was like that clock he kept hearing about that was wound too tight. That might have been the reason he was often throwing tiny white pills down his throat.

"But he is Comanch." The scout turned to the last page of the book. "And more's a'comin'. Right here."

Blomstrom cleared his throat, spit, and read each word carefully. " 'Look for the next roarin' adventure of the darin' half-breed avenger, Capt'n Dan'l Killstraight, in *Prince of the Prairie; or, the Demon of the Dakota Prairie,* by Colonel Titus Wheeler.' " He snorted. "Reckon the major got hisself promoted."

McLeish tapped his pipe bowl against a cedar post. "Half-breed. That explains the mustache."

Blomstrom laughed aloud, but a chill numbed Daniel, and the breakfast soured in his belly. *Half-breed.* They didn't know the truth of the word, but his mother had been Mescalero, captured by a raiding party that included Daniel's father.

"Is delivery of this penny dreadful the only reason you are here, Mister Blomstrom?" McLeish pointed at the novel with the stem of his pipe.

The scout squeezed the novel in his big right hand and said, "Well, I figured Capt'n Killstraight might wanna read it." But he did not hand the book to Daniel.

"Well, I have work to do," the agent announced. He stuck the pipe back into his pocket and opened the door, then looked back at Daniel. "I suppose you are here for your month's pay."

"Yes, sir," Daniel said softly, looking at his moccasins. "Mister McLeish."

"Come in, then, and get your Judas money." He pushed the door open and entered the building, muttering, "I don't know why we even need Indian policemen anymore. A waste of United States funds if you ask me."

Daniel removed his hat, wiped his moccasins, and followed the potbellied man inside. McLeish opened a drawer, pulled out a tin box, unlocked it, and counted out eight silver coins, which he slid across the desk, and waited.

Eight dollars. Daniel started dropping the coins into his rawhide pouch.

"Hell," McLeish said. "I almost forgot. I had to give you a new badge three weeks ago. To replace the one you lost."

Daniel raised his eyes, waiting. He did not lose that piece of cheap metal. Grass Eater, drunk on whiskey, ripped it off Daniel's shirt and threw it into a creek. Grass Eater almost ripped off Daniel's left ear, too, before Daniel clubbed him with the butt of the Remington.

"Badges are expensive, you know," McLeish said.

Daniel stared into his pouch. He found the dollar that looked as though someone had chewed on it. He had seen coins with scratches and nicks, but not teeth marks, though he had heard of men biting coins to make sure they were real. Was a damaged

11

coin worth less? He wasn't exactly sure, but he handed that coin back to McLeish, who took it without hesitation and dropped it into his tin box. "I ought to charge you more," the agent said as he returned the box to the big drawer.

When Daniel stepped outside, Blomstrom was carving a chaw from a brick of tobacco. He used the knife to bring the tobacco to his mouth, then folded the blade into the walnut handle. When the knife disappeared, he held out the paperback.

"You want to read it, Dan'l?" Blomstrom's teeth worked on softening the rock-hard tobacco.

Daniel didn't want to, but he could not taper his curiosity, and his blouse pocket jingled with silver dollars. He sighed, and finally answered, "I suppose."

The scout grinned. "I reckon Oajuicauojué would enjoy hearin' 'bout your adventures."

Homer Blomstrom was anything but stupid. Daniel had been thinking the same thing.

The scout wet his lips. "It ain't no dime novel, though." He waved the book until Daniel took it from him. "See." His head tilted. "Cost a whole twenty-five cents at the post sutler's." He voice went up an octave. "You don't get no money from this here writin'?"

"I haven't yet." Daniel found his pouch again and withdrew one of the coins, which Blomstrom snatched and struggled to finger into one of his pockets. But he sobered quickly and said, "I ain't got no change. I'm good for it, you know."

"I know." Daniel knew he would never see that seventy-five cents in this lifetime.

"You're a good injun, Dan'l. One of the best. Let me know how that story turns out."

He started walking to his horse when Daniel asked, "You didn't finish reading it?"

Blomstrom grabbed the reins to his horse and swung into the

saddle with a grunt. "Well, not exactly," he said as his right foot struggled to find the stirrup. "I read bits and pieces, but mostly just looked at the drawings and such. Thing is, that Wheeler, he just ain't much of a writer."

The horse turned around, Blomstrom applied the spurs, and Daniel, now two dollars poorer, walked to his horse.

Sitting by the firepit closest to what had become Daniel's lodge, they took turns reading chapters.

Oajuicauojué giggled; Daniel grunted.

Daniel had learned the words at Carlisle, seven long years that he often tried to forget. It had been at Carlisle where "Daniel Killstraight" had been born. Before that Daniel had been known among The People as Horn, till his father had given his name, He Whose Arrows Fly Straight Into The Hearts Of His Enemies, to his only son, and taken the name Marsh Hawk for himself. Shortly after Daniel's arrival in Pennsylvania, the *taibos* running the Industrial School had made the teenage boy pick out one patch of strange white scratches on a blackboard, and told him that from now on, his name was Daniel. Reluctantly, they shortened his last name to Killstraight—and most of the teachers at Carlisle despised that name, calling it savage, anything but Christian. But another had countered, "Let us give him this one victory so that, God willing, he shall not kill us all in our sleep or drive us insane." It was the woman teacher, Miss Brunot, who finally ended the debate.

"Let him be named Killstraight. He'll be dead soon enough, anyway."

Oajuicauojué had returned from the Indian school in the Kansas town called Chilocco. The People called the school "Prairie Light." Oajuicauojué had a new Pale Eyes name, too, but she vowed never to share it with Daniel. Only her family and the Pale Eyes at the agency knew it, and they had not told Daniel. Ben Buffalo Bone, Oajuicauojué's oldest brother, had not spoken much to Daniel in a number of years, though Daniel still lived across from Ben and his family.

The cabin had been built for Ben Buffalo Bone's father, a few years before he traveled to The Land Beyond The Sun. Oajuicauojué's oldest sister had traveled that road, too, years ago. Which was why Daniel's relationship with everyone in the family, except Oajuicauojué, had cooled. Ben Buffalo Bone blamed Daniel for his sister's death. Daniel blamed himself more.

Yet the more he sat and talked, the more at ease he felt. On this evening, Daniel did not even feel embarrassed when she giggled at some of the predicaments the writer Titus Wheeler put this particular Daniel Killstraight in, or what he had this particular Daniel Killstraight saying—out loud, to Pale Eyes and The People.

" 'The End,' " Oajuicauojué read. " 'Look for the next roaring adventure of the daring half-breed avenger, Captain Daniel Killstraight, in *Prince of the Prairie; or, the Demon of the Dakota Prairie*,' by Colonel Titus Wheeler. Available through subscription . . .' "

When she stopped reading, Daniel looked up, surprised to find her black eyes locked on him.

"You were shaking your head," she told him. "Did I read something wrong?"

He smiled. "No. It is the story that is wrong. It is Titus Wheeler who is wrong."

She tilted her head, studying him for a long while. Finally, she closed the book and handed it to him, but her lips had flattened and her eyes no longer danced with laughter.

"They taught you to read well at Prairie Light," he told her. He took the book and sat it near the hot coals.

14

She shrugged. "I learn fast. That is what they told me. But you read better than I do. That is why Quanah calls on you so often. They taught you well at Carlisle."

Daniel made himself smile. "They had to beat it into me."

Her next movement surprised him. She raised her right hand and reached toward him, three fingers landing on his cheek, and tracing the contours, the scars, the pockmarks, the crevasses, then grazed his lips, came down his neck, and settled on his shoulder.

"I am sorry for the pain they brought you."

His right hand landed on hers. "I brought much of it on myself," he said.

Their eyes met, held. Once he would have seen Rain Shower's sister. Now he saw Oajuicauojué. How could he ask her brother for the right to marry her? He had no horses to offer. He had six silver dollars—two less than his usual monthly salary.

A flap opened to the main lodge. Oajuicauojué's hand jerked away, and Daniel stood quickly, watching Ben Buffalo Bone storm toward his favorite pony, which he had left grazing near the circle of lodges. He did not even glance at Daniel, but shouted his sister's name.

"Tend to your mother. I have work to do."

Ben Buffalo Bone mounted the horse, and they thundered toward the Wichita Mountains. Daniel watched until the dust from the fine pony settled. Oajuicauojué's head had fallen, and she stared at the remnants of the fire.

"I must go," she said meekly.

Daniel let out a long breath.

"He rides to meet with Coals In A Fire," he said, not asking, but knowing. When Oajuicauojué did not look up at him or even open her mouth, Daniel sat back down. "It would be better," he said softly, "if The People did not fight among themselves."

15

She said nothing, but Daniel did not expect her to speak.

Coals In A Fire stood on one side for The People. Quanah led the other side. Neither would win. No Nermernuh could defeat Pale Eyes government, which now worked to bring an end to the reservation. That was another reason Ben Buffalo Bone rarely spoke to Daniel, even though thirty yards separated their homes. But Daniel and Quanah were Kwahadi. Ben Buffalo Bone and Coals In A Fire were Kotsoteka. Daniel let out a mirthless laugh. Taibos and The People were not so different after all. Instead of banding together to fight for a common good, they bickered like brothers and sisters.

"I will see you in the morning." Oajuicauojué rose, lifted her skirt, and ran to her mother's lodge. Daniel watched her until the flap closed. At least she had given him hope for tomorrow.

He reached down, picked up the copy of *Killstraight Returns,* and stared at the cover.

Would it not be a better world if life could work out as storybooks ended? Where right and wrong are easily distinguished. Where men could talk to each other with reason. Where good defeated the bad and the hero had a girl clinging to his arm and looking up at him with love in her eyes.

Daniel tossed the book onto the coals that glowed the brightest. He had lived too long in the taibo world. He had seen too much . . . *internecine* . . . strife. Ha! Evil Miss Brunot would drop dead if she learned that Daniel Killstraight had used such a big word without hesitation, and used the word correctly.

He frowned. Vocabulary did not interest him. There was no reason to laugh.

He watched the book burn.

CHAPTER TWO

Daniel awakened to the sound of Ben Buffalo Bone's new colt urinating in the neighboring stall.

As the hard stream continued without pause, cutting a gorge into the earthen floor, Daniel remained atop his bedroll, hands under his braids, staring at the ceiling and thinking as a taibo might. *I have a roof over my head.* He considered what the elderly father at the closest mission constantly told The People; that a good Christian should not complain about hardships, but thank the Savior for the blessings one had.

Ben Buffalo Bone's colt could have filled a whiskey keg. Daniel did not know what Oajuicauojué's oldest brother had been letting the piebald drink, but the smell stunk unlike anything that flowed down Cache Creek.

I have a roof over my head.

He sat up.

The roof belonged to a log cabin, which had been built for Ben Buffalo Bone's father many summers before, a present for one of the leading Kotsoteka peace chiefs. Ben Buffalo Bone's father might have seen the futility in The People continuing a war against the buffalo-slaughtering, ceaseless parade of *Tejanos* and Long Knives, but he never completely took the road taibos wanted him to travel. Until the morning the coughing sickness took him to The Land Beyond The Sun, he had never lived in the cabin. His lodge remained the teepee of buffalo hide, where Ben Buffalo Bone's now stood, and the old man had made the

17

cabin a stable for his horses. When Daniel had arrived on the reservation after years at Carlisle and those dark cities in the East, Ben Buffalo Bone had offered a stall in the cabin for Daniel.

It provided more protection than a blackjack tree. Even with the morning light shining through the cracks between the logs, which had not been chinked in years. Winters could be cold, but Daniel had a fine buffalo hide for warmth, and he had grown used to the scent of horses, even their dung and urine. Besides, The People loved horses.

The piebald's bladder finally emptied, and the horse snorted, twisted toward the window, and laid its ears back on its head. Daniel stopped counting his blessings and found the Remington revolver in the holster hung over a peg first. He pulled on the battered black hat, then cocked the revolver. The wooden door had been pulled off years ago and used for firewood, so Daniel stood against the wall and watched the trail.

Recognizing the blood bay gelding and its rider, Daniel lowered the hammer to half cock, and rotated the cylinder until the empty chamber would rest under the hammer—after he adjusted the cylinder with his fingers. The revolver was that old. For years, the approaching rider had been telling Daniel that he should buy a new one, or at least take that relic to Fort Sill and find someone there who could make it cleaner and, possibly, safer.

"A Pale Eye at the soldier-fort," Daniel kept countering, "might fix it so that it blows my hand off."

"But it might blow off the Pale Eye's whole arm while he was fixing it," Twice Bent Nose would argue with a smile.

Daniel glanced at the circle of lodges that housed Ben Buffalo Bone's family. Ben Buffalo Bone emerged, and stared at the rider. He turned his head and spoke to someone, likely his mother, wife, or Oajuicauojué, and disappeared, pulling the flap

18

closed behind him.

Before stepping into the morning sun, Daniel waited until Twice Bent Nose tugged on the hackamore and let the gelding stop.

"*Haa maruawe.*" Daniel raised his right hand and smiled.

Twice Bent Nose's black eyes did not look friendly at all, and his voice, brusque and guttural, matched the rest of his hard face when he returned the greeting.

But, Daniel understood, to be here this early in the morning, Twice Bent Nose had to have left his camp long before the eastern skies had started to welcome dawn.

"Quanah wants to see you," Twice Bent Nose said.

There was no point in asking what Quanah wanted. If Twice Bent Nose thought it important, he would have explained. Most likely, he did not even know. Quanah wanted to see Daniel. That was all that mattered.

"I will get my horse." Daniel pointed at the firepit. His battered enamel coffeepot sat on a stone at the rim's edge. "There is coffee from last night," he said. "It is cold, though."

Turning toward the pit, Twice Bent Nose asked, "Was the coffee cooked by you?"

"Yes," Daniel said.

The tribal policeman grunted, and swung out of the saddle. "Maybe I will wait to drink Quanah's coffee."

Daniel disappeared inside the cabin.

When Daniel led the dun colt out of the cabin, Twice Bent Nose was emptying his bladder on a patch of switchgrass. *Today is a day of piss. Perhaps this is an omen.* After the graying warrior shook himself off and turned while buttoning his blue trousers, Daniel said, "You piss as much as Ben Buffalo Bone's new colt."

The grunt of a reply could have meant anything.

Twice Bent Nose led his horse to the firepit, and he bent and raised Daniel's coffeepot, drinking most of the cold brew. Turning, he shrugged, saying, "Maybe I changed my mind," and extended the pot toward Daniel, who adjusted the saddle and shook his head.

"Long ride," Twice Bent Nose said.

Daniel conceded, and finished the coffee.

They leaped into their saddles, kicked their mounts into a trot, and rode out of the camp. Daniel looked behind him, but no one emerged from any of the lodges before the post oaks and that giant bigtooth maple shrouded Daniel's home and Twice Bent Nose urged his horse into a lope.

The house built for Quanah had not been turned into a horse barn.

They called this the Star House, named for the four white, five-point stars painted on the red shingles. Ten rooms and two stories, surrounded by a picket fence painted white, the house had cost two thousand dollars when it had been built years earlier. Daniel had tried to figure out, at eight dollars a month, how long it would have taken him to buy a home like this. Eventually, he had given up and had to ask the agent at that time, Joshua Biggers, for the answer. And that had taken the young minister a sizable number of minutes scratching his pencil on some paper before he had announced, "Almost twenty years—I think."

It had cost Quanah nothing.

The government had not paid for it. Cattlemen had. Texas cattlemen who wanted to graze their cattle on the land of The People. Texas cattlemen who wanted to keep Quanah happy.

Two of Quanah's wives, one young, the other older than Quanah, sat in rocking chairs on the long porch at the corner shaded by a large oak tree when Twice Bent Nose and Daniel arrived. Slowing their horses to a walk, they approached the large wooden mansion. Daniel could not help but smile at the sight of the women. Whenever he saw one of Quanah's wives, he remembered the story The People often repeated: Some government official had informed Quanah that he could have only one wife; the other five, six, seven, eight—it depended on who told the story on what particular night—would have to go. Quanah had nodded, looked solemnly, and said: "You tell my wives which ones must go." That taibo left in a hurry without even glancing at any of Quanah's wives. No agent, no bluecoat officer, no politician, and not even a Jesus Man had ever brought up the matter again.

Another wife sat on the second-story porch, sewing shells onto what appeared to be a blue dress. One of Quanah's sons stepped through an open window, and hopped off the porch, greeting the riders before taking the reins to both animals. As the boy led the horses around the side of the house to a corral, another of Quanah's wives came to the edge of the porch, folded her arms across her chest, and glared.

Before stepping up onto the wooden porch, Twice Bent Nose and Daniel wiped their moccasins on the mat on the ground. The old wife nodded, and turned, barking orders at the two younger wives, who dutifully stood and hurried through the nearest open window. The old crone gave the visitors a final glare before walking through the door.

Daniel and Twice Bent Nose moved toward the shade and Quanah, who had risen from his chair and smiled. Twice Bent Nose kept staring at the ceiling, listening to the wood creaking as the wife upstairs walked toward a window, or maybe the door. Daniel shot his companion a glance and whispered, "She will not fall on your head."

"How do you know?" Twice Bent Nose whispered back, and kept his eyes on the wooden planks above him until the creaking ceased and they stood beside Quanah, who greeted his guests with a pipe in his hands.

Unlike Daniel and Twice Bent Nose, Quanah was tall, thin, his eyes and face not as hard, but his hair just as black, parted in the center, and hanging in braids over his shoulders. His face was round, nose straight, lips full, with a gray scarf decorated with black diamonds, knotted at the center of his throat and hanging down the front of his beaded deerskin shirt as long as his braids and the beaded necklaces.

He held the pipe toward Twice Bent Nose, who was older than Daniel, and said, "It is good to see my friends again. We shall smoke."

Twice Bent Nose had fallen asleep.

Daniel strained to understand the last paragraphs in the final document Quanah had asked him to translate. He did the best he could, and slid the papers toward the tall Kwahadi and rubbed his eyes. Quanah reached over and filled Daniel's china cup with coffee his youngest wife, Co-by, had made. "She is not much to look at," Quanah had told his guests after she had left, "but she makes Pale Eye coffee better than any Pale Eye."

The joke ended. Quanah became serious again. "What does it all mean?"

Sighing, Daniel shook his head. For years, it seemed, he had been doing this, trying to comprehend all the movements, the parts and pieces, the strategies behind Washington City's latest plan to end the reservations, have The People take care of themselves. First had been this thing called the Dawes Act. Then came the Jerome Agreement, which Washington City kept trying to ratify but whose terms no one, taibo or Nermernuh, seemed to be able to agree to.

"One of your Tejano cattleman friends can tell you what this means better than I can," Daniel said. "They have friends who are great attorneys." Daniel had much experience dealing with taibo lawyers when he had to testify in court in Arkansas or Texas. Usually testifying against one of his Nermernuh brothers.

"They are not Nermernuh," Quanah told him.

"I am only half Nermernuh," Daniel said softly.

The tall man leaned forward, his eyes stern, and spoke in the taibo language he rarely used. "You forget, Brother, that my mother was white." He pushed himself back in his chair. "Do not speak of that again. You are of The People. You will always be one of The People. You will always fight for The People. That is what we do now."

"Tejanos know more than I do," Daniel said.

"Tejanos want The People to keep all of the land." Quanah shook his head. "And you know why as well as I do. They want to keep paying The People to graze their cattle on our land. When there is no more reservation, there is no more Big Pasture. They would have to find new grass. Or talk to countless Nermernuh for . . ." He snorted. "What is it now? Three hundred and twenty acres?"

"One hundred and sixty," Daniel told him.

Quanah's eyes blackened. "We asked for four hundred and eighty."

Daniel's head shook.

The hand flashed so fast, Daniel did not know what had happened until he heard the china cup smash against the wooden column in the corner. The old wife stuck her head out of the window, frowned, and disappeared.

Quanah turned and looked across the yard. For the longest while, he did not speak. At length, without turning back to Daniel, he said, "For years this *Great White Father* . . ." He snorted, and spit off the porch. ". . . and all his brothers have made promises to The People. To me. And each promise has vanished like one drop of rain on the hottest day of the summer. But one promise they will keep." He breathed in and out quietly, and a lone tear rolled down his cheek before vanishing like that drop of rain he had just mentioned. "Our land." He nodded. "Yes. They will take our land. Just as they have promised to do since the first Pale Eye rode into the land of The People."

The wind did not blow. Twice Bent Nose did not snore. Even the shattering of the china cup had not awakened him. Daniel lost track of time, until Quanah sighed and turned back toward him.

"Why have you not taken a wife?" Quanah asked suddenly.

Twice Bent Nose coughed and sat up, yawning, and looking right and left before realizing where he was. Quanah, though, kept his eyes locked on Daniel, whose lips moved but offered no answer.

"Oajuicauojué," Quanah said. "She has not married."

"No." Daniel got that much out.

"A Kotsoteka and a Kwahadi." He nodded. "It is a good match."

Daniel looked at Twice Bent Nose for help, found nothing there but a mischievous grin, and turned back to Quanah.

"I have nothing to offer . . ." He could not say Ben Buffalo Bone's name.

"I have more horses than I need," Quanah said, waving his right hand one way, then another. "I have more wives than I need. Which one would you like?"

Daniel thought he might be sweating. He swallowed, studied his coffee cup, flexed his fingers, heard Twice Bent Nose grunt, and looked back at Quanah. "I could not."

The Kwahadi leader smiled. "Good." He spoke English. "I make small joke. You make right answer."

But the levity ended, and Quanah pointed at the papers, and used The People's tongue. "What else must I know?"

Daniel pointed at the papers. "The Pale Eyes bicker as much as The People fight amongst ourselves. That works in our favor. Delays everything, at least. There has been no movement toward an agreement or . . ."

"Ratification." Quanah used the taibo word. "That is good."

"It will be ratified." Daniel spoke softly. "This much I know."

Quanah nodded. "So do I. But we must fight to get the best deal we can. We must know when to make the Pale Eyes happy. Because if we stall and fight this . . . *ratification* . . . for too long, the Pale Eyes will open up the country for one of those runs, the way they have done with the Cherokees. Pale Eyes, more than the Tejano cattle that graze now in the Big Pasture, will ride their ponies to death to stake out their own allotment. There will be more Pale Eyes than we can count. And The People will have nothing."

He stared at the timbers, the open prairie, and the pale blue sky for perhaps five minutes before he spoke again.

"To win this fight, The People must fight together. We will not win. We cannot win. We never could win, at least, not after the Pale Eyes brought The Rotting Face to us, to kill our ancestors."

Daniel was aware of the pockmarks on his own face, on his back, partway down both arms. "The Rotting Face still kills our people, young and old," he said.

"Yes," Quanah agreed. "But we are not fighting The Rotting Face now. We fight Pale Eyes, just without arrows and lances. We should not fight among ourselves. We must get what we can before the Pale Eyes steal everything from us."

Both men turned at the sound of rattling traces, and Daniel saw a buggy coming out of the road that led through the forest, and turned down the lane.

"You have visitors," Daniel said. "Twice Bent Nose and I will leave."

"No." Quanah kept his eye on the approaching riders. "There is another reason I have brought you here. Two days ago, a taibo came to talk to me. He wants to meet with you. His name is Titus Wheeler."

CHAPTER THREE

Daniel recognized the driver, a gray-haired former Buffalo Soldier. Since the old corporal had retired a few years back, he had been working for the stagecoach line that operated out of El Reno, running passengers on the Rock Island railroad south to the Wichita Agency or all the way to Fort Sill and back. Daniel remembered the man's name, Virgil Pry—Black Yellow Stripes, as The People knew him. But this was no stagecoach or mud wagon. Black Yellow Stripes drove a fancy surrey, wide-tracked with a canopy top and leather seats.

The thick-bearded trooper sat in the front, halting the team of matched sorrel Percherons in front of the Star House's long porch.

Black Yellow Stripes had shed his blue uniform for a fancy corduroy suit of dark gray, with a black ascot, black gloves, and a black, flat-brimmed hat of buckskin felt. As proof that this afternoon was much too hot to be wearing corduroy, sweat glistened on Black Yellow Stripes's forehead as he climbed out of the rig and helped the big man from the rear leather seat.

If the suit Black Yellow Stripes wore seemed ridiculous, the former Buffalo Soldier's passenger proved to be a man of even greater excess.

Excess height, weight, and, especially, excess clothes: gray trousers with black stripes stuck inside boots of gleaming black leather that reached all the way to the big man's knees; and the boots were adorned with silver-plated spurs with big copper rowels and jangling jinglebobs. He wore a black flannel shirt with a triangular bib embroidered with red, white, and baby blue stars; a large scarf of yellow silk; a high crown hat, creased in the top with pinches in the sides, with bound edges on the wide curled brim. The hat was also black, except for the dust after a long ride.

An outfit like that would have caused most men to have sweated out ten pounds, Daniel thought, but the man—who had to stand at least four inches over six feet, and must have weighed two hundred and forty pounds, had one more bit of costume.

He wore a long-fringed jacket of black leather, stitched in front and back and on the cuffs with beads of every color. Counting the fringe, the sides and tails of the leather coat reached the middle of his ample thighs. With those beads, Daniel figured, the coat might weigh close to ten pounds.

But the taibo carried himself as though he donned only summer undergarments. His green eyes beamed with a brightness Daniel had never seen in a taibo, and though he towered over Daniel, and the clothes seemed almost painted on him, no evidence of fat could be found. His legs were bowed as though he had been riding horses as long as The People, the sun had darkened his face to a rich bronze, the golden hair that hung in curly locks to the collar, also embroidered, of his leather coat matched the curled mustache and well-groomed goatee.

He was a man of confidence, until he removed his hat and bowed at two of Quanah's wives who had stepped to the edge of the porch to marvel at this strange taibo.

"Ladies, it does my eyes and heart . . ."

Those were the last words Daniel could understand, for what followed sounded not like words from a refined taibo, but one of the Long Knives at Fort Sill after being kicked, thrown, or dragged by a horse. Or Homer Blomstrom after several drinks of whiskey.

Quanah's wives giggled, Twice Bent Nose snorted, Quanah smiled, and over at the fancy surrey, Black Yellow Stripes frowned and shook his head.

Daniel did not laugh as the overdressed leviathan dropped to a knee and collected the wig that had fallen to the grass when he removed his hat and bowed.

His real hair, what was left of it just over the ears and in the back, did not match the golden wig. More salt, Daniel decided, than pepper.

The man made two attempts to return the yellow hair to his head, then gave up, turned, and tossed the wig to his driver. Black Yellow Stripes, by then, stood at attention, eyes facing ahead but seeing nothing, except the yellow hair that flew toward him.

"Keep that, Mister Pry," the man said, "till we get back to Fort Sill." He started to put his hat back on, stopped, and whipped it toward the old Buffalo Soldier, too. "And dust this off. Now get—"

He stopped to look at Quanah, who still sat in his chair. "Chief," the big man said, "is it all right if this boy here waters our hosses? Like you let us do on our last visit?"

Quanah's head bobbed once. "Yes." He spoke in English, and looked at Black Yellow Stripes. "You remember?"

"Yeah," Black Three Stripes said.

"One of my wives will bring food." Quanah picked up Daniel's coffee cup and raised it slightly. "And coffee."

"I appreciate your hospitality, Chief Parker."

Quanah nodded again, and looked at the big man, who stepped onto the porch, and made a beeline toward Daniel.

"Is this my boy, Chief?" the man bellowed, and now Daniel understood why the man was so easygoing after a long ride. The smell of whiskey almost slapped Daniel aside, and the man's green eyes showed not the brightness, but dullness, of a man who could not exist without whiskey. Daniel had seen that in the eyes, and smelled that on the breaths of far too many Kwahadis, Kotsotekas, and other bands of The People.

The man stared down at Daniel, who looked up at the tall *taibo*, and knew if he kept looking up, his neck would ache for days.

"Is this here my boy, Chief? Is this here the legendary Capt'n Killstraight?"

"It is what Pale Eyes call him," Quanah said, and then, for Daniel's sake, spoke in the language of The People. "But among Nermernuh, he is known as He Whose Arrows Fly Straight Into The Hearts Of His Enemies."

"What's that?" The giant's head turned to find Quanah, still in his chair, still holding Daniel's coffee cup. "Oh. That's how you say Killstraight in Comanch'. Mighty fine, mighty fine." His giant gloved hand grabbed Daniel's left shoulder—the man had the grip of a hawk's talons—and he herded Daniel down the porch toward Quanah. "I'm makin' you famous, Dan'l. I'm . . ."

For the first time, the big man spotted Twice Bent Nose. "And who might this savage-looking *hombre* be?" He paused, shot Quanah an apologetic look, saying, "That savage . . . that don't mean nothin', Chief. You know that."

Quanah answered, without acknowledging what the *taibo* must have considered an apology. "He is Twice Bent Nose," but Quanah gave the old Metal Shirt the same courtesy he had shown Daniel. He spoke the name in Nermernuh, not English.

The remnants of the cup Quanah had shattered crunched underneath the fancy boots as the man walked toward the others, stopped, turned, and beckoned Daniel. "C'mon, Dan'l, and let's have us a parley." When Quanah nodded, Daniel walked.

"I will make sure Black Yellow Stripes does not steal your horses." Rising, Twice Bent Nose slid his chair toward Daniel, for the big man had taken the one Daniel had been using. Twice Bent Nose stepped off the end of the porch and walked behind the house.

"Dan'l," the big man said. "You don't know who I am, do you?"

"You are Colonel Titus Wheeler," Daniel said. "Unless you have been promoted to General."

Wheeler's head tilted back and he let out a laugh that Daniel might have found infectious if he were not so disturbed by the man's writings, and the fact that Quanah had said Titus Wheeler wanted to see him.

When Wheeler stopped laughing, he reached inside a pocket of his jacket, and withdrew a plug, bit off a mouthful, and shoved the remnants into the pocket while his teeth worked at softening the tobacco. "You're a wise one, sonny," the taibo said. "I come all the way from El Reno to meet you, sonny."

"No," Daniel said. "You came from Fort Sill."

The man's jaw stopped moving. He glanced at Quanah, then smoothed his mustache and studied Daniel for several seconds. "How you figure that?" he asked.

Daniel pointed. "You rode in from the east. That's the Fort Sill trail." Daniel nodded toward the Wichita Mountains. "Had Black Yellow Stripes driven you from El Reno, he would have brought you in from the north. And the horses pulling your buggy, they have not come as far as El Reno." His head nodded firmly. He knew he was right. "You came from Fort Sill. You also told Black Yellow Stripes that you needed to 'get back to Fort Sill.' *Back to.* Meaning, you came from there."

Colonel Titus Wheeler let out a belly laugh, slapped his thigh, and shook his head.

"By thunder, Dan'l, you are a detective," he said.

31

Daniel's head shook. "No," he said. "I just see things. Hear things."

"Which is what a good detective does," Wheeler said. "We arrived at Fort Sill three days ago, so, yeah, you are right. But we came from El Reno. On account that's as far as the iron horse can take us into this country. For the time being, of course. And I come even farther. My home's in Kansas. Medicine Lodge. You might recollect that town."

Daniel did, though he had been just a small boy when some leaders of The People, and others from more tribes on the Southern Plains, had signed the treaty with the taibos.

This taibo reached inside the heavy buckskin jacket, and pulled out two of those dime novels that cost more than ten cents. Daniel recognized the lurid cover of *Killstraight Returns; Or, Captives of the California Trail,* but now he saw *Killstraight, the Magnificent Comanche: Or, Perils in the Indian Territory,* which made the cover of the book Daniel had burned the night before seem tame and, perhaps, even dull.

"These are about you," Wheeler said. "This one's called—"

"I can read," Daniel snapped.

"Yeah." Those green eyes twinkled. It came out as a test, a challenge.

Daniel opened the sequel, found the teaser to the next installment, and read: " 'Look for the next roaring adventure of the daring half-breed avenger, Captain Daniel Killstraight, in *Prince of the Prairie; or, the Demon of the Dakota Prairie,* by Colonel Titus Wheeler.' " He closed the book and slid both dreadfuls back to their creator.

"You seem to be offended, Dan'l," Wheeler said.

"I am no captain," Daniel said. "I have never been on the California Trail, never seen the Dakota prairie, and I am far from magnificent."

"Poetic license." The colonel returned the books to his pocket.

"I would not call your writing poetry."

Colonel Titus Wheeler straightened, turned, and spit tobacco juice off the porch. He wiped his lips with one end of the silk bandana, glanced at Quanah, then looked Daniel in the eye. "If I'd actually written those booklets, I might have taken some offense."

That caused Daniel to lean back in what had been Twice Bent Nose's chair. "You do not write these?"

Wheeler's head shook.

"Then why do they have your name on the covers?"

He laughed, then shifted the tobacco to his other cheek. "Because the name Titus Wheeler is recognized. Maybe not like that of Buffalo Bill Cody, but Colonel—we've been pards for some years, now—he and his Wild West are across the Big Pond now, and I got my own amusement planned."

Recrossing his legs, Wheeler worked on the tobacco, and hooked a thumb toward Quanah. "The chief and me have been havin' us a parley. I got big plans. Mighty big plans. Well, if you want the honest truth, or as honest as Titus Wheeler can make it, it was my grand scheme to have Quanah with me. Hell, if Bill Cody can put a mad-dog killer like Sittin' Bull, the very devil who took Custer's scalp, in his shindig, I wanted Quanah. But your chief—and the damned penny counters on this reservation—all said he was much too busy with all these here negotiations goin' on. But me and my press man, well, we come up with a plan. Since I've been writin'—well, since my press man has been doing the actual writin'—these here literary masterpieces about the Comanche copper Dan'l Killstraight, let him bring in kids and women and men by the hundreds into the tents I'll be settin' up across much of the great state of Texas. Summer through fall. Maybe even winter since it don't often get too damned cold in that infernal state."

He spit again, and the eyes seemed to change color. Leaning

forward, he said, "It is my heart's desire to pay you, He Whose Arrows Find The Hearts Of His Enemies, to play a large role in my show."

Those words came out in the unblemished tongue of The People.

"Shit," Daniel said in English.

CHAPTER FOUR

He was a drunkard, and a blowhard, but Colonel Titus Wheeler, Daniel quickly understood, was not an idiot.

Born in Newton, Illinois, where his father worked at a gristmill, Xavier Titus Wheeler III was fifty-six years old. Xavier Titus Wheeler III met his bride-to-be while she cooked up breakfast, dinner, and supper at the American House. He walked to Cairo, Illinois, in the summer of 1861 and joined the Eighth Illinois Infantry during the Pale Eyes war. "Seen the elephant at Fort Henry and Fort Donelson, and Shiloh and Corinth, and marched my feet raw around Vicksburg and Mobile. After that, Dan'l, I swore I'd never march ag'in."

Mustered out in Baton Rouge in May of '66, Wheeler took one steamer up the Mississippi River back to Cairo, another on the Ohio to Evansville, worked for his passage on a Wabash paddle wheeler to New Harmony, Indiana, then freighted for an outfit carrying goods to Effingham, but drew his time in Newton, and reunited with his ma and pa.

"But the war made me restless," Wheeler said, "and Newton was dull as Hades, though I reckon Hades ain't really so borin' if you're stuck there all the time. There were some settlers passing through from Kaintuck, bound for Kansas, so I joined up with 'em."

He paused, grinned, winked, and shook his head. "Right pretty redhead. With dimples. Lordy, how I can just dive right into a pretty gal's dimple."

He made it as far as Independence, Missouri, where he partook of too much John Barleycorn and woke up as a recently signed trooper in the Seventh Cavalry—"Gen'ral Custer's outfit, by grab!"—and rode west to help the bluecoats build a new Fort Hays, the original being washed away in a flood. "You'd think that a little thing called Big Crick couldn't flood enough to drown an ant, but, by thunder, those Kansas cricks don't fool around when there comes a good frog strangler."

According to the colonel, all he did for the next three years was ride after Indians, or try to follow Indian trails, or sweat in the summer, freeze in the winter, get blinded by dust, infected with lice, and sick from the foul stuff the Army called grub. Besides, tall as he was, and heavy as he was, he wasn't much good as a horse soldier.

"So they usually delegated me to ride with one of the scouts," Wheeler explained. "And that's how I learnt to be a scout. Rabid Wolf Jones taught me how to follow a trail. You'll meet him when you join us. He rides in our show. When he's sober enough not to fall out of the saddle."

His storytelling, Daniel observed, seemed much more authentic, realistic than the tripe he put in his novels. Or the tripe the colonel's press man put in those dreadfuls.

Once Wheeler's enlistment ended, he declined to re-up, but found work as a civilian scout. Mostly Kansas, into Nebraska, sometimes what then was Colorado Territory. Eventually, he followed some "fancy petticoat" into Texas, scouting at Fort Richardson. After they lowered the Stars and Stripes in 'seventy-eight at Richardson, he drifted back to Kansas, stopped in Medicine Lodge for a whiskey, found himself in his cups, without a copper to his name, and started working as a swamper to pay off his bar tab.

"Wound up buyin' the place," he said. "And folks started talkin' all 'bout the great treaty of Medicine Lodge. Now, I was in Hancock's War, as we called it, and helped bury many a fallen comrade, though, like I said, I hardly ever saw any war paint on any livin' injun. But it got me to thinkin'. That Western folks, and all Americans, love their past. Their history. And that this Wild West ain't gonna last forever. Buffalo Bill. He proved that folks like the glory that was and is the West. And Bill's got competition. And I said, Xavier Titus Wheeler The Third, this here is your chance to go down in history. By tellin' history. Showin' history. And why let 'em Sioux and Cheyenne bucks get all the glory? Just because they whupped up on Custer and his boys at the Little Big Horn. Hell, I knowed George Custer. He had a nice-lookin' wife, but he didn't know nothin' 'bout injuns. Not like Rabid Wolf Jones did. Or even me, after some years scoutin'. Or Bill Cody. And, by thunder, I'll tell you this: Comanches fought harder, rode better, and scared the hell out of me and many a white man and woman more than any Johnny Reb or Cheyenne buck I ever run up against." He laughed. "Or run away from!"

Wheeler turned to spit, then hooked out the well-chewed cud from his cheek with a thumb. After wiping his mouth and rubbing his teeth relatively clean of any remaining flecks of tobacco, he pushed back the brim of his big hat, drew in a deep breath, exhaled, and smiled that winning smile that made him so proud.

He resumed his speech: "So I'm roundin' up Comanches—the best I can get—for a four-month tour with my Wild Texas West. I asked the big chief here"—he nodded at Quanah—"but he said he's too busy. The head honcho at Sill agreed. So did your agent, and he's the one who said you'd be the best man to get."

Wheeler fished two double eagles from the pocket of his buckskin jacket, and slid them across the table toward Daniel.

"That's your bonus. Forty American dollars. Which is what you'll be makin' a month appearin' in my show."

Johnny D. Boggs

One more smile, then Wheeler withdrew the novels from his pocket and set them on the table before he pushed himself to his feet. "You'll want to talk about it with your big chief here, Dan'l. So I'll just mosey over to my boy Pry and maybe admire some of the big chief's hosses. Be back directly."

He moved gracefully for a big man with bowed legs, stepped off the porch, and rounded the corner of the house, the jingling of his spurs fading as he walked away.

Daniel looked at Quanah, his face showed no emotion. Then he reached for one of the two-bit "dreadfuls"—that's what one of the Pale Eye missionaries had called these types of books—and studied the cover.

SHUMAKER'S AMERICAN LIBRARY

And below that, in much smaller italic type:

Entered according to Act of Congress, in the Year 1891, by Gerald P. Shumaker, in the Office of the Library of Congress, at Washington, D.C.

Just above the dramatic title and silly illustration, Daniel read:

No. 083. / Complete / Gerald P. Shumaker, Publisher, 13 Rose Avenue, New York / Price 25¢ / Vol. 1

Issued Every Friday, New York, November 13, 1891

He looked at Quanah. "This was made in the Heading to Winter Moon," he said in the language of The People. He found the second book, frowned, and said, "This came in the Sleet Moon."

A tired smile briefly appeared on Quanah's face as he nodded. Weck-e-ah, one of Quanah's wives, stepped out of the window, scowled at both men, and dropped to her knees as she swept up the remnants of the broken cup, with her hands, onto a newspaper. Rising, she gave both men a steely look, and vanished through the curtains.

It took a moment for Daniel to regain his thoughts. He looked at the covers of the sordid books, and slid them away, though he wanted to throw them as Quanah had done with the cup. He felt the blood rushing to his temples, and he waited to speak.

But Quanah spoke first.

"They have been thinking about you for a long time."

Daniel rubbed his throbbing temples, shook his head. "Why?"

Quanah shook his head. He could not think of the right words of The People, so he spoke in English. "Seduce you."

Now Daniel laughed. So did Quanah.

"The Pale Eyes have strange notions." Quanah pointed at the covers of both books. "They think stories like that will make a man of The People think like a Pale Eye."

The smile died on his face and in his eyes.

"You know why they want you to go with them." It was not a question.

"The treaty talks," Daniel said.

Quanah's head bobbed once.

"I should not go," Daniel said.

"It is a choice for you to make. Forty Pale Eye dollars a month is a lot of money."

"They would have paid you more."

"But the Pale Eyes need me here. To sign the treaty. With you gone, and others like you, they think I will be forced to agree to their demands." He shrugged. "They might be right. Already we fight among ourselves. And as I have already told you, and as you have known for a long while, the Pale Eyes will get our land."

"I will not go," Daniel said.

39

Shrugging, Quanah said. "Maybe they will barter more. Like the Tejano cattlemen do sometimes. Maybe you can get sixty dollars a month."

"I would not go for one hundred dollars."

Quanah smiled. "Well, maybe they will pay me a hundred dollars to go. I go. Sleep in fancy hotels and eat big Pale Eye meals. You stay and deal with *sons of bitches* from Washington City and Agent Ugly Mouth."

Daniel laughed. The Pale Eyes thought The People were fierce warriors, brutal slayers of all enemies, and never realized that they could be uproariously funny, that they loved to laugh as much as they loved to be horseback. Or that the reason they fought so hard was because they loved their life and their families so much.

Quanah looked into the open window, barked out instructions in Nermernuh, and A-er-wuth-take-um, a wife he had taken while Daniel had been at Carlisle, mother of two precocious daughters, Ne-dah and Sunrise, and a small boy, Len Nehio, came out with Quanah's favorite pipe.

"We will smoke," Quanah said.

When Colonel Titus Wheeler returned, his eyes sparkled again, and Daniel knew the big man had been drinking whiskey while admiring Quanah's horses and talking to Black Yellow Stripes. The big taibo smiled broadly at Quanah and Daniel, slid into the chair, and found more presents in his jacket's inside pocket. He passed a cigar to Quanah, who took it gladly, and then one for Daniel.

When Daniel shook his head, Co-by, who had stepped out to fill the men's coffee cups—Weck-e-ah had replaced the one Quanah had broken—grabbed the cigar and quickly vanished through the curtains.

Wheeler struck a lucifer on the table's edge, lighted Quanah's

40

cigar first, then his, shook out the match, and dropped it in a saucer. They smoked in silence for a while, and Daniel heard the clomping of hoofs and jangling of traces as Black Yellow Stripes drove the fancy carriage back to the front of the house.

"So you've had time to talk about my generous offer," Wheeler said. "I'm hirin' Comanches for four months. I mean moons. That ain't a long time to be gone. Hell, Dan'l, from what I've been told, you was gone a lot longer than that."

"Too long," Daniel said.

"I figure this is a way to bring you red folks and the Texans together in a way. Let them see you Comanch for what y'all really is. Great horsemen. Brave warriors. I want to bring some squaws along, too. I mean, women." He tried to smile his way through his poor choice of words. "All y'all gots to do is dance, sing, and ride. And look ferocious. And make a right smart of money. I've got my press man—the one who penned this here blood-and-thunders about Capt'n Dan'l—down in Fort Worth makin' the final arrangements. And I got a slew of rich Texas investors. Money to spend. Glory to reap."

He paused to pull on the cigar again, blew out smoke, and turned to Quanah. "You ever been to Fort Worth, Chief? It's a fine ol' town. Best in Texas, if you was to ask me."

"Almost died there," Quanah told him in English.

Wheeler coughed. Found the coffee. Took a healthy swallow.

"Well, every town can be rough and rowdy. But, like I say, Buffalo Bill's fandango has done wonders on this side of The Pond and that side of The Pond. We're just gettin' started. Make my show in Texas this year. See what we can do next year. I ain't sure I want to cross The Pond, but I wouldn't mind a month or two in Chicago. Or New York City. San Francisco."

He had to stop to catch his breath, and Daniel took advantage of the pause.

"That will take longer than four months."

The colonel's head bobbed. "I know. This first run, it's just Fort Worth. Albany. Austin. San Antone. Then we'll see what my investors think and just go root hawg or die. Texas this time, then we tackle the whole blasted world. Let folks see what Comanches is really like. I'm all about makin' things right with you boys who ain't white."

Daniel nodded at Black Yellow Stripes, who leaned against the carriage, rolling a smoke.

"How about him?" Daniel asked.

Wheeler turned, stared, swallowed, and lost much of his bluster. "Well," he finally said. "I ain't sure Texas is ready to accept no darkies." He turned quickly to his driver. "No offense there, Sergeant Pry."

"None taken," the Black White Man said. But the look in his dark black eyes and the tone of his voice told Daniel that Black Yellow Stripes would love to drag the colonel behind the wagon all the way back to Fort Sill.

"But you'll be part of the greatest amusement in America, boy," the colonel called out. "I'm payin' you top dollar to be my right hand. Ain't that right, Virg?"

"Yes, sir," Black Yellow Stripes said.

"You spoke of He Whose Arrows Fly Straight Into The Hearts Of His Enemies," Quanah said in The People's tongue. "Some women. When we spoke yesterday, you mentioned no other names. You have been talking to our agent, and the leader of the Long Knives at Fort Sill. Who else do you want to bring along in your . . . amusement?"

Wheeler answered in Nermernuh. "I gave you a list yesterday."

Quanah smiled. "I speak your tongue. I do not read your words. And the wind blew your paper away after you left."

The big man frowned, but quickly recovered.

"Well, that buck that came in with Dan'l here," he said in English. "He'll do. I don't recollect his name."

42

"Twice Bent Nose," Quanah said, this time in English.

"That's an apt name for that ol' boy." Wheeler patted his pockets, likely hoping for another list of names, but soon gave up and said, "Well, there's Lone Wolf."

Quanah's head shook. "You mean White Wolf."

White Wolf was a leader of The People, but that did not make sense, since White Wolf led the Yamparika band, and usually opposed Quanah. The Pale Eyes would want to keep White Wolf close by for any negotiations on the future of the reservation.

"No, not White Wolf. Lone Wolf."

"Lone Wolf is not of The People," Quanah said. "He is Kiowa."

The man's head bobbed. "Yep. But everybody knows that the Kiowas are fast pards with the Comanch'. Y'all have been fightin' alongside each other as long as I can recollect. Like when y'all attacked that wagon train at Salt Crick back in 'seventy-one."

Daniel looked at Quanah, who nodded in understanding. Yes, of course, the taibos would want Lone Wolf with the big man's "amusement." Lone Wolf had been as big a thorn in the taibos' side as Quanah during these negotiations.

The big man rose, stuck the cigar in his coffee cup, and extended his hand toward Quanah.

"Tell you what, Chief. Me and my boy yonder, we've got to get back to Fort Sill. Speak to the colonel, and the agent. Why don't you talk things over, then ride to the agency in the morn', and we'll firm up our talks? It's gonna be one crackerjack amusement, and it'll make a bunch of your braves and squa— wives and daughters and nieces, I mean, rich beyond their wildest dreams. What do you say?"

Quanah accepted the man's hand.

"We will talk." Again, Quanah used the taibo tongue.

Wheeler whirled and shook Daniel's hand. It was a hard grip.

43

"And, Dan'l, since I've made you famous beyond your wildest imagination, I might be willin' to go up to fifty dollars a month for your wages. We'll do our final palaverin' at the agency tomorrow. Say . . . when the sun shines straight up?"

Quanah's head bobbed again, and the big man stepped off the porch and made a beeline to the fancy carriage.

Black Yellow Stripes helped him up, and the man found the jug on the floor, pulled out the cork, and took a pull. He was still drinking when the Black White Man flicked the lines and carried Colonel Titus Wheeler back from whence he came.

CHAPTER FIVE

"He is strange," Quanah said after the coach had disappeared. "But he laughs. I like a man who laughs, especially at himself." He shook his head and drank coffee. "Most Pale Eyes think that The People never laugh, that we are demons from this hell they talk about so much."

A-er-wuth-take-um came out and refilled their cups with coffee. "There is not much for The People to laugh at anymore," she said, and left through the open window.

For the longest while, no one on the porch spoke. Twice Bent Nose drank his coffee. Quanah just stared at his cup. Finally, he reached into his satchel, a gift from one of the Tejano ranchers, and withdrew a piece of paper, which he slid toward Daniel.

"This," Quanah said, "is the list of names the colonel says he wishes to go with him. You tell me what names he has written."

Daniel smiled at the wry leader. "The paper did not blow away?"

"It blew away," Quanah said. "A-er-wuth-take-um chased it before it escaped. That is why she is so bitter this day."

Daniel read the names. His was first.

"There are no women on this list," Twice Bent Nose said after Daniel finished, then slid the paper back to Quanah.

Nodding, Quanah said, "The colonel said for me to pick the women. As long as they were pretty. And can dance."

"Pretty?" Twice Bent Nose said. "In the eyes of a Pale Eye? Or the eyes of The People?"

"In the eyes of The People, all women are pretty," Quanah said. "The Pale Eyes?" He shrugged. "They probably mean young."

Twice Bent Nose shook his head. "My wife . . . she's not so pretty anymore. Or young."

It felt good to laugh, but that lasted only a minute before Quanah frowned and said, "Do you know why those names are on the list?"

"They are friends of yours," Daniel replied immediately. "They fight for you. They fight for The People."

"I fight for what I think is best for The People. Am I right?" He shrugged.

"Titus Wheeler did not come up with those names," Daniel said.

"No, he did not." Quanah shook his head. "The names were given to him by Agent Ugly Mouth. Probably with some suggestions by the Long Knives chief and others."

"They want us away so you will not have as many friends and followers," Daniel said.

Quanah smiled. "The People are not as many as when I was a child. And when I was a child, The People were not as many as when my father was a child. But there are not many names on that paper, and the Pale Eyes are still frightened enough by The People to send no more. I will have enough voices behind me. And the Tejanos . . . they still want the Big Pasture. The Pale Eyes think they can get what they want, but they are wrong. The voices of all The People will still be heard."

Silence followed. But the wind felt good on the porch. A-er-wuth-take-um returned with more coffee, but all except Twice Bent Nose had had enough.

"There is another way this colonel might help The People," Quanah said.

Daniel and Twice Bent Nose looked at their leader, waiting.

"The colonel is much the way the Lakotas to the north talk about his Buffalo Bill," Quanah said. "They say he is like many Pale Eyes. He gets crazy by drinking too much of the Pale Eyes whiskey. They race horses and shoot guns that cannot kill, but they also show the Lakotas as human beings. This Buffalo Bill . . . he does this for the money, yes. But most of the Pale Eyes have never seen a Lakota before. Just seen drawings in the newspapers or storybooks. If a Pale Eye sees a man with a different colored skin, sees a man with a wife, then maybe even a Pale Eye can understand that we breathe and bleed the same as he does. That as much as we are different, we are alike. And that maybe we can reach an understanding."

"This Wheeler," Daniel said, "is not Buffalo Bill."

"No." Quanah said. "He just wants to be." He breathed in till his lungs could hold no more, exhaled, and looked into Daniel's eyes. "It is a choice for you to make. We will smoke on it. You will sleep on it. I will honor your choice. But if the men who tell their stories for the newspapers in these Tejano cities that you visit with the colonel, perhaps they will talk to you. You speak their language as well as you speak your own. You tell them the way things are."

"They write what they want to write," Daniel said. He pointed at *Killstraight Returns.*

"Even that affects the Pale Eyes," Quanah said. "This . . . character . . . he is a hero. Most writers, I am told, depict The People, the Lakotas, the Kiowas . . . all of us . . . *Indians* . . . as the evil enemies of the Pale Eyes. A colt walks before it lopes, and before it walks, it must stand."

"We have been taking small steps for years," Daniel said. "Now they ask us to step backwards."

"As I say. It is your choice."

"Maybe . . ." Twice Bent Nose rose and stepped to the side of the porch, opened his trousers, and began to urinate. ". . .

Maybe . . . I show the Pale Eyes in this colonel's *a-muse-ment*
that The People piss like the Pale Eyes, too . . . Only bigger.
And better."

Quanah almost fell out of his chair laughing, and several of
his wives peeked out of the windows and giggled.

Twice Bent Nose slept outside, near the front porch, and Daniel
wished he had done the same when he woke up on the
hardwood floor shortly after sunrise. He rolled off the blanket,
sat up, his back, thighs, and shoulders aching. What revived him
was the smell of coffee brewing, and he made himself stand,
and worked his leg muscles as he moved out of what taibos
would call a parlor and found the front door. He had lived too
long in Carlisle to go in and out through open windows.

Twice Bent Nose and Quanah stood in the large front yard,
saddling horses. Looking over a fine piebald stallion, Quanah
grinned at Daniel, then cracked a joke to Twice Bent Nose.

"How late would he have slept if I gave him a bed?" Quanah
said.

Chuckling, Twice Bent Nose grabbed the latigo as he worked
on his horse.

"Coffee is on the table," Quanah said.

Daniel nodded his thanks and creaked his way to the waiting
pot and cup.

The trail from the Star House to the agency was easy to follow,
worn down over the years with the tracks of men and women in
moccasins, and soldier boots, unshod ponies, shod horses of the
Long Knives, and wagons—carriages like the one of Colonel
Titus Wheeler, and the freight wagons of the taibos. As young
as Daniel was, even he could remember a time when this land
belonged only to The People and the Kiowas, when the only
tracks one saw were of horses without the metal shoes—except

those that had been stolen from taibos in what the Pale Eyes called Texas or Kansas. Or the tracks of the *cuhtz*, but those were hard to find these days, almost wiped out by those foul-smelling men with the far-shooting rifles that had slaughtered the great herds that fed The People, taking nothing but the hides.

Never pushing their horses, for Quanah loved to make the Pale Eyes wait, they came out of the Wichita Mountains and followed the broken prairie to where Medicine Junction and Cache Creeks joined, and passed the soldier-fort. Daniel was just a boy when the Long Knives arrived and began building what would become Fort Sill. The Long Knives who began building the fort were the first Black White Men Daniel had ever seen. He remembered Ugly Badger complaining that the scalps of those Black White Men were not worth taking, but his father countering that those Black White Men fought harder than any Pale Eyes he had come up against, and that he had heard from a Creek trader that many of those Black White Men had once been slaves to many Pale Eyes.

"Then they should fight with us," Ugly Badger cried out.

His father's voice had sounded sad that evening. Daniel remembered the words. "That time has passed."

The soldier-fort had grown much since those early years. Twice Bent Nose always seemed frightened at its size, and Daniel wondered how his friend would react had he seen Carlisle or Philadelphia or even Fort Smith. Daniel tried to picture how this country would look if the Pale Eyes got their wish and rushed across the country from the Red River to the south or the Washita to the north, pounded a wooden stake into the ground, and started building their own Star Houses, their own corrals, their own barns, and dug their own wells and grew their wheat or raised their pigs or cows or chickens.

This had once all been Indian Territory. That's the name the

Pale Eyes gave it, but to Daniel it was one of his homes. He was lucky. He knew that. To the east, the Chickasaws, the Choctaws, the Creeks, the Cherokees, and many others had been moved here from their homelands many, many, many miles away. He remembered trading with a Seminole, who told him: "This is your country. It is not mine. I never wanted it to be mine. I live here, true, but I have no home. I am a stranger here. A stranger where I live. A stranger where I will die."

Then they turned and took the road to the agency, where many fancy wagons parked in front of the log and stone structure, including the extravagant rig owned by Colonel Titus Wheeler. Black Yellow Stripes stood beside it, talking to the drivers of other carriages.

Athol McLeish stepped outside, followed by a Long Knife in a fancy suit. Other leaders of The People sat underneath a shade tree, talking among one another. Lone Wolf, the Kiowa, was there, too, with three of his followers.

"Chief Parker," McLeish called out. "It is good to see you this morning."

Quanah reined up and swung out of the saddle. A young Kwahadi ran over and took the reins to Quanah's horse. Another boy waited for Twice Bent Nose and Daniel to dismount; that boy then led their horses to a corral.

McLeish reached Quanah and extended his hand.

Quanah looked at it, making no move to accept the hand, and turned toward the trees. "Are we here to talk about this Colonel Wheeler's amusement? Or do you bring us here to ram your lies down our throats?"

The man backed up as though he had been punched.

Colonel Titus Wheeler stepped in, grinned, tilted his head back, and let out a loud laugh, and when he brought his head up, he sang out with a bellowing war cry.

"By grab, Quanah, you don't beat around the bush, and that's

50

somethin' I admire in a man, red or white." He caught a glimpse of Black Yellow Stripes out of the corner of his eye, and said, "Or that fine old darky that drives for me. Yes, sir, yes, sir. I bet you're hell on wheels when it comes to dickerin'."

He turned, and pointed at the porch of the agency building. "I don't have no truck with 'em boys up yonder, or these blue-coats. They ain't here on my behalf. If Mister McLeish and the head honcho at Fort Sill wanna talk to you about somethin' I don't know about, by grab, they'll have to wait. I drawed the lottery on you, and I wanna finalize my deal so we can get my Comanches loaded up and move us all out to Fort Worth. Time is money. And money is time. And my investors is gettin' antsy. And I'm 'bout out of time, money—and damned rich inves-tors—if this show don't get started." He drew his breath and shouted at the taibo leaders. "And I need injuns to star in my show."

And so the two men talked in the shade of the cabin, with McLeish and the Long Knives leader making suggestions, and Daniel translating whenever Quanah needed help.

Daniel admired how Quanah would make a suggestion, changing one name on the list to another, offering a reason for the switch. McLeish might not have liked the substitute, but by now Daniel began to digest that Colonel Wheeler really believed that time was money, money was time, and he was running out of both.

Under the trees, The People and the Kiowas paced, frowned, smoked, and kicked pebbles. Two others threw knives into the dirt, some kind of game. Twice Bent Nose went inside the build-ing and Daniel smiled when he heard coffee being poured into a cup.

So it went for three more hours, according to the chimes on the clock that hung on the wall across from McLeish's desk.

"We wait no more," Lone Wolf called out.

McLeish turned, started to say something, but quickly understood that when a Kiowa had lost patience, the best thing to say was nothing at all.

A cloud of dust swallowed the Kiowas as they galloped away, and Daniel started to turn back, but a rider rode straight through the departing riders, splitting them. Only one of The People could ride like that, Daniel realized. He did not recognize the rider at first, but as he drew closer, Daniel knew he was of the Yamparika band—a grandson of Ten Bears, the wise leader whose death had led to the decline of power in that group of The People.

He did not slow down, but raised a hand to his mouth and yelled.

One word. Just that. Not a word of The People, but a taibo word. That every person at the agency understood. That they all feared.

A word that made Daniel's heart sink.

CHAPTER SIX

"Smallpox!"

Naruʔuyutasiʔa.

Red Wolf leaped off his horse before it had fully stopped. His knees bent, but he did not fall, just staggered and righted himself, slid to a stop, and called out in the Yamparika dialect:

"The Rotting Face! The Rotting Face! The Rotting Face!"

Red Wolf kept running, but Daniel heard the metallic clicking of a revolver behind him. He heard Agent McLeish sing out, "Don't let that buck get any closer. He might infect us all." The agent quickly reached into his pocket, and Daniel feared he might pull out a small revolver, but his hand emerged with one of those dark bottles, and he quickly unscrewed the cap and tossed some white pills down his throat, chewing them for he had no water, his face tightening.

Fear numbed the marrow in Daniel's bones, but he made himself rush toward the Yamparika. He held his arms high over his head and shouted in his own tongue: "Stop! Stop! Do not come any closer."

A shot rang out. Daniel cringed. He heard the whine of a bullet as it struck ground. He yelled harder.

Red Wolf stopped, stunned. His right hand reached for a sheathed knife.

"No," Daniel said. "Do not. They will kill you." He had to catch his breath, but somehow, some way, Red Wolf did not pull the knife from the fringed leather. But his face showed nothing

53

but hatred for these Pale Eyes.

"Killstraight . . ." Daniel heard McLeish's voice, an octave higher, panic mixed with hatred. "Tell that boy to get on his pony and get out of here right this damned minute. Major, you put that next round in that boy's heart. Troopers. Kill the horse, too. If he isn't out of here instantly."

It was the Long Knives leader who spoke sense.

"Christ a'mighty, McLeish, get your wits together, man. Lieutenant Lodge, if one of your men touches a trigger without my order, I'll have him shot right after I hang you. Savvy?"

"Yes, sir," a voice squeaked.

"Major Martin!" the agent yelled, and again he found his bottle of pills.

"Horses don't spread smallpox, McLeish," the Long Knives leader said. "We know that much after all these years. Gather your wits together, sir."

The major breathed in deeply, exhaled, and looked again at Daniel. "Killstraight," he said. "Who is this friend of yours?"

Red Wolf wasn't a friend, but he was one of The People. Daniel told the Long Knife the name, adding, "He is a grandson of . . ." He hesitated, hating to call out the name of someone who had gone to The Land Beyond The Sun. But there was no way around it, for even years after his passing, Ten Bears remained a name known among Pale Eyes. "Ten Bears."

"Ten Bears, Lord almighty." It was Colonel Titus Wheeler who whispered the words. "They don't make 'em like that anymore."

Again, Major Martin drew in a breath, held it, exhaled. Daniel wondered if the Long Knife still held the revolver. The Long Knife looked at The People and Twice Bent Nose standing closer to Red Wolf, but inching back slowly, carefully, though they had to be at least twenty yards from the Yamparika. And the wind was blowing away from them.

54

"Ask him," the major told Daniel, "if he is sure this is smallpox. I mean, chicken pox, other diseases, I'm told, have the same symptoms. At the beginning anyway."

Daniel called out Red Wolf's name. The young man turned, his eyes filled with hatred, and waited.

Daniel said, "The leader of the Long Knives asks a stupid question, Red Wolf. But we must answer him. Are you sure what you have seen is The Rotting Face?"

The boy spat. "I have seen it. I know what I see. Have you ever seen it?"

"Look at my face." Daniel could not hold down his anger. "And you will know that I have seen The Rotting Face much closer than you ever have." Now, it was Daniel's turn to spit gall out of his mouth.

The boy stared at his moccasins, ashamed.

As he should be.

Daniel gathered his composure. "It is . . . smallpox," he told the taibos.

"Where?" Major Martin asked.

Daniel repeated his question in Nermernuh.

"Our camp," Red Wolf said. "Near where the Tejanos still graze their smelly beeves with the crooked, ugly horns."

There were many pastures where Tejanos paid The People to let their cattle eat grass and fatten themselves, but Daniel knew where most of the Yamparikas camped, and this was the Big Pasture the Tejanos favored, for it lay just across the Red River. It was also land that, so far, the Pale Eyes had not considered opening up for one of those land runs. Because Tejanos who owned cattle wanted very much to have rights to graze their cattle on that land for a long, long time.

"It is near the Big Pasture," he said in English. "Just across the river. Closer to Texas than here."

"Well, if it kills more secesh, that's fine with me," the major

55

said, and exhaled.

"But not to me," Colonel Titus Wheeler said. "I've got business in the Lone Star State, and my press man has been booking appearances for my fine exhibition across Texas, Major Martin."

"I'm joking, Titus," the major said.

Though Daniel found nothing comical about The Rotting Face.

"How many of The People are sick?" Daniel asked, and heard Major Martin demand:

"What did you just say, Killstraight?"

Daniel waited. Red Wolf held up one hand, extending all fingers and thumb. He brought up his left hand, and held up two fingers.

"Seven." Daniel felt sick. "Seven of his band have smallpox."

"Are they absolutely sure it's the pox?" Titus Wheeler asked. His voice came across as childish. The major had already asked that question, and Red Wolf had answered. Daniel did not need to ask Red Wolf again.

"We have seen enough of The Rotting Face to know what it is. It has killed . . ." Daniel did not continue. He did not want to think about that.

"How about the other bands?" McLeish asked.

"I have seen nothing among the Kotsotekas," Daniel said.

"But you're Kwahadi," Major Martin said. "Or so I'm told."

"But I live near the Kotsotekas," Daniel said, feeling again that he had no home, not even among The People. Mescalero mother. Kwahadi father. Spent most of his youth in the taibo schools in Pennsylvania, learning to be a taibo. Don't kill the Indian, they loved to say. Just kill the Indian in the man. And save the man.

Save him from what? For what? This?

"Nokoni?" the major asked.

56

"No." McLeish had calmed himself. Now he seemed to be in deep thought. Planning his escape? Daniel wondered. Or what? "At least not as of yesterday. Big Bull was up here. You know . . . talking about . . . things."

Things, Daniel understood, meaning the future of the reservation.

"He would have mentioned it," McLeish continued. "That smallpox wreaked havoc on those boys a year or two back."

"Wish it had wiped all them bucks out," whispered a voice among the Long Knives.

"Mister Lodge," Major Martin said, "have that man put in irons and thrown in the sweatbox till I decide to court-martial him or just let him rot."

The lieutenant called out: "You heard that order, Sergeant Wilson."

Daniel realized he was holding his breath again. He let it out and thought about Oajuicauojué. He had not seen her in almost two days, and The Rotting Face could spread like a fire on the prairie on a hot, windy day.

"Killstraight," the major said, and Daniel waited.

"Tell . . . Red Wolf . . . tell him to go back to his band. Tell him to leave now. That we will have help sent immediately. Tell him that no one is to leave the village. The way to beat smallpox is to catch it quickly, and not let it spread. Tell him that. Tell him to separate the sick from the healthy, if they haven't already done so. Tell him that we will do all we can."

While Daniel was translating the major's orders, he was listening to the Long Knives leader give other instructions to the agent.

"Sergeant Wilson. Get to the telegraph. First thing is send a warning to the federal marshal. No, hell, make it the Texas Rangers. They act faster than any political appointee. Hell, telegraph both Rangers and the U.S. marshal. Tell them that there's a smallpox outbreak among the redskins just north of the Red, and if Texas doesn't want to get wiped out, they had better put patrols up all along the south side of that river from, hell, Childress to Spanish Fort."

He stopped to breathe again, and the young lieutenant said, "What about inoculations, sir?"

"Don't be daft, Mister Lodge." The major paused to determine his next orders.

Titus Wheeler took advantage of the pause.

"Major, I have been at the agency and your fort and a short visit to Chief Parker's fine house. Just me and my boy yonder."

Daniel glanced at Black Yellow Stripes, who was smoothing his beard, and staring at Red Wolf as he galloped south. The Black White Man paid no attention to the Pale Eyes talking about him. He just watched Red Wolf ride.

The major kept barking orders. "Lieutenant Ryman." Another younger bluecoat stepped forward and snapped a salute.

"Write down these orders so there will be no confusion. And write so that you and Captain Baxter can read them. Find Captain Baxter, have him lead his troop south at once and surround the northern perimeter of the Yamparika camp near the Big Pasture. Do not engage. Do not enter the camp. Also, locate that Hun major we have for a surgeon. Tell him about the outbreak. Tell him . . . Hell, tell him to do what he can. *I'm not finished, Mister.*"

The young officer muttered an apology and stepped back into line, found his pencil and his paper, and waited.

"Telegraph the railroad at El Reno and Colonel James at Fort Reno. Inform them what is going on here. Tell the railroad there is to be no civilian travel to Fort Sill or anywhere south of the Wichita agency without military permission. Let Major König know what is going on here, too. Send telegraphs to the War Department and the Department of the Interior. Ask for any medical assistance to be dispatched here and tell them I await further orders. Also instruct them of what I have already ordered. Have you got all of that?"

"Yes, sir."

"Good. Get to it, Mister. Get to it and don't make any mistakes in what I've told you to do."

The lieutenant saluted and hurried to the string of horses. The major seemed to be thinking about what he should do next, when Titus Wheeler said, "Major, I've had the pox. So I can't get it no more. But I also got an expensive enterprise and must get to Texas. With my Comanches." He laughed, and pulled out his pants pockets inside out.

"Or else, I'm bust. Busted. Kaput. Bankrupted. Ruined. Wiped out."

"Wheeler. Your finances and your reputation are the least of my concerns at the moment." He suddenly sounded as if he were forty years older, and twenty miles away.

"Harry." It was the agent who spoke, and when the major turned, McLeish tilted his head toward the open door to the cabin. Daniel watched the agent enter first, then the Long Knives leader. The door closed behind them.

The bluecoat soldiers whispered among themselves, those that had not been ordered to do something. Faces bronzed by the prairie sun had paled. Deep voices no longer sounded so stern. Even Daniel felt beads of sweat forming on his brow. Again, he pictured Oajuicauojué. But he could not think about her for long, because the door to the agency opened, and McLeish and Major Martin stepped out.

"Major," Titus Wheeler whined.

"Wheeler," the weary bluecoat said, "get with McLeish and Chief Parker. Pick your Indians and report to the parade ground at Fort Sill. I know that Hun doctor I have. He'll insist on examining anyone before we turn them loose to the civilian population, even if the civilians are traitorous secesh."

"The war ended a long, long time ago," Titus Wheeler said jovially.

"Not in my book. *Officers!*" The major waited just a minute. "We return to Fort Sill, where you will fall in front of the corrals immediately to receive your orders. You will fall into two groups. Those of you who have had the pox. And those of you who are damned unlucky virgins."

"Thank you, kindly!" Titus Wheeler shouted. "Lord bless you."

But Major Martin wasn't listening. He was walking ramrod straight for his horse, which was held by a pale bluecoat whose hand that held the reins shook like he had no bones in his left arm.

Everyone, except for Daniel, seemed to move like ants. The agent hurried toward Wheeler, but found himself standing next to Black Yellow Stripes. The colonel hurried to the major, who did not appear interested in anything the showman had to say. Most of the young taibo soldiers looked like they wanted to be anywhere but where they stood.

Daniel did not blame them.

A few minutes later, the soldiers raced back to Fort Sill. The colonel stood alone, found his scarf, and wiped his sweaty face.

"Killstraight!" McLeish yelled.

Daniel saw the agent waving him over, so he turned and motioned for Twice Bent Nose to follow. They walked to the shady spot. Wheeler yelled Black Yellow Stripe's name, Virgil, and the Black White Man sighed and headed after the buckskin-clad scout.

"Get to the fort," he told Black Yellow Stripes. "Send a telegram to Billy in Fort Worth. Tell him not to worry. Tell him our show will not be stopped. Tell him not to cancel nothin' or let nothin' get canceled. Tell him our injuns is healthier than he is."

Titus Wheeler walked away, mopping his face again. Daniel wondered how the colonel could say all his "injuns" were healthy when none had yet been chosen to go with this Wild West show.

Usually, a talk of this sort would start with speeches, then pipe smoking, then presents, then more pipe smoking, more speeches, and end with the taibos getting exactly what they wanted. McLeish had been talking to Black Yellow Stripes, but now he walked away from the Black White Man and the fancy buggy, and approached Quanah.

"Chief Parker," McLeish said, "I have a list of names of men that Colonel Wheeler has asked to take part in his show. Mister Killstraight can read the figures, and you can see that the salaries being offered are extremely good—good even for a white man. For an Indian, it's more than a fortune. These men will go. You can send four women. The women of your own choosing. Those . . ." He laughed like a child. "Those who you wouldn't mind being shed of for a few months."

Quanah did not look up.

"Killstraight. Read those names."

"No." Quanah still did not look up.

"Chief?" Rejection from an Indian was something the agent had not expected.

"I will tell you who will go," Quanah told him. "Men. And women."

"Well, Chief, ol' pard." Colonel Wheeler started his act again. "I respect your opinion. Surely, I do. But this ain't 'bout nothin' but showmanship. And I've been a-ganderin' at your folks, and I can say who's got that look, that feel, that special somethin' that grabs a white man and a white woman, even a Mex, or, by golly, a darky, too, like my boy Virg.

"It's a good list. You won't miss these men at all. And I'll have 'em back. I'll keep 'em safe. Safer than you can what with the pox goin' on here. I'd love to have you, too, you know, ol' boy, but with all these talks a-goin' on, and your men and kids and women needin' you close with the . . . what's that they called it . . . Rotting Face. You can't be spared. But these men I want, they can. And like we've agreed to. You get to say which women go."

Quanah turned. "We go," he said. Daniel turned, moving toward their horses, Quanah behind him, and Twice Bent Nose falling behind.

"Chief!" the showman and the agent cried out in unison.

"We go," Quanah said without breaking his stride. "Yes, we may die here. And your *amusement* will die in Texas."

CHAPTER SEVEN

"Damnation," Athol McLeish whispered. "All the bands to come down with smallpox, and it has to be the Yamparikas. God just couldn't help us by infecting the Kwahadis."

The agent waved his hands in exasperation, cursed underneath his breath, and then shook his head.

"He's got you licked," Colonel Titus Wheeler said, sighed, and suddenly chuckled. "Hell of a leader, I reckon. Hell of a man. I'll take what I can get, Mister McLeish, and remember, you get a percentage of what we make on this tour of Texas. So it's your call. Hell, I can always hire Mexicans and Italians and have 'em dress up like the red devils."

"Go," Quanah told Twice Bent Nose, "and return with your wife. Huuhwiya is wise and strong. Prettier and younger than you think she is. She will be of great help with the other women I send with Wheeler."

"Huuhwiya thanks you, Quanah," Twice Bent Nose said, and hurried to his horse.

"You will go back to your home," Quanah told Daniel. "Return with Oajuicauojué. She is very pleasing to look at." He watched Twice Bent Nose put his horse into a gallop. "Unlike Huuhwiya."

"Ben Buffalo Bone might not wish for his sister to go," Daniel said softly.

"Ben Buffalo Bone wants what Coals In A Fire wants for The

People," Quanah said. "But Ben Buffalo Bone wants his family to be safe more than anything else. Because he is Kotsoteka. It is Ben Buffalo Bone's choice, of course, and he must grant permission, but Ben Buffalo Bone will not wish for his sister to die of The Rotting Face. Because he is of The People. He will let her go with the colonel."

Daniel also thanked the Kwahadi leader, and left to find his horse, but Quanah stopped him.

"You will also return with Ben Buffalo Bone." Daniel's face must have shown something, though he had tried to hide his feelings. "If Oajuicauojué goes, her brother must go. We know how Pale Eyes look upon our women, especially one as lovely as Oajuicauojué. Her brother—and not you—must be there to protect her. You know this as well as I know this."

Daniel swallowed down any protest he might have tried.

"This also shows that I speak for all of The People. Not just the Kwahadis." Again, Daniel knew Quanah was right. "They will not let us take any of the Root Eaters," Quanah continued, using the nickname of the Yamparika band. Let Etzapuinit pick a Nokoni and ask Inap to choose a Penateka. That will be enough women. Tell Inap and Etzapuinit why we send these women. Tell them that The Rotting Face is among The People again."

"You do not wish to send Co-by?" Daniel asked. "Or To-nar-cy?"

Quanah stared at his moccasins. "I cannot." He did not look up. "Many times I have wished the Pale Eyes never made me this . . . *chief* . . . as they like to call me. But never more than this moment. You understand."

He did not look up, and Daniel felt the coffee from this morning roiling in his belly. "Ebicuyonit is the best dancer among the Nokonis," Quanah said, his eyes still trained on the moccasins Mah-cheet-to-wook-ky had beaded for him just last spring, but

Daniel doubted if Quanah saw anything at this moment. "See if Etzapuinit will let him come with us. And suggest Ecahcueré to Inap. His voice is as strong as his heart."

Quanah looked up. "I have never wished The Rotting Face on anyone, but I am glad it touched you long ago. And glad that you did not die. You survived, I now know, because you would be needed for this journey."

Daniel nodded.

Quanah sighed, and lifted his head toward the skies. Daniel saw the moisture in the man's dark eyes. "My father," Quanah said, "told me of the time when The People covered this country like the Tejano cattle do now. And my father said that his father remembered a time when The People outnumbered the buffalo." His head shook and tears began rolling down his cheeks.

"The Pale Eyes did not defeat us with their long knives and cannon. They beat us with The Rotting Face that they spread among us.

"Go." Turning, Quanah wiped away the tears, and stared at the agent and Titus Wheeler. "Return with those as quickly as you can. I will choose the others."

It wasn't quite that easy. By the time the men and women selected to join Colonel Titus Wheeler's amusement had gathered at Fort Sill, the surgeon from the soldier-fort was waiting, chewing on an unlighted cigar and spouting out *taibo* profanities at his ridiculous assignment.

"Smallpox epidemic's breaking out, and here I am making sure I'm sending healthy Indians out to mingle with the masses for a stupid, son-of-a-bitching medicine show run by an ignorant, self-absorbed old Army scout who thinks the world is big enough for two damned Buffalo Bills." The major had called König a Hun, but the little man spoke just like most of the Long Knives Daniel had known.

65

A long-fingered right hand jerked the cigar from the surgeon's mouth. König threw the cigar against a tree. "When one damned Buffalo Bill Cody's too damned many."

He pulled spectacles from the pocket on his white coat, adjusted them over the bridge of his nose and his big ears, and said, "Killstraight. You ready to translate for me?"

Daniel stepped forward. "Yes, sir."

"You've had the pox. I know that. Ask for anyone who has had smallpox to step over to the right." He turned to a pockmarked assistant. "Corporal Canton. You'll check them out. You know what to look for, right?"

"Yes, sir, Major."

"And if you miss something, just remember that you'll have a herd of angry Texicans wanting to pound your face till it's nothing but jelly."

"I understand, Major."

"Don't call me, Major, boy. I'm a *doctor.*"

"Yes . . . *Doctor.*"

Daniel spoke the orders in the language of The People, then signed to the Kiowa, Apiatan—Lone Wolf had refused to go, saying his place was with his people, but had recommended Apiatan. His name translated into Lance, and Daniel knew him as a strong hunter with bow and arrow, a fine rider who wore his hair in braids, who had survived eighteen winters, and whose face remained young, unblemished.

Twice Bent Nose and his wife walked to the Two Stripes assisting the doctor-major, along with the Kwahadi holy man, Red Buffalo. Their faces bore the scars from The Rotting Face from two winters back, during the most recent scourge of the disease taibos had brought to all tribes in the West. The Nokoni woman Tamasual held her head down as she joined the Kwahadis and Kwasinaboo, which meant Rattlesnake—the perfect name for this quick-to-rile Kotsoteka.

Counting Daniel, that made six of those who would be traveling with Colonel Wheeler's show who were, as far as everyone
knew, immune from The Rotting Face.

Half the group. The others—the Kiowa Apiatan; the Penateka
woman Tuhuupi, whose name meant Blackjack Oak; the Nokoni
dancer known as Roadrunner; the Penateka singer, Ecahcueré,
or Woodpecker; Ben Buffalo Bone and his sister, Oajuicauojué—had to pass the doctor-major's examination.

Colonel Wheeler had wanted more Comanche men with
him—so had Athol McLeish. But the Secretary of the Interior
had insisted no more than a dozen, and four of those had to be
women. And all had to be healthy.

"Ask them if any of these have had any interaction with
anyone from the Yamparika band south of here," Doctor-Major
König instructed Daniel. "In the past two weeks."

None had. Well, none said they had. The mistake here, Daniel
thought, was having the doctor of the Long Knives ask this
question. The People would not lie to each other. Lying to a
taibo was a different matter entirely. Daniel decided to correct
this oversight.

When the doctor-major asked the next question, Daniel
started with his own plea. "We must know the truth to all these
questions asked by this Pale Eye." Not that any Kotsoteka might
be interested in anything a Kwahadi had to say these days, but
Red Buffalo repeated Daniel's statement, agreeing with the
urgency and the need for honesty. Red Buffalo might have been
Kwahadi, too, but he had saved many lives among the Kotsotekas, Nokonis, and Penatekas. And had Quanah not insisted that
he travel with this group, Red Buffalo would have been on his
way south, to save as many Penatekas that he could.

Ben Buffalo Bone barked back: "You think we would lie
because we do not agree with much of what Quanah says? You
think we would lie and risk killing more of The People than the

Pale Eyes and The Rotting Face have already killed?" He didn't look at Red Buffalo when he spoke, but his black eyes bore through Daniel. "You lived with the Pale Eyes far too long, Brother. But then you never were truly one of The People. Your mother—"

"No," Red Buffalo said. "This ends. It ends or I will tell the White Coat healer that we all have seen the Penatekas, that we all might have The Rotting Face. That it is our wish to take the sickness to the Tejanos and kill as many of them as they have killed of us. We are all of The People. We shall always be The People. You children need to learn how to be men—and not boys. The People now need men. True men. Now more than ever."

Daniel hung his head. The grass below him blurred.

The wind blew. Horses snorted.

"I am sorry." Ben Buffalo Bone's voice reached Daniel, who shook his head.

"No," he said. "It is I who am sorry. It is I who was wrong."

"You were both wrong," Red Buffalo said. "It is now forgotten."

A long silence held before the doctor-major asked, "Am I interrupting something?"

No answer came.

"Then do you think it's possible for us to get this over with so I can do what I'm paid to do? Save lives. Save white lives, colored lives, red lives? If I can."

König asked the next question. Daniel translated.

And so the medical examinations went, if one wanted to call them examinations. A thermometer placed underneath the tongue. A stethoscope used to make sure the patient's heart still beat. And a cursory examination to make sure no red sores had appeared on the face, hands, forearms.

"Have you felt ill?" the doctor asked each person. "Tired?

Bad pain in your back? Or just overall, not yourself?"

Doctor-Major König cleared every one free to go with Colonel Wheeler.

"My friends," Colonel Titus Wheeler shouted, but he surprised most of his recruits by speaking in the language of The People. "Each of you fine warriors get your best pony. Have your women gather your finest buckskins, which we'll load up on some wagons, and we'll make our way to the train station—you are going to ride on an Iron Horse."

The People looked shocked, but Daniel smiled at Colonel Titus Wheeler, who grinned like a mischievous boy. The colonel had impressed his hirelings by speaking their language, but he had done something else that he didn't realize. He had warned them, too. Now that they realized Wheeler spoke their language, they would be careful of what they said.

The surgeon cleared his throat. "What did you tell them, Wheeler?"

Colonel Titus Wheeler translated, accurately, in his casual dialect.

"No possibles," Doctor-Major König said.

"Doc . . ." Wheeler pleaded.

"Smallpox can be transmitted not only by face-to-face contact, but through infected items. Bedding, clothing . . . that can be contaminated. These people go, but they go without anything else."

"Doc," Wheeler pleaded. "You've already said these ain't sick. Their clothes then—"

"I'm not taking any risks, Wheeler."

"We'll be gone for three months, Doc." The colonel shook his head. "I know injuns ain't much on keepin' clean, but that's a mighty long time to be wearin' the duds they got on."

"They can make their own or you can buy them clothes." Doctor-Major König began walking away. "I'm not even keen on the idea of letting anyone leave the general area, but I have my orders. If it were up to me, I wouldn't even let you off the agency. But nobody here seems to care what a damned doctor has to say about this. Get out of here before I decide all of you are infected with smallpox."

"Damned Hun," Wheeler muttered underneath his breath. He shook his head, cursed again, and called, "You heard the doc, folks. Let's get out of here and put some miles behind us." He repeated the order, truncated but effective, again using The People's tongue.

"Horses?" Ben Buffalo Bone asked. He could not believe The People would be allowed to bring something to ride.

"Damned right. Bring your horses," Wheeler said. "They're part of the show. But just for you bucks. The women'll have to walk."

"Our women," Red Buffalo said. "Will ride. They ride better than any of you."

Wheeler chewed on that a moment, smiled at last, and made his big head bob. "Course. Course they'll ride. But only to El Reno. Not in my show. It'll make the Texans feel insulted, seeing how a Comanche squaw can outride the best cowpuncher there is. But we might need the spare mounts."

He seemed to forget about any setbacks, and grinned. "Folks, y'all be in for a treat. Wait till you see the way Colonel Titus Wheeler tells the story of the West." This time, he spoke in the taibo tongue but used his hands to sign.

"You will be escorted by soldiers to the railroad in El Reno," McLeish said. "That is for your own protection. Word about a smallpox outbreak spreads faster and louder than a beer fart. Lieutenant Lodge will be in command."

Daniel stared as the agent joined the doctor-major and they walked across the parade ground.

He heard soft footfalls behind him and caught the scent of

70

Oajuicauojué. His heart leaped with excitement, and he turned to see her. She smiled, and Daniel forgot about everything for the moment.

Until Oajuicauojué said, "I am happy that you are not sick. I am happy that I am not sick. But I am not sure I want to go."

"You do not have to go," he told her. "Only if you want to go."

"Do you not wish for me to go?" The shine left her eyes.

He wanted to reach for her, but he saw Ben Buffalo Bone glaring a few yards away.

"Of course I wish for you to go. This place will not be safe for . . ." He did not know what else to say.

"Our holy men will help The People," she said.

"As they do always." Daniel tried to make his smile and voice seem reassuring, confident.

"I feared I would be told that I have The Rotting Face," Oajuicauojué whispered.

Now he reached over and touched her face, and did not give a white man's damn what Ben Buffalo Bone thought.

"Your face will always be beautiful," he said.

"Sister! Come! You ride with me. And I leave now!"

Oajuicauojué sighed, but gave Daniel a sheepish grin as he lowered his hand. She turned and hurried to join her big brother.

McLeish started toward the soldier-fort hospital, but stopped, turned, and said, "Corporal Pry, could you spare a few minutes?"

Black Yellow Stripes stifled a yawn, and took a step toward the agent. But Colonel Titus Wheeler stopped him.

"Boy, you know who's payin' you top dollar, don't you?"

The Black White Man stopped, and stared at Wheeler, who was smiling at McLeish.

"Sorry, hoss, but we ain't got no time. We gots to catch a train in El Reno and introduce Texas and then the world to the

71

wonders of the Wild West and the glory of the Comanche Nation. C'mon, Pry. There's work we gots to get done."

"Something troubles your mind, my son."

Daniel turned to find Red Buffalo standing beside him. He must have seen seventy summers by now, though only his face and hair revealed his age. He could still sneak up on a person like a gliding falcon.

"Yes," Daniel said. "My mind is troubled."

The holy man turned briefly toward Oajuicauojué, shook his head, and looked again at Daniel. "But you are not troubled by women." His head shook. "You are too young not to be troubled by pretty women."

Red Buffalo grinned a toothless smile.

Daniel looked at Oajuicauojué, too. "She is worth much trouble," he said.

"What is it that troubles you, my son?"

Daniel breathed in, and out, and turned again to McLeish, who was walking back to the agency.

"What troubles me is that they are letting us leave," he said. "When they should not."

"That troubles me, as well," Red Buffalo said. "I wanted to stay here, to fight The Rotting Face. But Quanah is more often right than he is wrong. And we will be safe, except for all the other sicknesses the Pale Eyes give us." He shook his head, then spit in the dirt.

"Come on!" Wheeler yelled. "All y'all." He then spoke a calmer solicitation in The People's language.

"We must make the Pale Eyes happy," Red Buffalo told Daniel, and he turned. "And we should be happy. For we are well."

Are we? The outbreak of The Rotting Face had just been discovered among the band near the Red River. But Daniel knew that symptoms such as those the doctor-major had asked about—fevers and headaches and back pains—often were not spotted until many days later. And the ugly sores would not first appear until long after that.

CHAPTER EIGHT

Above the snores of Colonel Titus Wheeler, Daniel heard Black Yellow Stripes rise from his bedroll, pull on his boots, and walk to the string of horses. Daniel rolled over on his side and in the moonlight watched the Black White Man grab the bridle of the bluecoat leader Arnold. The man called Pry led the black gelding away, carrying one of those flimsy saddles the Long Knives put on the backs of their ponies.

Black Yellow Stripes had a good eye for horses. The black was the best of any of the Long Knives' mounts, and the old man was smart enough not to steal one of The People's horses. Horse and man walked softly to the south, maybe fifty yards. A few minutes later, just enough time to saddle the black, Daniel heard the horse walking away. Yes, Black Yellow Stripes was smart. Walk the horse first, then kick the gelding into a gallop. Ride fast and hard. Ride away from The Rotting Face.

Daniel did not blame this man for his desertion. He bet most of the Long Knives "guarding" The People and Colonel Titus Wheeler wanted to leave, too.

A few feet away, Red Buffalo laughed. Perhaps the holy man was dreaming, or perhaps he, too, admired Black Yellow Stripes's plan of retreat.

Daniel rolled back over, hands behind his head. He stared at the moon, and closed his eyes. It had to be past midnight. But

74

he did not sleep.

He remembered.

The Wichita Mountains were holy to The People, but the canyons of the Llano Estacado became home to the Kwahadi band.

Pale Eyes found it barren, rough, uninhabitable. The People thought it a beautiful land worth keeping.

Canyons dark as vermilion, with streaks of gypsum and caliche like the white clouds in the blue skies. Junipers, mesquite, and hackberries added green to the country, with cottonwoods shading the creeks. Buffalo could still be found here, along with mule deer and whitetails. The giant herd of horses owned by The People fattened themselves on thick grass, and Daniel— then called Oá, or Horn—loved when the Kwahadis made camp in the caprock. For he could get fat as the horses and buffalo. His friends gorged themselves on wild plums, but none could ever eat as many as Daniel. Not even Boy Who Comes Last To Eat's stomach could hold as many plums as Daniel's.

So, later that day, Daniel told his mother that he must have eaten a bad plum because he did not feel well.

Smiling, she traced the stains of plums along his lips and to his chin with her fingers. "I do not think bad plums grow in these canyons," she said. "Perhaps it is not a bad plum, but too many plums."

He made himself smile. "There is no such thing as too many plums."

"You will feel better after you throw up."

"I do not want to throw up."

"But you will. But you will not do it here. Run to the creek."

His father, He Whose Arrows Fly Straight Into The Hearts Of His Enemies—the name he would give his son two summers later—was sitting nearby, watching, listening, while making arrows. Daniel did not want to run to the creek, but his mother had told him to, and his father's face seemed stern, and Daniel did not wish to feel his father's bow against his backside.

He ran.

Running, he thought later, is what caused him to throw up. His mother must have known that, too.

He washed his face, scrubbed the plum stains off his face, rinsed the foul taste from his mouth, and rolled over to let the sun dry his body. For a while, he thought his mother was right, that vomiting had cured him of his illness, that maybe next time he should not try to eat more plums than any of his friends, especially, Boy Who Comes Last To Eat, whose belly, arms, thighs, and neck suggested that he needed a new name. By the time he returned to his lodge, his head hurt, while no matter where he found shade, he could not cool off.

His mother made him bark tea, and sent him to bed.

But he could not sleep. His mother and father whispered. He tried to hear what they said, but could not. When he woke, Huukumatsumarʉ knelt over him waving a rattle and singing softly.

Dust Off By Hand was young for a holy man, even younger than Daniel's father, but he had healed many Kwahadi women and men. He had protected many men when they went off to steal horses, and four days ago he had told Sit In The Sun that she would bring three Kwahadis into the world—at the same time—which she had. Daniel could hear all three crying right then.

Huukumatsumarʉ lowered the rattle and stopped singing. He smiled. "How many plums did you eat?"

Daniel wanted to return the grin, but his skull seemed to be crushing his brains. It even hurt to swallow, but he could mouth, *Too many.*

"I know," he said. "I tried to find some for my breakfast.

76

They were all gone."

Daniel could not laugh at the holy man's joke. He ached all over.

"I will be back tomorrow," he said. "Sleep. Stay away from plums."

"I want no more plums in my belly."

He closed his eyes, and heard Huukumatsumaɹu walk out of the lodge.

"Let me know," he heard Huukumatsumaɹu tell his parents. "Immediately. If the red spots appear on his face."

His mother gasped.

"Then it is true," his father said, "of what they say of Ekawoni's family."

"It is true. And Puhi Tubi, as well. Ahra is moving his teepee to the top of the bluff. Sit In The Sun's face is almost all red spots. That is why her babies cry."

"What will become of them?" Daniel's mother cried out.

"They will die," Huukumatsumaɹu said. "As will Sit In The Sun."

Sores dotted Daniel's face, hands, and forearms within a few days. Later, he had to sleep on his side because the sores spread to his back. His fever refused to break. He could barely keep down water. Huukumatsumaɹu visited him every morning, though, praying, covering his lesions with a cold salve, shaking that rattle, and singing his healing songs.

By then the sores had turned into blisters, and a stinking, ugly pus leaked when the blisters burst. But one day, Daniel woke to find the holy man smiling, and showing a small stone to Daniel's parents. When Huukumatsumaɹu realized the young Kwahadi was awake, he held the stone close to Daniel. "I have cast out the spirit that made you sick," the man whispered.

"A rock?" Daniel whispered.

"A spirit. A bad one. That I have turned into a pebble. You, my son, will live."

He had awakened every morning to the cries of Sit In The Sun's sons. And the morning he woke and did not hear the wailing, Daniel cried.

"Where is Dust Off By Hand?" Daniel asked when he awaked to find his mother cleaning his sores, humming a song.

"He cannot come." She read the fear in his eyes, and reached down and pushed his sweaty hair off his forehead. "He is well, my son. There are just . . ." Her eyes fell. "Too many sick."

"Mother," he told her. "I do not want to die. I am afraid to go to The Land Beyond The Sun. And I do not want to be afraid."

She leaned forward and kissed his nose, which had avoided the lesions, the pus, the rot.

"Hear me, Oá," she said in a gentle voice. "You will not die. Dust Off By Hand has said so. Remember the spirit he turned into the pebble. You will not die. Not of The Rotting Face. I did not carry you in my body all that time for you to die like this. That is what I told Dust Off By Hand. You will grow up to be an important man among The People. I know this. It was whispered to me by the wind when you decided it was time to be born. Your father will give you his name, and take another. And you will go away from us. That was whispered to me, too. But you will return. And when you return, you will help The People. Perhaps even my first people, the Mescalero. Remember that."

He had forgotten. Till this night when the moon shined and Black Yellow Stripes rode away.

Ekawoni died first. Then Ekawoni's mother. His two wives followed after his three daughters. Sit In The Sun's babies went next. Dust Off By Hand said the mother might have survived, but the loss of her babies broke her will to live. Her husband begged to die, but his wish would not be granted until the Long

Knives killed him at Yellow House Canyon. Ahra survived, though his face was horribly disfigured. He said the wind blew the sickness away because he was a thousand feet higher on the bluff. He would outlive Daniel's father, but not by many years. The Long Knives said he died of something called dysentery at the soldier-fort prison in the faraway place called Florida after Quanah had led the remnants of the Kwahadi band to surrender at Fort Sill. Puhi Tubi lived, too, but mourned for her husband and son, and wandered away from camp that winter during a savage blizzard. By the time her body had been found, the wolves had left nothing of her but scattered bones.

The Rotting Face claimed seven other lives. It would have been more, Quanah said, if not for Dust Off By Hand's powers.

So when the holy man visited Daniel when it was apparent the sickness had waned, and Daniel's life had been spared, Daniel thanked him.

"Do not thank Huukumatsumaru," he said. "For the next time The Rotting Face strikes The People, Huukumatsumaru will have need of you."

"It will not strike us again, will it?" Daniel asked.

"It will not strike Oá," Huukumatsumaru reassured the worried young child. "Oá will never be sickened by The Rotting Face again. That is your blessing, Oá. I have scared away The Rotting Face from you forever. Remember the spirit I made into a stone, a tiny rock I crushed with my heel. But surviving will also be your curse. Because The People will never be done with The Rotting Face. The Pale Eyes have brought this curse to us. And you will feel the curse because you were not taken to The Land Beyond The Sun."

Daniel did not understand, and Dust Off By Hand did not explain. Three years later, when The Rotting Face returned to The People, he learned what the holy man had meant.

For it was Daniel, and Ahra, and others who had survived

the disease who had to bury the dead, and burn their teepees, and kill the best horses for the journey of the dead to The Land Beyond The Sun.

He could not speak their names, but Daniel would always remember them.

Tshuni. Daniel's uncle. Daniel's father chopped off his left pinky finger in mourning. Tshuni's wife slashed her face, and cursed herself for living when The Rotting Face had taken so many others.

Esitoyaabi and all of his family, and Esitoyaabi had many wives and many children.

Beautiful Pasahòo.

Ohapia.

Animui and all of his family.

Kabitsi and his young wife.

Yupusia and his oldest son.

They were the first Daniel would help bury.

He did not sleep that night. He barely closed his eyes. When dawn began to break, he rose, stoked the fire, and waited for the Long Knives to wake, eager to hear their curses when they learned that Black Yellow Stripes had run off. Ben Buffalo Bone joined him, but did not speak until he looked at the string of horses.

"One is missing," he said.

Daniel smiled. "Yes."

Ben Buffalo Bone looked around. His eyes had always been sharp, and he quickly whispered, "The Black White Man is gone." He looked at Daniel. "Did he steal the leader of the Long Knives' pony?"

"He rode away on him," Daniel said.

Ben Buffalo Bone grinned, and Daniel felt a pang, for it had been many years since Ben Buffalo Bone and Daniel had shared such a moment. "This," he said, "will be fun to see."

"Not," Daniel whispered, "for the Long Knives leader."

But it was not to be, because when the troopers began to waken, and Colonel Titus Wheeler had started making his coffee, Black Yellow Stripes rode back into camp.

"Sergeant Pry!" Colonel Wheeler roared. "Where the hell have you been, boy? And what the Sam Hill are you doing on the lieutenant's hoss?"

The lieutenant shot up from underneath his covers. "What?" He climbed to his feet, and tripped over his blanket.

His men tried not to laugh. Twice Bent Nose, Ecahcueré, and Oajuicauojué did not hold back.

The Black White Man swung out of the saddle, and led the gelding to the line, jingling the way taibos often made music with their spurs. He removed the saddle and blanket and began rubbing down the snorting horse.

"Well?" Lieutenant Lodge demanded.

"Beggin' the lieutenant's pardon," Black Yellow Stripes said, "but since the lieutenant did not see any need in posting a sentry, I thought it might be wise to cover our back trail."

"What on earth for?" Lodge shouted.

"Because we're leavin' a smallpox outbreak behind us," the man drawled, then yawned beneath the thick gray beard and mustache that covered his face. "I don't want no sick injuns comin' up behind us. I don't want no angry white folks comin' up after us once they hear that we're leavin' this country for Texas."

"And you take my horse? Without my permission?" Lodge tried to puff up his chest and look like an experienced soldier. "You have horses of your own, former Sergeant Pry."

"Well, Lieutenant Lodge, sir, you went to sleep right early. And I didn't think about this till sorta late. And I also figured that, well, if there was a whole lot of Comanches, or a whole lot of angry white folks, I'd want a hoss that could take me out of harm's way in a heartbeat. Colonel Wheeler's big draft hosses ain't much for gallopin'."

Titus Wheeler almost doubled over laughing. "He's got you good, Lieutenant. Good indeed. That's my boy, there, yes sir. Yes, sir-ree."

"Trooper Briggs," the lieutenant said. "Help Colonel Wheeler get breakfast started. Mister Pry, the next time you think of something on your own, run it past me as I am in command until you and the colonel's troupe are aboard a train for Texas. Is that clear, Mister Pry?"

"Clear as can be, Lieutenant, sir. Clear as can be. I'm gonna give your hoss here a good rubdown. He might be a bit sleepy, sir, and a bit stiff. He ain't used to pullin' nighthawk duty, I reckon."

"He better get me to El Reno, Mister Pry. Or I'll have your ass in the guardhouse."

"Oh, I don't reckon he'll let you down, sir. He's a good hoss."

"How much longer till the coffee is cooked, Colonel?" the lieutenant asked.

"Depends on how strong you want it, son."

Daniel waited, but when he realized no one was going to ask, he cleared his throat and called out, "Any sign that we're being followed?"

Black Yellow Stripes stopped rubbing the cloth over the gelding's neck. He studied Daniel for a moment, then shook his head.

"Probably could've gotten a good night's sleep after all that worryin'. Didn't see much of nothin' except darkness."

"And," Colonel Wheeler shouted, "if we were followed, they couldn't have seen you or that black horse because of darkness."

He slapped his leg as his joke. Some of the soldiers joined

him, but Black Yellow Stripes just kept on rubbing down the gelding.

CHAPTER NINE

The women of The People made breakfast for the men. A soldier cooked for the Long Knives. Colonel Titus Wheeler simply drank coffee, and Black Three Stripes ate beef jerky and sipped coffee by himself.

They had just finished when another bluecoat rode from the south into camp.

Colonel Titus Wheeler tossed out his coffee and stood, grunting as he rose from the ground, and muttered, "If that damned major has changed his mind and plans on makin' us return to Fort Sill, he'll rue the day."

The soldier was a two stripes. Daniel remembered him from the previous day. Canton was his name. He had been helping the doctor-major. He rode extremely well—for a Pale Eye—and pulled hard on the reins, stopping the horse before the circle of Long Knives.

"Lieutenant Lodge, sir!" the horseman said, and snapped off a salute.

"What is it, Corporal?" Lodge did not return the salute, but rose, holding his coffee, waiting.

"Major König ordered me to accompany Mister Wheeler's entourage for the duration of the performances with the Comanches." He slid from the saddle, dropped the reins, stepped forward, and reached inside his blouse. The horse, a wiry sorrel gelding, had been kept at a hard run, so it wouldn't be running off.

Two Stripes withdrew a piece of paper and held it out. "Here are my orders, sir."

Lodge finished his coffee, tossed the empty cup into the grass, and stepped closer. He took the paper, read it, folded it back, and handed it to Corporal Canton.

"I suppose the Hun has his reasons," Lieutenant Lodge muttered.

"He thought it best to send someone with medical experience with the Comanches." Canton returned the paper to the pocket.

One of the Long Knives sniggered. "I've seen prettier nurses."

Another said: "I'd hate to have to be nursemaid to a bunch of prairie—"

"Keep your comments to yourselves," Lodge said. He considered saying something else, but shook his head, and turned around. "All right, let's get these Indians to El Reno so we can return to Fort Sill—and do some real soldiering."

The first soldier who had spoken laughed as he crawled over to pick up the lieutenant's coffee cup. "Ain't been no real soldierin' done since Wounded Knee."

"And we weren't nowhere near that foofaraw," another said.

Red Buffalo called out in the language of The People, and Lieutenant Lodge and the other soldiers looked at him.

Daniel, now standing, translated. "Red Buffalo asks if there has been any change?"

"Nobody's gotten sick, if that's what you mean," Corporal Canton answered. "At least not at Sill. No word from anything at the infected Indian camp. At least not before I left. But I left before daybreak. Had to ride like hell to catch up with you boys."

"You just enjoy nursin' these bucks," a wiry bluecoat with a thick cinnamon mustache said. "Hope you don't come back with holes in your face."

85

"It'd look a damned sight better than yours does now," Canton said, and started for the coffeepot.

That was a mistake, because Cinnamon Mustache stood at the coffeepot. He found a mitt, gripped the handle, and poured the remaining liquid onto the coals.

Most of the soldiers—even a few of The People—laughed, and Canton lunged toward Cinnamon Mustache. "You bastard. You—"

"You asked for it, Corporal," Lieutenant Lodge said. "Leave it be. And thank your lucky stars, Canton." The Long Knives leader looked at Cinnamon Mustache. "You're getting a free pass from the Fort Sill hospital. I'm betting the beds will be full of soldiers and Comanches alike before this is all over."

As the sun rose overhead the following day, Daniel reined in his horse and looked at the taibo town of El Reno. Beside him, Ebicuyonit stopped his pinto, and gasped.

"I have seen the drawings," Ebicuyonit said. "Pale Eyes drawings. But never have I seen a Pale Eye village in person. This is bigger than the soldier-fort."

Daniel looked at the Nokoni in surprise, until he realized that Ebicuyonit had not left his teens, barely too young to remember when The People raided Tejanos and other Pale Eyes, when The People roamed from as far north as what the taibos called Kansas and could follow the trail to annoy the Mexicans.

"Are all Pale Eye villages like this?"

"No." Daniel's head shook with sadness. "This one is small."

"Small?"

"Yes. Fort Worth, to where we travel, is much bigger. As is Dallas to the east of Fort Worth. And those villages are like an anthill compared to where Pale Eyes live in the east." He pointed in that direction. "Philadelphia. Pittsburgh."

"And where the Pale Eyes sent you?"

Daniel shrugged. "It was too big for me. But I hear it has not grown as much as Fort Worth."

"And all these people—they will come to watch us ride horses and act like fools?"

"Not all. But many. I think."

He heard Oajuicauojué's excited shriek, and twisted in the saddle to see her pointing at the thick black smoke. She screamed at her brother, and Ben Buffalo Bone barked for her to stay quiet.

Colonel Titus Wheeler laughed at her as Black Yellow Stripes stopped the wagon. "That's an Iron Horse, little lady," he said. "But not the one we'll be taking. C'mon, children, let's head to the station."

"Iron Horse?" Ebicuyonit asked Daniel.

"It is the name Cheyennes and others call what we call a Fire Wagon," Daniel said.

"Ahhhh." He kicked his horse into a trot.

Daniel sat in the saddle, staring.

He could remember when there was no Fire Wagon in this country. He could remember when there was no El Reno. When there was no soldier-fort here, either. Now he saw a smoking Fire Wagon. Three springs ago, Pale Eyes had arrived. Chaos came with them.

"Lieutenant," the colonel said. "Any time Colonel Titus Wheeler rides into a town, he does so in style. I'd like you boys to form a column of threes. I ain't playin' El Reno, but maybe one of these days I will. You don't mind, do you, Lieutenant? It'll be a good show for the Army, too."

The lieutenant most certainly did mind. Daniel could read that in the young officer's face. But he knew the quicker he obeyed, the quicker he would be shed of Titus Wheeler and his Comanches.

Daniel rode alongside Twice Bent Nose and Huuhwiya, feeling the stares as taibo men, women, and children stopped on the boardwalks, the dirt streets, or peeked out of windows to stare at this . . . circus. The building of two floors, made of red brick—now City Hall—stood where an old warrior, Isa Nanaka, now living in The Land Beyond The Sun, had helped young Oá skin a deer.

El Reno had grown even more in the months since Daniel had last visited. He remembered the First Hotel, but it was now called the Hotel Del Monte. Fancier, Daniel figured, though the building looked old now after just three years. The newspaper, the *El Reno Herald*, remained, but its name had been changed to *The Oklahoma Herald*. He also saw an office for the *Oklahoma Democrat*, where a boy in blue denim and a funny hat stood in front, yelling for people to buy the *Canadian County Courier*, which he carried in a satchel slung over his shoulder.

"Come and get your money," the boy called out. "Read about which of y'all has got script coming. Four bucks. Two bucks. Seventeen dollars and eighty-nine cents. Twenty-four dollars and seventy-two cents. If you don't claim it, they burn it all up in a year!"

When Colonel Titus Wheeler's group reached the west side of town, another boy was screaming:

"Another daring and deliberate train robbery by the notorious Dalton Gang. The Katy's Number Twenty held up at Adair. Cool as cucumbers they were. See who died. See who lived. Read all about the Daltons in the *Globe*."

The teen selling the *Courier* was doing much better business, but Corporal Canton rode over, tossed the *Globe* kid a coin, was handed a paper that he shoved in his pocket, and spurred his horse to catch up with the lieutenant. Once he fell back into line, he dropped his reins over his horse's neck, opened the paper, and began reading.

His horse was trained well enough to follow in line, the way all Long Knives liked to ride. Enough people crowded the narrow streets of El Reno to prevent a horse from spooking and taking off at a gallop.

People stopped to gawk at this parade. Three Long Knives at the head. Next came the carriage driven by Yellow Black Stripes in front, Colonel Wheeler in the back yelling greetings to men and women on the boardwalks, his voice jovial, his words just a little bit slurred.

Then came Lieutenant Lodge, Corporal Canton, and another Long Knife. Daniel rode behind them, still alongside Twice Bent Nose and Huuhwiya.

Daniel continued to study the taibo city. He saw shingles hanging over doors for attorneys and counselors at law. He wondered if there was a difference. He passed a blacksmith shop, and a restaurant that bragged that it was "Best in The City—Everything's Neat, Clean, & Wholesome."

More banks had opened, and there was a big sign over a small building:

**The Great Railway Center
And Future Commercial, Educational and
Manufacturing City of the Southwest is
EL RENO, OKLAHOMA TY.**
**Gateway to the Cheyenne and Arapahoe
Indian Lands
A few Cohice Residence and Business
LOTS FOR SALE**

It took him a moment to figure out that *Cohice* should have read *Choice*.

There was also a sign proclaiming:

BEST DENTIST
IN EL RENO
Open first and third
Tuesdays and Wednesdays
Each Month

"Which depot do we want, Colonel?" one of the soldiers at the front of the column called out when he reached the railroad tracks.

"Not the Rock Island," Titus Wheeler answered from the back of his buggy. "The Choctaw Coal and Railway Company. We'll take her to Oklahoma City, then the Katy into Texas. But that ain't the train—the one that's smoking blacker than the hearts of the most notorious villains I have ever encountered— we're taking. We don't leave till this evenin'."

" 'Smoking blacker than the hearts of the most notorious villains I have ever encountered.' " Corporal Canton shook his head. "He must be reading from one of his blood and thunders."

Daniel reined in his horse at the narrow alley, twisted again, and looked back at El Reno. Three Pale Eye soldiers rode past him without much of a glance, as did Ben Buffalo Bone, Oajuicauojué, and Roadrunner, the Nokoni dancer. Cinnamon Mustache, a taibo too fat to be much of a Long Knife, and another pony soldier with a cheek filled with tobacco, trailed the last of The People, Ecahcueré and Red Buffalo, and the Kiowa Apiatan.

The Kwahadi holy man stopped his horse. Apiatan and Ecahcueré kept their horses at a walk.

Cinnamon Mustache glared as he reined up, and his two comrades also stopped, putting their right hands on the stocks of their carbines. He opened his mouth and started to growl, but his gelding decided to take advantage of the break and began urinating in the street.

The Long Knives with him laughed. A taibo woman in a pink

dress and carrying a white umbrella that did not look like it would do any good during a rainstorm drew in a long breath and said, "How disgusting," before disappearing into a dressmaker's shop. That left Cinnamon Mustache's companions giggling like schoolchildren.

"Shut up," Cinnamon Mustache said.

"What are you thinking?" Red Buffalo asked Daniel.

Daniel exhaled slowly before he looked at the old Kwahadi. "I think this," Daniel said softly. "Is what I see here on this day what I will soon see in The People's country?"

"You two bucks keep movin'," Cinnamon Mustache ordered. His horse had finished its business.

Ignoring the ugly taibo, Daniel glanced at Red Buffalo, but the sadness in the old man's eyes made Daniel wish he had not revealed his thoughts to the holy man. Sighing, he turned his horse around and followed the rails to the Fire Wagon.

CHAPTER TEN

Corporal Canton wadded up the *Globe* and threw it on the platform of the Choctaw Coal and Railway Company depot. "There isn't one word about anyone dying in that train holdup. There's not even one word about anyone getting shot."

"Good salesman." Colonel Titus Wheeler turned from the open window and laughed. "I ought to sign him up as a barker for my Texas tour." Then he turned back and talked to the man behind the window.

Two men whose skin color matched that of Black Yellow Stripes walked out of a cattle pen and spoke to Lieutenant Lodge, who nodded and called out to Corporal Canton.

"Canton, we'll be taking your horse with us back to Fort Sill." For the first time, the leader of these Long Knives seemed happy. "The Indian ponies are to be put in this cattle pen till the next train is ready for loading."

"And Colonel Wheeler's team, sir?" Canton stepped off the platform, loosened the reins, and walked them to the nearest mounted trooper, who took the leather.

"The colonel is not my concern. Just Army property. Our mission here is done."

"You're not going to wait to make sure we get off, sir?"

"That was not in my orders. My orders were to get Colonel Wheeler and his bucks and bitches here, and they are here. I guess that leaves you in command, Corporal." He laughed.

"Lieutenant," Canton said, his face paling. "I'm a hospital

orderly. I'm—"

"In charge. Hope you enjoy the theater, Corporal."

"Mount up!" Lodge yelled, and stepped to his horse, put a boot in the stirrup, and swung into the saddle. "Colonel Wheeler!"

Once again, the showman turned away from the ticket window.

"I wish you luck, Colonel."

Titus Wheeler seemed to have lost his voice. He just stared as Lieutenant Lodge trotted his horse to the street, waited for his men to fall into a column of twos, and then led them at a trot out of El Reno. But he quickly regained his composure.

"Well, Canton, it looks like it's just you and me and my boy yonder." He nodded at Black Yellow Stripes. "And a couple of handfuls of the most notorious injuns these United States have ever known." He laughed, found a cigar, started to light it with a match, but withdrew the Havana and laughed again.

"And I've always heard, and known for a number of years, that just one Comanch is a handful."

The Choctaw Coal and Railway Company engine was a 4-6-0 model, one that had seen many years on the rails. As it pulled away from the depot, churning out huge clouds of black smoke, the ponies in the pen began stamping their hooves, rearing, running around their square prison.

Ecahcueré climbed to the top and began singing to try to soothe the animals' fears. Quanah was right. Ecahcueré had a fine voice. Huuhwiya joined him. The man who had been sitting behind the window stepped out and listened to the singers, and Daniel leaned forward and looked down the street. No one else in El Reno paid any attention. Perhaps they could not hear the song or the horses because of the clanging, belching, and groaning the Baldwin locomotive made as it eased its cars eastbound.

When the noise of the train faded, the horses settled down, and the songs ceased, Man Who Sits Behind The Window did not return to his place. He walked to the unhitched carriage where Colonel Titus Wheeler sat, eating fried chicken from Best in The City—Everything's Neat, Clean, & Wholesome.

"Are those redskins going to sit there all day?" the railroad man asked.

Daniel watched Colonel Titus Wheeler toss a chicken bone toward the trash bin at the corner of the platform. He wiped his fingers on his trouser legs, turned, and looked down at the little man with no hair on the top of his head and spectacles.

"The eastbound leaves at five-oh-eight," Wheeler told him. "Providin' your fine railroad runs on time." The colonel pulled out his watch, studied it for a minute, and slipped the Elgin back into its pocket. "Which your first train, alas, did not. But only twenty-two minutes late. Not bad, I guess. I've seen railroads run later. But even if we leave here forty-four minutes late, those Comanches will not be sittin' here all day. Just five, six hours or thereabouts."

"They're scaring away customers," Man Who Sits Behind The Window said, not bothering to lower his voice.

"Sir," the colonel said. "The only train runnin' east-west out of El Reno is your fine Choctaw Coal and Railway Company. The Chicago, Rock Island, and Pacific Railroad runs north-south, but not into Texas—yet. And Texas is where I—and my loyal Comanche subjects—are bound. Therefore, I believe you have a monopoly on anyone wishin' to travel to Oklahoma City. Good day, kind sir. If you will let me enjoy my dinner in peace, I will gladly autograph a copy of *Killstraight, the Magnificent Comanche: Or, Perils in the Indian Territory.* A twenty-five-cent masterpiece that I will let you have for eight bits."

Man Who Sits Behind the Window bristled, turned on his heel, and hurried to the steps.

94

Daniel laughed underneath his breath.

Twice Bent Nose leaned over and whispered, "What did they talk about?"

"Us," Daniel answered.

"That much I knew," his friend said.

"It is nothing we have not heard before when we rode as Metal Shirts," Daniel said. "And had to take our friends to the iron cages in the Pale Eye villages."

Twice Bent Nose grunted.

"Sometimes, I do not know what to think of . . ." Daniel had to think of the name The People had given Colonel Titus Wheeler. "Man Whose Mouth Is Bigger Than His Belly."

Twice Bent Nose waited.

Daniel shrugged as in explanation. "Sometimes I think he is a fool. But then there are times when I cannot help but like him."

Twice Bent Nose stared at Daniel, yawned, and turned to talk to the Kiowa Apiatan.

So The People and the Kiowa and Black Yellow Stripes sat in the dirt, some in front of the pen that held their horses, others against the wooden bottoms of the platform where the Fire Wagons came. Black Yellow Stripes sat cross-legged away from them all, playing the game Daniel had seen Pale Eyes spend hours at.

The Kiowa asked, "What is that the Black White Man does?"

"It," Daniel explained, "is a game that is called . . . *chess.*" There was no word for this game in Nermernuh.

"Who does he play against?" Apiatan asked in the singsong cadence of the Kiowas.

"He plays himself."

"Why?" Apiatan asked.

"Because when he loses," Twice Bent Nose said, and paused just long enough to stop grinning, "he also wins."

Daniel laughed. Apiatan shook his head, stood, and walked to the pen holding the horses.

The singing wires at the other end of the depot began causing the clacking. The old man who made the wires talk, and understood what the wires said, hurried out the side door when the singing died down. He yelled something at Man Who Sits Behind The Window, waving a yellow piece of paper at him. His feet bounded down the steps of the platform like a much younger taibo. He crossed the Fire Wagon Road and disappeared behind a brick building.

Titus Wheeler stepped down from his shady seat in his carriage, and climbed up the steps to the edge of the platform. "What has Clarence in such a fit?" he yelled at Man Who Sits Behind The Window.

The answer came quickly. "I will gladly tell you . . . for eight bits."

The colonel laughed. "*Touché,* my good man." He went down the steps, shaking his head, and returned to his seat in the carriage.

Long afterward, the old man returned. But he no longer ran. And he was not alone.

Those sitting against the loading pens saw them first. Ben Buffalo Bone jumped to his feet, and opened the gate. He yelled for the women to get inside, and when they had, he closed the gate behind them.

By that time, everyone had risen. Black Yellow Stripes yelled that the colonel had visitors, and then he inched his way back to the edge of the platform. Cursing, Colonel Wheeler stepped out of the buggy again, but he stopped and stared.

Daniel watched him wipe his mouth. He saw the Adam's apple bob, and the colonel reached inside the carriage, found his hat, and put it on his head as he walked toward the visitors who had not crossed the lane that separated the depot from the nearest buildings.

"What do they want?" Twice Bent Nose asked.

Daniel's head shook. "I do not know." But he could guess.

He counted twelve men, including the old man who understood the singing wires. Three of them wore gleaming stars with six points on their vests. Two of those carried shotguns. The biggest one, with a thick beard the color of mud, stood beside the old man. This one had to be their leader, for he wore the finest clothes among the dozen, a large hat the color of a summertime cloud, a black tie, black boots that came up to his knees. He carried no shotgun, but his right hand rested on the handle of a shining revolver holstered on his right hip. His left hand held the yellow paper that the old man had carried from the far corner of the building on the platform.

"Marshal," Titus Wheeler said jovially, though his eyes betrayed his voice. "I didn't know the turkey shoot was today."

Without turning away from the group of men, Wheeler spoke to Daniel in a whisper, using the language of The People, his voice serious for once. "Tell this to your men, Daniel. You need to just stand like you are standing now. Do not make any sudden moves. Do not run. Don't say a word. Let me figure out what has these fools riled up."

"What's that you're telling your injuns, Wheeler?" the marshal demanded.

"To keep the peace, Marshal," Colonel Wheeler said. "Unless you'd like me to tell 'em somethin' else." The joviality had vanished.

Daniel repeated the colonel's instructions, and signed the message to the Kiowa.

"You've brought the smallpox to El Reno, you stupid son of a bitch," the marshal said. The shotguns had been held loosely. Now the three men brought them up.

"Easy," Wheeler said in English. "Daniel, you boys just keep your wits."

Daniel's guess had been right, but there was no triumph in that.

"Corporal Canton," Wheeler said. "Tell these righteous citizens about the medical examinations performed on my injun friends yesterday."

A curse from the marshal cut short Canton's words. "I've got a telegram here, Wheeler, that says Comanches are infected all to hell. And these bucks sure look like Comanch to me."

"Healthy Comanches, Marshal," Wheeler tried.

"Yeah. And here's a story for you. Something I read in a newspaper. Up in Idaho. Place called Nampa. A bunch of Japanese railroad workers come down with smallpox. And you know what the citizens there done? They run a hundred and fifty of them Japs out of the camp. Chased them into the mountains. Before any decent white folks got sick. Well, we're doing the same thing here. I've read what the pox can do to a town, and I've seen a couple of cases of it before. What I ain't gonna see is smallpox wipe out this town."

"You could inoculate yourself," Corporal Canton said. "Get everyone in El Reno vaccinated."

The marshal laughed, and spit in the street, and Colonel Wheeler turned slowly, looked up at the doctor-soldier on the platform, and said, "You ain't rightly helpin' us here, Canton, talkin' like that."

"Yeah, soldier boy," the marshal said. "You ain't helping at all. Give myself the smallpox. Do I look like a damned fool?"

"Yes," Canton said. "You do."

Wheeler sucked in his breath.

"Colonel Wheeler," Canton said, "and these Indians have permission to travel off the Kiowa, Comanche, and Apache Reservation. As do I." He reached inside his coat and withdrew the paper. "Permission granted by Agent Athol McLeish, acting post commander Major Harry F. Martin. Not to mention Secretary of War Elkins and Secretary of the Interior John W. Noble. And, I might add, endorsed by President Benjamin Harrison."

"Guess what, Yank," the lawman said. "I didn't vote for that blackhearted Republican."

"It doesn't matter. If you interfere with the United States Army, and these Indians who have been granted permission to travel with Colonel Wheeler, you will feel the wrath of the military and the weight of Washington City. Oklahoma is still a territory, sir. Under federal control. And every one of these Indians passed a medical examination. They show no signs of any illness. Not even a head cold."

Daniel felt himself breathing again.

Colonel Titus Wheeler's shoulders straightened and he smiled at the lawman. "Marshal, I've got a few bucks and squaws. We're takin' the eastbound in a few hours. Be out of your hair. I know a bit about smallpox, too, and not from readin' some malarkey a'bout Jap railroad workers in Idaho. We're just sittin' here, waitin' on a train. Now it's gettin' near *siesta* time. I'd like to take my nap. If it makes you feel better, leave a couple of your boys with their scatterguns here on that side of the street. The train'll come. We'll get on 'er, and we'll be gone like yesterday's clouds. Or you can try to turn this into El Reno's very own Wounded Knee. And then we'll all be dead. And you soon will be. Because these here are friendly Comanch." He snapped his fingers, turned to Apiatan, gestured with a smile, and added. "And a Kiowa."

The grin vanished. "You kill us, and Quanah will lead his Comanches and Lone Wolf will grab his Kiowas, and you'll end almost twenty years of peace here. And there won't be nothin' left of El Reno but two railroad tracks, ashes, and bones."

In the end, the marshal left the three men with shotguns. They stayed on their side. The rest of the men hurried back to the main part of town.

Eventually, Ben Buffalo Bone opened the gate, and the four women came out. Black Yellow Stripes lighted his pipe. Daniel and the others settled down to sit and wait.

And Colonel Titus Wheeler held his hand up toward Corporal Canton.

"What's your Christian name, Corporal? I want to know the man I'm thankin' for my business, my reputation, and my life."

"Tobias," the man said. "But most folks call me Toby."

"Toby Canton," Wheeler said. "I'm gonna have my press man make you a hero in my next literary masterpiece."

CHAPTER ELEVEN

The Choctaw Coal and Railway Company locomotive arrived at the time it was scheduled to leave. Two brave taibos with shotguns crossed the street, stepped up to the platform, and met the four passengers—two drummers, by the looks of them; a red-haired woman in a green dress; and a mustached man in a cornered sack suit and tan fedora.

Daniel and the others had left the bottom of the platform to the shipping pens, to lead their horses to the livestock car when the train was ready. Over the hissing of the Fire Wagon and the excited talk among The People, Daniel could not hear what one of the shotgun men told the passengers and the black-hatted conductor. He didn't have to.

The woman covered her mouth, and one of the drummers covered his mouth and nose with a handkerchief. The guards led the passengers off the boardwalk. Two porters helped with the luggage, and they got away from the depot as fast as they could.

As the engine pulled ahead into the brick roundhouse, the conductor talked to Man Who Sits Behind The Window and the old man who understood the singing wires, and Daniel stopped Ben Buffalo Bone from opening the gate.

"It will take a while before they are ready to load our ponies," Daniel explained. "Let them breathe fresh air instead of smoke for as long as they can."

To Daniel's surprise, Ben Buffalo Bone made no argument.

He turned, stared hard, and said, "Fine." Then he opened the gate anyway, but only slightly, slid inside, and pulled it beside him. "I would rather stay with horses and fill my lungs with their scent than the stink of the Fire Wagon."

"Colonel Wheeler."

Daniel turned to see the conductor, still by the window in the depot building, waving at the carriage. The colonel leaned out, and looked up.

"A moment of your time, Colonel," the conductor said.

"Of course, my good man, of course," and Titus Wheeler climbed out of the carriage, slapping his hat against his britches as he walked to the steps, waving good-naturedly at Daniel and the others, and then climbed up to the platform and pulled the hat on his head.

The conductor stared at Daniel and the others, opened the door, and held it open for Colonel Titus Wheeler to enter. The door closed behind the showman. Daniel kept looking at the building.

"What do they talk about?"

Oajuicauojué's voice surprised Daniel. He turned quickly, saw her smiling up at him, and he realized what a favor Ben Buffalo Bone had done by opting to stay inside the loading chute with the horses. So did Oajuicauojué. She started to walk down the pens, toward the roundhouse, though she stopped at the end of the wooden pens.

A giant longhorn bawled from the last pen.

"Are these part of our show?" she asked.

Daniel did not think so. Cattle could be found by the scores in Texas. "No," he said. "It is not likely. They ship cattle on the railroads."

"With us?"

"No. Most often, they have Fire Wagons that bring people, and Fire Wagons that bring cattle and supplies."

"But they will let us bring our ponies?"

"Yes." He pointed. "That is an express car. It carries the mail. Sometimes much money." He pointed again. "That is the caboose." He had to use the English word.

Oajuicauojué giggled. "That is a funny word."

Daniel smiled. He started to forget about The Rotting Face, Ben Buffalo Bone, and the feuding between The People.

"When you went to the boarding school, you did not travel on the Fire Wagon?" Daniel asked.

Her head shook. "Wagon and mules. But where I went, in Kan-sas, it was not as far as where they sent you."

"That is true," he said.

"Does the Fire Wagon travel fast as they say?" Oajuicauojué asked.

"It is fast, yes. It rocks. It is easy to sleep on these things. The rocking, the noise the iron wheels make. You fall asleep. And they wake you up when they have reached the place where you must get off. Sometimes, they have cars where passengers can sleep in little beds." He frowned. "Those cost extra though. I never slept in one of those beds."

"You and Quanah are the only ones among The People that I know who have traveled on Fire Wagon," she said.

She smiled at him. He just focused on Oajuicauojué.

But such pleasures, Daniel had observed over the years, never lasted long.

"Daniel, ol' pard," Titus Wheeler called. The big man was beckoning with that enormous hat of his. "A moment of your time, *amigo.*"

Wheeler and the conductor had left the office, and stood near the center of the platform.

A taibo curse slipped off Daniel's tongue, causing Oajuicauojué to giggle. He stared into her dark eyes, and made himself smile. "Girls of The People should not know the meaning of such words," he said.

"Boys of The People should not use such words," she told him. "It is what the master and the teachers at Prairie Light often said. Did your master and teachers also say that at . . . Carlisle?"

"They did," Daniel said, but did not tell her that the teachers there sometimes had harsher methods than scolding.

He walked her back to where the other women sat staring at the activity going on outside the brick roundhouse. Twice Bent Nose and Kwasinaboo passed a cigarette between them. Black Yellow Stripes smoked a cigar as he sat at the foot of the wooden steps. He did not look at Daniel, just stared across the path at The People standing in front of the pens.

Once Daniel had climbed the steps, he read Colonel Titus Wheeler's face and realized that the scowling conductor had given him unpleasant news.

"Daniel . . ." The colonel shook his big head.

Steeling himself for the worst of news, Daniel waited. Titus Wheeler shot an angry glance at the conductor, shook his head, and must have seen the look in Daniel's eyes.

"It ain't nothin' from down on the reservation, son. Not at all. Nothin' that grim, but . . ." He turned back and spoke to the conductor. "It's damned annoyin' and uncivilized and repugnant."

The conductor's scowl did not change.

Wheeler turned back to face Daniel. "Son." He put his hat on his head. "I promise you this. I have my own set of rollin' stock waitin' for us in Texas. Bought and paid for by me . . . well, businessmen who have invested in my show. You know, men who got too much money, men who are richer than God." He turned back to the conductor. "And a whole lot holier than these sons of bitches that run or work for the Choctaw Coal and Railway Company."

"Go to hell, Colonel," the conductor said. "This is not my idea. I have orders." He waved one of those yellow sheets of paper at Wheeler.

"Yeah. At least I was man enough not to obey plenty of orders I was given." His face relaxed, and he put his arm over Daniel's shoulder and turned him away from the conductor.

"Maybe it ain't this gent's fault," the colonel whispered. "Maybe he is just followin' his instructions, his orders. Don't rightly matter. But this son of a bitch won't let Indians ride in the passenger cars. You and the others will have to ride in the stock car."

Daniel felt the pain he knew would hit Oajuicauojué when she learned this. He saw her excited face when he had told her about sleeping cars and the songs the wheels made that put one to sleep. He caught the scent of tobacco, and looked down to find Black Yellow Stripes still sitting, his back against the wood, legs crossed at the ankles, one elbow on the steps.

"Once we get to Fort Worth, you got my word, son. My word of honor." Wheeler shook his head again. "You and your squaws and your braves will be in a car just like me and my white players. Even got Pullman sleepers." He withdrew the arm. "Maybe, there's a chance anyway, that once we get to Texas and change trains in Dallas, they might let you ride with us. But I promise you, son, you won't be treated like dirt when we get to Fort Worth. And for the rest of my tour. Whenever we're on my train, you'll be treated like kings and queens, princes and princesses."

Daniel turned to the conductor. "Do you know where you are, sir?" he asked.

The man moved his lips, wondering if he should answer.

"Well, do you?" Wheeler roared. "What's the matter? Cat got your tongue? You wasn't so damned silent when you was tellin' me all about those damned orders you got. Askin' me to tell my injuns. Well, answer him, damn you. Do you know where you are?"

"I'm in El Reno," the man bit back.

Wheeler nodded. "Yes. In old *Indian* Territory."

The conductor looked at his city shoes, slid the yellow telegram into his pants pocket, and turned away. "Like I say, this isn't my idea." He started walking toward the open door to the depot. "Company policy. That's all."

"I am sorry about this," Colonel Wheeler said again after the conductor disappeared inside the building. "Truly. I am."

Daniel was not aware if he nodded his head or even verbalized an answer to the colonel.

"Can you, Danny, explain this to your injun pards?" Titus Wheeler no longer sounded like the big hero, the blowhard and champion. His voice reminded Daniel of a frightened child.

"I will tell them," Daniel said.

"Colonel, what about me?"

The voice came from below, and Daniel looked down toward the steps, saw Black Yellow Stripes pulling himself to his feet, tossing the last bit of his cigar to the ground, and crushing it out with his boot. He slapped his weathered hat on his trousers, pulled it on his head, and put his hands on his hips. "I ride with the hosses, too, Colonel? Or in the baggage car?"

Colonel Titus Wheeler stared at the old buffalo soldier for at least half a minute. The clanging and screeching and grinding became louder in the brick roundhouse, and Daniel noticed that the shotgun-carrying taibos had returned from escorting the passengers on the westbound train to wherever they needed to go. He wondered how long they would have to wait until they loaded their horses, and then themselves, into one of the stock cars. At least it wasn't cold. And no dark clouds threatened. There was a roof over the top of the stock cars, but the walls were picketed like the white fence surrounding Agent

106

Athol McLeish's house behind the agency building. A hard rain would soak all of those inside a stock car, and hard rains were common in Indian Territory this time of year.

"You ride in the smokin' car, Virgil. Like always." He walked to the steps, down them, and said, "I'll be in that saloon a few doors down. Fetch me when the train's loadin'."

But Colonel Titus Wheeler did not get close to the saloon. The three shotgun men aimed their weapons at him. The biggest of the three said: "You can get back there with your redskins and your darky, or you can go to hell in a hurry with a belly full of buckshot. What'll it be, Colonel Titus Wheeler?"

The colonel did not answer, but he turned around and came back up the steps, where he pulled out paper and pencil from his coat and began scribbling.

"Well, somethin' good has come out of this day of nothin' but gettin' shat and pissed on." He spoke as he wrote, 'Get back across this street or get sent to . . . Hades . . . in a hurry with a belly full of buckshot.' " He smiled, returned pencil and paper to his coat pocket, then looked at Daniel and said, "I'll have Billy put this in my next Killstraight masterpiece. "Hades in a hurry. Belly full of buckshot. Great alliteration."

Daniel did not smile. Nor did Black Yellow Stripes below. When he reached the pens, Ben Buffalo Bone had slipped out and closed the gate.

"How much longer till we leave?" he demanded.

"I do not know," Daniel said. He realized all of The People and the lone Kiowa were looking at him. He recognized the concern in Oajuicauojué's eyes, and hated to disappoint her. He hoped that Colonel Wheeler was not lying to him, that The People and Apiatan would be treated as human beings, not livestock, when they reached Fort Worth and the colonel's fancy train. He looked at Ben Buffalo Bone.

"We will be traveling with our ponies." Daniel had to shout

107

above the pounding of the taibo machines in the brick roundhouse. "That is what The Man Who Runs The Train told the colonel. We will be in the cars that carry the horses. At least until we reach Fort Worth. Then the colonel says we will have our own car." He looked at Oajuicauojué. "And another car in which we shall sleep."

Some of the men spoke in anger. The women, even Oajuicauojué, seemed to have expected this.

"As I have said before." Ben Buffalo Bone opened the gate, and pulled it behind him as the horses of The People, frightened by the unnatural sounds of El Reno and the railroad machines, snorted, whinnied, and stamped hooves. "I prefer the company of horses than that of any Pale Eye."

The Choctaw Coal and Railway Company train pulled out of El Reno at six-thirty-one. For most of The People, traveling in a stock car with good horses was fine. The women sang songs. Ebicuyonit danced. The men laughed, smoked pipes, and tended to their horses.

Roughly two hours later, they pulled up to a depot in Oklahoma City, rode their horses in the darkness to another depot, found a pen for their horses, and slept on the ground till dawn.

The women cooked breakfast, and Colonel Titus Wheeler brought them "bear sign," the sugary snack most taibos called doughnuts. At first, the women were angry at the colonel and the men because the men loved eating "bear sign" more than what the women had cooked. Their anger vanished, replaced with laughter, when they saw the whiteness left on the lips and chins of the men. And when the women tasted the "bear sign," they understood why the men had been so pleased. This time, the men pointed and slapped their thighs, and laughed at the white powder that covered the women's fingertips, and their lips, chins, cheeks, and even the tip of Oajuicauojué's nose.

So they boarded the livestock car of the southbound Katy in the middle of the morning, and sang to their horses as the Fire Wagon slowly pulled out of Oklahoma City. This trip lasted much longer, and their full bellies and the clacking of the wheels put most to sleep.

Kwasinaboo, the hotheaded Kotsoteka, woke and complained that the "bear sign" had poisoned him, that the taibos had tricked them and that they all would die.

Red Buffalo smiled. "Perhaps you ate too many."

"You laugh at me now. But you won't laugh . . ." Kwasinaboo did not finish. He sprayed the hay with a chunky liquid that resembled coffee and "bear sign." But he felt better afterward. He even joined Ecahcueré in a song.

"What are you thinking?" Red Buffalo asked Daniel a long while later.

Daniel sat with his back against the west side of the livestock car, a blanket covering his legs, his fingers locked behind his head. He kept watching the women across from him, although horses moved around, forcing him to tilt his head one way or the other to see them underneath the bellies of the ponies.

"I think that if The People laugh now," Daniel answered. "Then perhaps this trip will be worthwhile."

"It is so." Red Buffalo nodded.

That was all Daniel remembered. The rhythmic rocking of the Fire Wagon made him close his eyes. When they opened, the sun was behind him, the smoke stung his eyes, and he turned and stared through the slatted wall.

The plains, so green and vast, raced past him, and he saw hundreds of taibo cattle—longhorns, yes, but also fatter cows with shorter horns, and some with no horns at all.

Red Buffalo was looking at the great herds, too. Without looking away from the pastures, he asked, "What are you thinking, my son?"

"I have no thoughts," Daniel answered. He smiled. "I just woke up."

Red Buffalo's laugh did not last long.

"What does Red Buffalo think?"

The old man shook his head. "I have no thoughts, either. I just remember. I remember a time, not that long ago, when this prairie was covered not with the long-horned, miserable-looking cattle of the Pale Eyes. But with buffalo. Nothing from here to there but buffalo."

He sighed, turned around, and looked at the horses and the sleeping women, and Ben Buffalo Bone, smoking a taibo cigarette with the Kiowa.

"There was buffalo. And there were The People. And it was good. And I, a young man, thought that this was how it would always be."

Smiling, he turned his creased face at Daniel. "And I am not that old, my son. I had seen The Rotting Face. I knew, the old ones knew, we all knew that the Pale Eyes were coming and would keep coming. That they outnumbered the sprigs of grass. I was young enough then to think that The People could beat them, would beat them."

He sighed, shook his head.

"Nothing lasts forever," he told Daniel. "Perhaps, not even The People."

CHAPTER TWELVE

The Katy pulled into Dallas before dusk. The Fire Wagon had traveled more than two hundred miles from early in the morning to before the sun set. The Pale Eyes had much power to create such things. A taibo on a horse could travel two hundred miles in four days. One of The People . . . make that two days.

Daniel smiled at that thought, stepped out of the car when a Black White Man opened the door. Daniel stiffly walked, his smile fading, to where Colonel Titus Wheeler stood barking orders.

"Where's Billy?" the colonel barked at a man in a tan suit and straw hat.

The man looked one way, then the other, turned and stared behind him, and shook his head and faced Titus Wheeler again. "He's around here somewhere."

"What track are we on?"

"The T&P," the man answered. "Billy's already greased the wheels, you know, in Fort Worth. And he's lined everything up with Albany."

"Albany!" Wheeler roared. "That burg sprang up not too far from my ol' stampin' grounds. Near Fort Griffin. Wasn't you stationed there at one point, Virg?"

Black Yellow Stripes turned toward the colonel, but Wheeler had seen Daniel now, and the showman painted on that thick smile.

"Danny, lad, good to see you, son. We're gettin' the train . . .

my train, by thunder, that plays by my rules . . . ready to take us to Fort Worth, for a three-week engagement. The Texas and Pacific. Good train. We'll be in Panther City before dark. How does that suit you, son?"

Daniel stopped. "Have you telegraphed Fort Sill?"

"Fort Sill? What on earth for?" He turned and thrust a thick finger at the man in the tan suit and straw hat. "Dan'l, this is Ivy Inman. My two *eyes.*" He slapped his hand on his thigh. Ivy Inman smiled the smile of a man who has heard this joke far too many times.

"Ivy . . . this here is the one and the original Daniel Killstraight."

Ivy Inman studied Daniel curiously. "He's shrunk a bit," he said, "and put on some weight around his paunch."

"Ain't we all, Ivy." Colonel Wheeler tapped his own large gut. "Ain't we all. Now—"

"I would like for you to telegraph Fort Sill," Daniel said. "And let us know how The People are doing. If the sickness has spread."

Ivy Inman's two eyes turned and bore hard down on Colonel Titus Wheeler.

"Sickness?" the man said.

"Oh, not much of anything. Colds. Maybe influenza. You know. But, Danny boy is right." Wheeler put his arm around Daniel and steered him to the nearest telegraph office. The big man looked over his shoulder and called out, "I'll fill you in on everything after I take care of the star of my novels and these upcomin' shows, Ivy. Meanwhile, find Billy Kyne. Have him find me. If I ain't in the telegraph station at the corner up yonder, I'll be with Danny in that beer garden on Pearl Street. Or I'll meet you at the T&P depot. What time do we leave?"

A train whistled drowned out Ivy Inman's answer.

★　★　★　★　★

"How long do you reckon it'll take to get a reply?" Wheeler asked the telegraph operator.

The bespectacled man counted out the coins and slid the change across the counter. "No telling," he said. He read back the message the colonel had dictated. *KONIG FT SILL HOSPITAL ARRIVED DALLAS SAFE HOW FARE INDIANS QUICK ANSWER PLEASE REPLY HERE OR HOTEL CHRISTLIEB FT WORTH.*

"That it?"

Wheeler looked at Daniel, whose face showed nothing. "That's it, my good man," Wheeler said, though without much of the accent or any of the usual enthusiasm.

"Something wrong up in the Indian Territory?" the telegrapher asked.

"No," Wheeler said, laughing. "The boy's . . . wife." He slapped Daniel's shoulder hard. "She's in the family way. You know how first-time daddies get."

"Not at all, mister. I never married."

"A wise choice, sir."

It cost Wheeler a five-dollar note to get Daniel into the Pearl Street Beer Garden, and they were seated in the remotest corner, and the owner came over and said, "If this buck causes any commotion, Wheeler, I'll sue you for damages."

"This buck, Mullins," Wheeler said, "is Daniel Killstraight, hero of my most popular prose. He'll have coffee. I'll have the tallest pour of pilsner."

The man looked down at Daniel. "How you want your coffee?"

"Black," Daniel answered.

The man snorted. "Funny. I figured you'd want it red."

"Ever been to Dallas before, Danny boy?" Wheeler asked.

113

"Yes."

"Keeps growing," Wheeler said just to fill seconds. "Tried to get a show here, but when the city council realized I was showin' in Fort Worth first, they blackballed me, said it would not happen, that Dallas would never hold a show that performed first in the Panther City." The beer and the coffee arrived. Wheeler paid the man, and lifted his stein in cheer. "That's a rivalry for you. Cities can be worse than cousins."

Daniel stared at his coffee.

"Don't matter. San Antonio's a better place for my Wild West. And Austin'll be just crackerjack. Might even get the governor to come down. Bet he'd enjoy ridin' in a stagecoach that gets attacked by Comanches till Colonel Titus Wheeler and Rabid Wolf Jones ride to the rescue."

The colonel had finished half of his pilsner.

"Daniel."

He looked at the colonel. "You worry too much." Titus Wheeler pointed at the pockmarks on the left side of his face. "See these."

They were different from the pocks that scarred Daniel's face. Not as many. Some smaller, but a few larger. Chicken pox, Daniel knew, not The Rotting Face. But he did not correct the colonel's lie. "That Hun's a good doctor. And I know we've got a good medicine man in Corporal Canton."

"Why did not you tell the telegrapher and your associate Inman . . . ?" He stopped, changed his question. "Why did you not tell the telegrapher or your associate about . . . ?"

The colonel raised his free hand and tensed. Daniel did not finish the question. He didn't have to. Wheeler leaned forward and whispered, "Because you've seen a buffalo stampede, I'm bettin'. You know what kind of damage that can do." He lowered his voice even more. "Smallpox. That'll cause more carnage than even a thousand chargin' shaggies. You know that's the

114

truth." He sipped his beer. "We get through the Fort Worth show, I think everything'll be fine. We'll see what else Kyne has lined up for us. And I promise." Another sip. "I promise you, Danny, that as soon as I hear from Fort Sill, I'll share the news—good or bad—with you."

"Kyne." Daniel tested the name.

"Kind indeed. I got a heart, Danny. I ain't just about makin' a name for myself or a fortune so that I can sail around the world and find me an island like Stevenson."

"No." Daniel thought about the name again. "You said 'Billy Kyne.' "

"Oh." Wheeler laughed. "Kind Kyne. More alliteration. I'll tell Billy to fit that in somewhere, too." He drained the last of his beer. "Billy's an old inkslinger. Well, he ain't that old. I hired him to write my books for me. He's also my press man. Ivy, he's the manager. Thinks too much. But Kyne can write fast. Not good. But fast. And I can tell a story fine, most folks say, especially after . . ." Winking he lifted the empty stein and then called out for a young man carrying a tray of filled glasses to a large table that he'd like another.

"I can talk up a story, Dan'l," Wheeler said. "But I can't put two words together on a sheet of paper that make sense. Exceptin' when I write down what someone said. Like Kind Kyne." He found the paper and pencil in his coat pocket.

A few minutes later, another stein of beer was brought to the table.

He stopped after two beers. Daniel barely touched his coffee. They returned to the telegraph office, but the man said it was too early to have gotten a reply. Wheeler left him instructions to bring any reply to the Texas and Pacific depot before the Number Nine left or have the message relayed to the Hotel Christlieb in Fort Worth. He dropped two silver dollars on the counter to encourage the man.

When they reached the new depot, Ivy Inman was talking to a T&P conductor, and Titus Wheeler, perhaps feeling happier after two steins of pilsner, bolted to the tracks, turned, and waved at Daniel.

"Hurry, Danny. Come see this."

Daniel did not hurry. The People hurried only when they were horseback. But he covered the distance in good time, and saw Wheeler pointing at an assembly of rolling stock that backed up on a siding all the way to the end of the track.

"That, Danny, my noble red man, is what made me become a showman. Get your boys, and your women, and let me give you a tour."

Most did not want to see anything. Ben Buffalo Bone came just because his sister and the three other women wanted to see. Red Buffalo and the Kiowa and Twice Bent Nose went, too. So did Ecahcueré.

Two boxcars housed the tents, stands, and everything that would be needed to seat five hundred spectators. Three livestock cars followed. Before those was a Pullman sleeper.

"This is where my noble red friends will sleep," the colonel explained. "And you, too, Pry." He looked around. "Where the hell is my boy? Virgil! Virgil Pry!" He turned and shouted, "Sergeant Pry. Sergeant Pry." Shook his head, cursed, and then forgot all about it.

Two passenger coaches, another Pullman—for taibos only, Daniel guessed—a smoking car, and the colonel's private coach.

"You must be richer than all white men," Red Buffalo told him.

"Not yet," Wheeler said with a wide grin. "But if this makes the money I think it will, I'll be set for life. Even after my investors get most of it."

"All this belongs to you?" Twice Bent Nose asked.

"Well . . . it's . . . leased, let's say. Rented." He straightened. "Belongs, actually, to some rich railroad gent in San Francisco. Understand, that it takes a hell of a lot of greenbacks and gold and good liquor and better cigars to get an operation like this going. I have to pay that damned Choctaw railroad, and the Katy that got us here, and the T&P that'll take us to Fort Worth. Pay them a damned sight of money. They say they're just rentin' me the tracks, you see, the iron rails so that the Iron Horse can get us to where the sun will set." He paused, perhaps thinking to write that down and hand it to Billy Kyne to incorporate into one of his books.

"How far will we go?" Ben Buffalo Bone asked.

"Miles, I don't know," Wheeler said. "Months . . . ummm . . . moons . . . that'll be four, so I'll have y'all back home on the reservation long afore Christmas." He paused, but saw no reaction. "Lessen we get belted with a norther, which, in this part of Texas, ain't out of the question. Remember once when I woke up sweatin' in September and went to bed colder than a witch's tit."

The colonel led them through the Pullman where the Indians, and Black Yellow Stripes, would sleep. Most did not think they would be able to sleep in such a place.

"I will sleep with my horse," Ben Buffalo Bone said.

"You might get tired of smellin' like hoss apples, pard," Wheeler said, and stepped off onto the ground, and helped the four women down first, and waited till the men had climbed down.

"What exactly is it that we will do?" Ben Buffalo Bone asked.

Wheeler laughed. "Well, that's why I want to have a parley with Billy Kyne. He's writin' all this down for us. Ivy'll want final approval. But mostly, the way I got it figured, is that you'll ride around the arena first off, whoopin' and rarin' and raisin' your lances and bows—don't do no shootin', that'd scare the hell out of my ticket buyers, and you might even accidentally hit one on purpose, you know. And I want a rain dance or a war dance, and I want the women to sing and dance and just look lovely."

"For four moons," Ben Buffalo Bone said.

Daniel had not heard him talk this much, ask these types of questions in a long time.

"Give'r take. I wish to hell Kyne was here."

"You can stop wishing, old man."

Daniel turned toward the voice behind him.

"Hello, Killstraight," Billy Kyne said. "It's been a long time."

CHAPTER THIRTEEN

Memories flashed back before Daniel could draw another breath.

As did the pain.

The scars of mourning seemed so fresh, he thought the wounds had opened, and he bled again. His heart shattered into more pieces than he had learned to count at Carlisle.

"Hello, Killstraight."

The voice rings out, booming, somehow above all the clatter—bells from streetcars, a steamer's horn, the taibo songs of God, of Jesus, of salvation, songs being sung to the man on the gallows, Charles Flint, who wears a new suit as he steps onto the trapdoor that will drop him and, if he is lucky, his neck will break and he will die instantly.

Instantly. A man is alive. Then he is not. The concept becomes hard to fathom.

A new suit. Odd. Taibos think that a man, even one of The People, should wear a new suit before he is hanged. They will put him in a box, and bury him in his new suit. But they will leave the rope around his neck. The rope that killed him.

But . . . if he is not lucky . . . he will dance and kick, trying to touch the ground that lies just inches below his toes. He will choke. He will strangle. The taibo doctor and the deputy marshal, Harvey P. Noble, will wait until the man breathes no more. At some point— Daniel remembered one man took seventeen minutes to die—the doctor will declare the man dead. And the hangman, big, silent George Maledon, will go home, until he is needed again.

Which will not be long. Not in Fort Smith. Not where Judge Isaac Parker determines who hangs and who rots in prison.

Hello, Killstraight.

Before Daniel stands Billy Kyne. A sober Kyne, not the rye-breathed newspaperman Daniel had met in Texas. Kyne has lost weight. He wears a nice suit. His face has been shaved this morning. There is no stubble, but a well-trimmed beard.

Billy Kyne smiles, finds a card stuck in a vest pocket, and passes the piece of small, hard paper to Daniel. The card has Kyne's name, and a bigger name: Cincinnati Commercial. *An address.*

Billy Kyne speaks over the whispers and the noises of the city about his new job. Above them, on the gallows, Charles Flint's death sentence is read. Six old taibo women begin singing. But no one really pays attention to the hymn. Most look at the frightened young man who is about to die.

Billy Kyne speaks: "I hate to do this, partner, but it's my job."

Partner. It is a word that Daniel finds hard to translate. Notsa?ka? *comes closest, but that word can mean one's wife, or sweetheart. Billy Kyne is neither to Daniel, and the thought of sweetheart—even wife—makes Daniel's heart ache, crack, disintegrate for the countless time. The reporter finds another paper, a telegraph, and Billy Kyne explains that these are the words from Captain Pratt at Carlisle. Where Daniel had learned the Pale Eyes way. As had Charles Flint. Charles Flint had learned much about the taibos, more than Daniel. He had learned to murder his own people.*

Including Rain Shower. And an old man of The People. But the taibos would not hang a Nermernuh for murdering two others of the same tribe. They hanged Charles Flint because Charles Flint had killed a taibo in cold blood. At least, that is what the man reading the death sentence pronounced by Judge Parker tells spectators.

All these years later, Daniel has forgotten the name of the taibo Charles Flint killed. He remembers the names of Charles Flint . . . of Rain Shower . . . of Yellow Bear. Remembers their names. But cannot speak them again.

Daniel is reading the telegram when the trapdoor opens and drops Charles Flint—the name given him by the taibos at Carlisle—to his death. Mercifully, the hangman has done his job well this morning. The legs bounce. The bowels release. Charles Flint lets out a soft gasp. And then . . . he is no longer in this world.

"Well?" Billy Kyne asks now that Charles Flint is making his journey to The Land Beyond The Sun and Daniel has read what Captain Pratt has to say.

Daniel has nothing to say to any newspaper reporter, and this is what he tells Billy Kyne. And Kyne's smile is like nothing Daniel has ever seen on a taibo. It is the sad smile, of a man who knows and has seen far too much, and Billy Kyne says more words.

What Billy Kyne said on that spring morning in Fort Smith, the years have washed away from Daniel's mind.

And now, here stood Billy Kyne, older—the hair not as far down on his forehead as Daniel remembered, the creases around Kyne's eyes deeper, longer, and the eyes revealing the years, hardships, the wandering journeys of a reporter. But Billy Kyne no longer dresses as a newspaper reporter from the *Cincinnati Commercial*. Kyne wears boots, and a hat not quite as big as Colonel Titus Wheeler's. But he still has pencils above his ears, and a notepad in one hand.

"Hungry?" Billy Kyne asks.

"A Comanche," Daniel says, "is always hungry."

It is an excuse to walk away from the depot, where the colonel directs and yells and laughs, and Ivy Inman yells but does not laugh—sometimes in one sentence—and men and women run around like ants, and the engines belch black smoke and hiss, and streetcars clang, and The People and the Kiowa that have traveled from Oklahoma Territory stand close together, unsure, and watch the people of the city gawk and stare and point and gasp.

121

The food is parched corn, bought from a man pushing a cart, and a sweet beverage, not alcoholic, but dark brown, almost black, that foams and burns on its way down Daniel's throat. Burns. But tastes wonderful. Taibos have some magic.

"You are no longer a newspaperman?" Daniel asks.

"For the time being." Billy Kyne sips his drink. "I wrote a few articles about Titus Wheeler, and he offered me a lot of money. Man's gotta look after himself."

Daniel nodded. "Then . . . would you . . . not have any news . . . from . . . our home?" He wondered why the words took so long to form.

Kyne gulps down the rest of his drink, crushes the cup of paper, and pitches it into a keg next to a hitch rail.

"Smallpox." Kyne shook his head. "The *Herald*—my old newspaper—did not have much on what's happening on the Comanche reserve. Just a sentence. No numbers, no reported deaths, just that the soldiers at Fort Sill are handling the situation, and that the outbreak is contained to one village."

"Yamparika," Daniel said. Well, that was good news—containment, anyway—unless one was Yamparika.

"Biggest concern in Texas is some cases rising in Daingerfield. They haven't quarantined the town, and at least one man has died there."

Daniel moved to drop his cup and the rest of the hard corn into the keg. "I do not know of this Daingerfield," he said.

"It's pretty far east of here." Kyne pointed. "Better than a hundred miles. I don't think we have to worry about it spreading here. And we're heading west in a couple of hours. To Fort Worth. The papers say the pox was brought to Daingerfield by some man named Stroman who came up from South Texas." Kyne found the makings of a cigarette and began rolling one. "You wouldn't want to be named Stroman these days."

"It is not his fault that he caught The Rotting Face," Daniel said.

Kyne stopped licking his cigarette, and stared over the paper in his brown-stained fingers. "The Rotting Face?" He put the cigarette in his mouth but did not light it. "Is that what you call it?"

"Naru̱ʔu̱yu̱ tasiʔa," Daniel said.

"I don't think I could pronounce that in a month of Sundays." Kyne lighted his cigarette, then immediately pulled it from his lips. "Or spell it. And I think most of my newspaper bosses would have said 'The Rotting Face' is too grotesque for a newspaper." He started to return the smoke, but stopped.

"You look worried, Killstraight. It can't be this show you signed up for. Or is it?"

Daniel shrugged. "I do not want The People to look like fools," he said. "We are not fools. We are not amusements."

"It won't be like that at all." Kyne took two drags on his smoke. "Mostly you'll dance and sing. Beat some drums. Ride around on horses at a full gallop."

"Riding horses, the men will like."

"The guns are loaded with blanks. No lead balls, no bullets. Except Colonel Blowhard does some target shooting. For a fat old bastard, he's got a pretty good aim. And he rides better than that damned fool Jones. Come on, Killstraight. Before Colonel Blowhard blows himself to smithereens. We've got a train to catch to Fort Worth. And . . ."

He took another drag and stopped, pitched the half-finished smoke on the boardwalk, and crushed it out with the toe of his boot.

"You're still worried."

Daniel said nothing.

"Smallpox?" Kyne let out a breath as though he was relieved. "You're miles away from that, Killstraight. We'll be in Fort

Worth in a couple of hours, and we'll be there for a few weeks. Advance ticket sales have been brisk. Folks want to relive the old days. You're going to go home with a veritable fortune in the Comanche world. And I bet that money will come in handy. Besides, this is going to be a hell of a lot of fun. You're famous, Killstraight. Thanks to ol' Blowhard . . . but mostly because of me."

He reached inside his coat and withdrew one of those thin but vibrant books, and Daniel read the title: *Prince of the Prairie; or, the Demon of the Dakota Prairie,* and saw Colonel Titus Wheeler's name. And he felt disgust when he saw the likeness of one of The People, presumably Captain Daniel Killstraight, rising over the prone body of an Indian, and holding the scalp triumphantly in his hand.

"You," Daniel said, and turned the book over so he could see the advertisements for the other titles recently published or coming out in the next two months from Gerald P. Shumaker, Publisher of 13 Rose Avenue in New York, New York. "You wrote these."

Billy Kyne let out some sort of laugh that sounded more like a cough. "I wouldn't exactly call it writing."

"I am no captain," Daniel told him. He thrust the book out. "And I would not scalp another—"

"I get no say in what Shumaker's son, who runs the business, puts on the cover, partner. I just write forty-five thousand words, most of them descriptions of guns blazing and wild whoops. Put Captain Killstraight in some adventures. Shumaker, the old man, not his punk son, made me turn you into a half-breed so some of our readers wouldn't be offended if you happened to be with a white woman."

The sweet dark drink soured in Daniel's stomach.

"I wish you would not write such things about me," Daniel said.

"I just happened to mention your name to Blowhard," Billy Kyne said. "He liked the sound of it. Said it rang. Thought if we had success in getting some Comanches in our show, at least for the Texas run, we might do some good. Wheeler, as much as I like to run him down and give him hell, has a heart. He lived with some of your people for a spell."

Daniel just stood there, watching the people stare at him as they passed. Point at him. Whisper about him.

"I do not like these books," Daniel said softly.

"Killstraight," Kyne said, "if you want to know the God's honest truth, I'm not crazy about them, either. It's a long way from writing for the *Commercial* or the *Herald*—or the *New-York Tribune*—but the money's good, and I'm not clawing my way over dead bodies or telling some poor sob that I'm an investigator with the city water works to get the story my editors want or else lose my job. You aren't the only ones who've had a hard life, Killstraight. So what I write might be horse apples, ol' boy, but in one way, these dime novels are important."

They let a city policeman push a handcuffed drunk past them.

"That Captain Daniel Killstraight. He's the hero. Not the bad injun that gets killed in the last chapter by Buffalo Bill, or Wild Bill, or Texas Jack, or Kit Carson or Colonel Blowhard himself. It took Shumaker about a month of my arguing before he agreed to let me give it a whirl. I have no delusions of becoming Mark Twain. Or Emerson, Poe, Stevenson, Austen, Dostoyevsky. But maybe folks will look at a Comanche different after he reads that blood and thunder."

Daniel was not convinced. "I wish you would not write about such things," he said.

"Well, the sales will determine that." Kyne sighed. "And the old man. Shumaker. Not Wheeler. This one." He held up the latest novel. "Might be the last ride for Captain Killstraight. But . . . we'll see. This show, and you being part of it, might boost some sales. But I don't know how many folks in Fort Worth actually read. And after that, we're in Albany. San Antonio and Austin might play a bit better."

A young boy ran up and stopped, staring at Daniel.

"Here." Billy Kyne handed the kid the copy of *Prince of the Prairie; or, the Demon of the Dakota Prairie.* "This is the latest book about this Comanche hero."

"Hero?" The kid stared at the cover, and looked back at Daniel. "He don't look like much in person."

"Better watch it," Kyne said. "He's Comanche as they come. And he wears a badge so he can do anything he pleases. Especially to little white boys."

The boy raced across the street, causing a man in a freight wagon to jerk hard on the brakes and reins and send a string of curses and spittle chasing after the kid as he reached the far boardwalk and disappeared in the crowd.

"You," Daniel told the reporter, "are as big of a liar as the colonel."

Kyne laughed. "I know. Can't help it. Let's head back and keep Colonel Blowhard from blowing his top." He titled his head toward the depot, and Daniel turned.

"Do you want to know what a tribal policeman does on the reservation?" Daniel asked.

"I'm sure you'll educate me."

"For much of the last month," Daniel said, "I have guarded the school at night."

They walked around a woman complaining about the quality of cornmeal at Baker's Mercantile.

"Well," Kyne said. "Schools can be dangerous."

It was a sentence that meant nothing, a joke or an attempt at a joke. And Billy Kyne meant nothing when he said it. Likely, Daniel would not have even remembered what the newspaperman turned press agent had said had Daniel not fallen asleep on the T&P train on the way from Dallas to Fort Worth.

CHAPTER FOURTEEN

Ben Buffalo Bone shoves him awake.

Daniel stares, rubs sleep out of his eyes, mouths, "What?"

"Do not speak like a Pale Eye," Ben Buffalo Bone snaps. "No, I guess you cannot. You are no longer one of The People. But, then, you never were."

Daniel rises. He feels the blood roaring to his head. He also realizes that he is not on the train to Fort Worth. He is somewhere else. Alone, for the moment, with Ben Buffalo Bone.

"I am Kwahadi." Daniel speaks in his native tongue.

"Yes, you are Kwahadi. I am Kotsoteka. Like I say, you are not of The People. When you joined us, they treated the Kwahadis like kings. They let you keep many of your ponies. They did not throw you in the icehouse."

No, Daniel no longer is riding a westbound train. He lies on a thin blanket. Ben Buffalo Bone has vanished.

Huukumatsumaru kicks Daniel's moccasin. It is dark, stormy, but Daniel sees the Kwahadi holy man clearly.

"We have work to do," Huukumatsumaru says in a toneless voice. He turns, takes six steps, then waits until Daniel rises and follows.

This is the icehouse at Fort Sill. The one the Kwahadis avoided when Quanah surrendered. This is where the first to surrender were imprisoned. Where the soldiers forked over raw meat, and The People ate it. Raw. For fires were forbidden. And it is where many of The People died.

Huukumatsumaru stops. Daniel stares down at his dead mother.

He and Rain Shower move toward the woman, her face disfigured by The Rotting Face. Rain Shower grabs the dead woman's legs. Daniel lifts his mother by the shoulders. They raise the body over their heads, grunting, standing on tiptoes, and throw her over the wall. Her body thumps on the other side.

Daniel dams the tears, for he is Nermernuh. He starts to leave, but Rain Shower says, "No." Turning, he sees that Rain Shower is looking at his feet. Daniel looks down, and finds his mother's rotting head. It must have fallen off. So he bends over, grabs the hair, raises the head, and throws it over the wall.

"Is that all?" Daniel turns and looks at Huukumatsumaru.

"No." The holy man points.

Daniel sees the dead, stacked like the Long Knives pile their firewood in winter. He sees his father. His grandfather. He sees his sister. There is Charles Flint, before he became Charles Flint. There lies Quanah. Yellow Bear. Co-by. To-nar-cy. There is Rain Shower. The Nokoni dancer named Roadrunner. The Kiowa called Apiatan. There is White Wolf. Huuhwiya. Two pockmarked Yamparika women walk over and dump another body, that rolls off the top, and down, toward Daniel, stopping at his feet. And looks down into the dead eyes and ravaged face of Oajuicauojué.

"Bury her deep."

He jumped awake. Breathing heavily, feeling even sweat, and his heart thundered inside his chest. It was a nightmare. Just a horrible dream. That is what he tried to tell himself. But then, as the train rattled westward, and a few seats behind him Ecahcu-eré sang softly, he began remembering a similar scene, from another nightmare, but that one, Daniel knew was not a dream. Just a memory that would never leave him, never let him have peace.

"Bury her deep," Miss Brunot said. Behind the teacher at Carl-

129

isle, two burly taibo men held lanterns.

The night air felt damp. And Daniel could never get used to how the air felt, heavy, thick, impossible sometimes to even breathe. Taibos called it humidity. Daniel thought it was the hell the Jesus Men were always yelling about.

He stared down at the girl. She was taller than Daniel, pretty, black-haired and thin. Her name was Kimimela in her native tongue. Which The People would call Ueyahcoró. And taibos? Butterfly. No matter the language, it was a beautiful word. And Kimimela had been a beautiful girl. In life. But in death, she looked old, cold, pallid, and the sickness that killed her and reduced her to little more than a skeleton.

Daniel remembered hearing her coughing, wheezing, fighting for breath. Maybe, in The Land Beyond The Sun, or wherever it was that Lakota girls went when they were no more of the Earth, she was pretty again. At least, she had not died of The Rotting Face. Miss Brunot, who Daniel had decided was not a teacher but a taibo witch, said pneumonia had killed Mary Alice, the name Captain Pratt had given Kimimela. The girl had gotten sick, and never improved.

"Start digging her grave, Daniel," the witch said. "We don't have all night, boy."

I am Nermernuh, Daniel tried to tell himself. The girl who lies at my feet was not. I do not know much about Lakotas—except that my father told me they were fine horsemen, just not as fine as The People—but I do know some things about these beautiful people.

He knew much, because at night, when they were supposed to be sleeping and when the guards had decided that the schoolboys at Carlisle were too tired to run away, they would roll over on their uncomfortable beds, and one would open the curtains to the window, so that the moon and the stars and the lights from the Industrial School and the city of Carlisle,

Pennsylvania, would give them just enough to see.

In sign language, and later when they had learned enough of one another's tongues, they could whisper and tell stories about their lives, their cultures, their own wars against taibos and Long Knives.

"She was Lakota," Daniel said softly. Too soft for Miss Brunot or the two men to hear.

"Speak up, boy," the witch said. "Lord have mercy, I thought you Comanches whooped and screamed all the time."

"She was Lakota." They all heard him that time.

"Yes. She was a Sioux. And now she's dead. Start digging."

He had been just a young boy. Barely having seen thirteen summers. He tried to summon the words, swallowed down fear, and pointed at the shovel and pick on the ground before him.

"We . . . my people . . . Comanches. We bury like you do. Underground." He nodded at the young, thin corpse before him. "But she . . . Lakota. Sioux."

He hated calling her Sioux. He remembered Chayton—Falcon to the Pale Eyes—telling one of the male instructors, "I am not Sioux. That is a name the enemies gave us. I am Lakota." He also remembered the instructor knocking Chayton, now Jim Falcon, to the ground, and kicking him until the boy cried.

"They do not bury their dead under dirt." He pointed to the sky. "Above. On . . ." Carpenters were working on one of the buildings, and he had heard the word that best described how the Lakotas sent their dead to The Land Beyond The Sun.

"Scaffold."

He remembered other customs Butterfly and Falcon had told him.

The dead might not be dead, so it was best to wait between one and two days before burying them. In case they were not ready to join their ancestors. Life was precious. Death was

131

inevitable. But death meant no more suffering. So Kimimela no longer coughed and fought to breathe. She was beautiful again. Her name would not be spoken here—The People had a similar custom—but she was Kimimela again, young and beautiful and with those who had traveled the path before her.

"We're not putting her up on one of those heathen altars," the witch said. "She goes underground. Deep. Now."

He wanted to explain that, from what he had learned from his Lakota friends, that they could be buried under rocks, or stuck in a tree. Kimimela had a necklace she loved, one given by her mother, and she would want to take that with her. She should also be sent with food and water, for no one knew how many days and nights it took to reach The Land Beyond The Sun. It would be good, too, to kill a horse, and tie its tail to the scaffold.

Chayton would be singing, crying, cutting off what hair the taibos had not hacked away when he first arrived at Carlisle and became Jim Falcon. He would be cutting his arms and legs with a knife. And, since Kimimela was so young and so beautiful, and a girl, Chayton might also cut off part of one of his little fingers.

When he tried to explain all this to the witch and the two men, he was knocked down. He did not see which of the two big men picked up the spade, but he felt it slam into his back, and he landed beside the dead Lakota girl, fighting for his breath, hoping he would not join on her journey to that unknown place.

He rolled over, and vomited. He almost fell into what he had wretched. At last his vision cleared, and Miss Brunot knelt before him. She grabbed what little remained of his fine black hair, and she jerked his head up.

Yes, there could be no mistake. She was a taibo witch.

"Bury her," the evil woman whispered. "Deep."

132

CHAPTER FIFTEEN

It was not, Daniel thought after the first performance, terrible. It just was not . . . good.

Fort Worth's "Cowboy Band" opened with an overture that included "The Yellow Rose of Texas," "The Star-Spangled Banner," and some tune he recognized as Stephen Foster's but he could not recall the title. Taibo songs pretty much sounded all alike. But, Colonel Titus Wheeler said he felt the same way about songs The People sang.

Then the band struck up something new, and Colonel Wheeler, riding point, rode through the opening in the massive tent, pulled off his hat—he had made sure his yellow-haired wig was on tight—and waved it at the crowd. Following the colonel came a handful of veterans of the Grand Army of the Republic, who were long in tooth and graying, or balding, but kept their old blue uniforms clean. They were also greatly outnumbered by the two dozen riders of the Confederacy, a few of whom broke out singing "I'm a Good Ol' Rebel," to the delight of the packed seats.

After that came the stagecoach, with passengers like the mayor, the publisher of the newspaper that had been the kindest to the colonel, two local preachers, and a young boy, waving their hands and yelling huzzahs and hurrahs. Rabid Wolf Jones rode a fine pinto pony beside the wagon, leaning this way and that on the saddle. Taibos in the stands cheered him for his athletic ability in the saddle. What they did not know, but what

Daniel and everyone else in the show did, was that Rabid Wolf Jones was drunk.

Mexican *vaqueros* came next, only six, and then it was Daniel's turn. He did not feel that he should ride out first, but Twice Bent Nose said he must. "They will shoot you first," he said. "Then we might be able to escape."

Does he make a joke?

"We will avenge you, of course," Twice Bent Nose added, but did not grin.

Behind The People and the lone Kiowa rode local cowboys that the colonel had hired for the performance. They slapped their quirts against their chaps, or twirled lariats this way and that. Two covered wagons followed, and finally a fiddler, a banjo player, and a fat redheaded woman singing "Dixie."

Daniel did not think this was the way Buffalo Bill Cody opened his show.

He did not wave to the crowd as those in front of him did. Nor did Twice Bent Nose or Oajuicauojué. They stared in silence, and possibly in fear. The pale faces in the lower stands—those close enough for Daniel to see with any detail—clapped slightly when the vaqueros rode past them, although the Mexicans in one section cheered their friends loudly. Taibos went almost completely silent, however, when Daniel led The People and the one Kiowa past them.

He remembered when the instructors at the "school" in Carlisle decided it would benefit the "savages" to see the greatness and compassion of the White Race. So Daniel, six Lakotas, two Ojibwes, and a Cheyenne boarded a Cumberland Valley Railroad car shortly after dawn and arrived in Philadelphia at 10:30 that morning, just twenty minutes late.

The power of the taibos became overwhelming there. The rush of white-faced people, the noise, the tall buildings, the streets that were not dirt. A wagon carried them across the Girard Avenue Bridge, and Daniel realized the power of taibos, for the river that flowed beneath the massive bridge was wider than any body of water Daniel had ever seen. And massive boats steamed underneath the bridge. But the Philadelphia Zoo, he found comforting . . . at first. It was the first to be established in America, he was told, and President Grant had visited a few years back. The gatehouse frightened him, but he was Nermernuh, the only one of The People at this "industrial school," and he would not let six Lakotas, two Ojibwes, and a Cheyenne think him a coward.

Once inside the zoo, however, he saw wild animals the likes of which he would never forget. The kangaroos, which made all of them laugh, were new, they were told. Brigham Young had given two bears to the zoo. William T. Sherman donated the cow, which had marched to the sea with him during the recent unpleasantness. Daniel did not find the cow very interesting. He thought he had never seen a beast as ugly as the rhinoceros, and wondered what kind of man would ride a zebra.

"I did not like the bars that imprison these animals," the Ojibwe girl signed to Daniel. "But I am glad this beast is kept behind the iron rods."

Yes, the elephant, was huge, Daniel agreed.

The monkeys made them all laugh.

And when the "students" were told it was time to leave, Daniel did not think he was happy, but felt pleased that he had been blessed to see this zoo, even if the cages made him think of his own people. Yet as they walked to return to the wagon that would take them back across the big bridge over the big river, a Zoo Man was leading a string of horses past them.

Except for the zebra, he could not recall seeing any horses in the zoo. The horses were not much. Old, worn out, heads hanging down—horses that would not carry a man, even a child, very far.

"What are those nags for?" Miss Brunot, the witch, asked.

"Supper for the carnivores," the Zoo Man said. "Horses are cheaper than buying beef, and it takes four a week to keep the bears and lions and tigers from eating us."

Daniel was new to Carlisle, so the words meant nothing to him. But on the train back to Carlisle, the smart Lakota girl told them what the Zoo Man had said.

The train ride home turned silent.

Now Daniel recalled how the elephant had looked at him through the iron bars. Even the fierce lion. He understood how the animals had felt. He wasn't in a Wild West "amusement." He was a caged animal in a zoo.

After they exited the tent, more chaos began.

A horse race. A recreation of the Pony Express, where Ben Buffalo Bone and Apiatan were told to chase one of them around the arena twice, then ride back out. "Yip like you're devils who want to kill them," Billy Kyne told them. "Put the fear of Comanches into the audience."

"He is Kiowa," Ben Buffalo Bone pointed out.

Rabid Wolf Jones passed out. The manager named Ivy kicked him, but Rabid Wolf Jones felt nothing.

The cowboys rode back out, then the colonel rode to the center of the arena and began a shooting display.

Billy Kyne wiped sweat off his face. "You know, Killstraight," he said, "if I could get a decent news story, a massacre, a fire, a train wreck, a tornado, I could land a job with a first-rate newspaper and never have to write another blood-and-thunder for Gerald P. Shumaker or that old blowhard again."

Daniel paid scant attention. He was looking at Black Yellow Stripes, who sat on a block whittling.

"Is there no part for the Black White Man in the colonel's show?" Daniel asked.

Kyne turned, confused, saw who Daniel meant, and shook his head. "He can have my job." Kyne removed his hat and wiped his forehead. "No. No, hell, no, he can't have my job. He has to be at Wheeler's beck and call. I wish to hell I had someone to keep me lubricated with whiskey."

"You Mexicans," Ivy Inman screamed. "Get mounted. Now. You're up next. Hurry, damn it. *Vamanos.*"

The wagons rolled out after the vaqueros. Kwasinaboo and Ecahcueré got to chase one of the wagons. And finally the stagecoach took off, and all of the male "Indians" got to chase them, whooping, working their bows but without arrows, or waving their lances.

Daniel forgot all about that feeling of the Philadelphia Zoo when he galloped after the stagecoach, circling the arena floor three times. Riding a good horse at a gallop could make one of The People forget about most of their troubles.

The colonel rode back into the arena when they were done, talked and yelled, and then Fort Worth's "Cowboy Band" struck up with some song Daniel did not know.

"Ride back out there," Billy Kyne told them. "Slow. Act like you did during the Grand Review. They're cheering for you-all. Go take your bows."

They would not bow to any taibo, but they rode around twice more; the show was over, and as they unsaddled their horses, Rabid Wolf Jones woke up, and Tuhuupi said, "This Pale Eyes event is stupid. You could have killed them all, burned the stagecoach, the wagons, taken their scalps and their horses."

"Ever seen one of Cody's Wild West exhibitions?" Corporal Tobias Canton asked as they walked back to the train.

"No," Daniel answered.

"It's something to see." The corporal pulled a pewter flask

from his coat pocket, unscrewed the lid, and drank. He offered the liquor to Daniel, but Daniel shook his head. Canton took another drink, and let the flask disappear. "Whereas this show . . . well . . . it's something."

And so the week continued.

Sleep in the railroad cars on the railroad siding. Or try to sleep. The siding was not far from the main congestion of railroads and streetcars and hacks and pedestrians. The men and women who lived in Fort Worth did not appear to need sleep.

Wake in the morning, or well before morning, and wait till dawn broke, then step off the train and make their breakfast. Billy Kyne would send over a young boy in the early evening with a bag full of "makings" for a meal. Not buffalo, but sometimes beef, usually bacon. Sometimes onions. Pecans were abundant, and Red Buffalo found a beehive and returned with honey. The Nokoni dancer found a large patch of prickly pear, which Oajuicauojué prepared one morning.

It was all right.

By noon they were at the Big Tent. The colonel said it was important to be there hours before the "amusement" began, so people could come by—after paying their fifty cents for a ticket for adults and two bits for children thirteen or younger—and get a glimpse at Comanche culture.

Rabid Wolf Jones was drunk by two o'clock. The exhibition began at five-thirty in the afternoon Mondays through Fridays. On Saturday there was a matinee at two, then another show at five-thirty. The colonel's "amusement" usually ran two hours, but could be unpredictable, such as the Wednesday when the stagecoach lost a rear wheel. Or when the drunken Rabid Wolf Jones was thrown by his horse and dragged about two hundred yards before two old men from the Grand Army of the Republic stopped the horse from running.

The People and the Kiowa found that funny. So did everyone else inside the Big Tent—except for Rabid Wolf Jones.

When the day was over, and they were back at the siding, Daniel would walk to the calendar that hung on the wall of the car where The People and the Kiowa did not sleep, and he would take the big marker and scratch through the date. He scratched through every square when they returned to the siding, or on Sunday, their one day off, when the bells rang throughout town in the morning and sometimes in the evening. When they did not have anything to do but tend to their horses and themselves.

"Why do you do that?" Oajuicauojué asked on one Friday.

"I count the days," he told her, and sat in one of the chairs that taibos said were comfortable but just made Daniel's back ache.

"Are you sad to be here?" she asked.

"I am glad you are here," he told her.

That was not an answer. He said, "The show is all right. We get to ride horses. Some of the Pale Eye children are nice." He shook his head. "It is safer, I think, than trying to arrest a Choctaw selling Choc Beer to The People. Everyone here shoots powder only. No bullets. They do not let us even shoot arrows."

"And we make money," Oajuicauojué said.

Daniel nodded, but while Athol McLeish paid eight dollars a month, the colonel paid in promises. Eventually, he said he would hold the money for all the Indians so they wouldn't lose it. They'd get all their salary after the last show of the season. Gold coins, he said, were too heavy to be packing around for four moons.

"How much longer will we be in this town?" Oajuicauojué asked.

Daniel looked at the calendar. He counted the crosses he had made in the squares. "Three more days," he said.

"And then we go home?"

His head shook. "Albany."

She waited.

"It is a town northwest of here. A fort used to be nearby, but the Long Knives left it. They do that often." He looked at the calendar again, and counted the marked-out squares.

"You are smiling," Oajuicauojué said.

Daniel turned to her. She looked beautiful.

"I have not seen you look happy in some time."

"You make me happy," he told her, and while that was true, he smiled for another reason.

He had counted eighteen squares. The taibos all said that if one had been exposed to The Rotting Face and no sickness had started after two weeks, that person was safe—until being in contact again with a sick one. A week was seven days. Two weeks, fourteen. Eighteen days. Just in Fort Worth.

They had escaped The Rotting Face.

CHAPTER SIXTEEN

They left on a westbound Texas Central train after spending three weeks in Fort Worth—" 'bout five days too many in this damned ol' cowtown," the colonel complained to Ivy Inman and Billy Kyne.

They arrived in Albany, the Shackelford County seat, around one in the afternoon on another clear Texas day.

A band played "Dixie" on the lawn in front of the massive courthouse, a three-story structure made of stone that stood in the center of Albany's town square. A buckboard, driven by a burly man in a big Texas hat, holding a repeating rifle, with a local lawman sitting next to him, carried Daniel and the other "Indian guests" from the depot. Colonel Titus Wheeler rode his big horse, waving his hat—likely, Ben Buffalo Bone joked, praying to his God that the wind did not scalp him of his yellow hair in front of the hundreds of people gathered on the boardwalks of the square. Kyne, Inman, and Rabid Wolf Jones rode in a carriage in front of the Indian wagon.

When they reached the center, the driver pulled the mules to a stop, and the lawman turned around.

"You-all just get out, sit on the grass yonder, and don't cause no ruckus till this shindig is over. Savvy?" He looked at Daniel.

"We will sit on the grass and behave ourselves," Daniel said.

"That's a good buck." The man nodded, but his expression never changed.

Daniel told his companions what was expected of them, and

they stepped off the back of the wagon and started for the closest patch of green.

"Wait!" the deputy called.

Daniel turned and waited. The taibo pointed in the back. "Take them blankets with you. You can sit on them."

"We will not kill your green grass," Ben Buffalo Bone said, "by sitting on it."

"Don't sass me, boy," the lawman said, and shifted the barrel of his rifle to make his point. "Folks here probably expect some sort of injun stuff. The blankets are that. I hope to hell nobody gets the bright idea of lettin' y'all put up teepees in front of our courthouse."

Daniel looked at the building. "It is big," he said.

"Gonna be bigger," the driver of the wagon said. "Folks want to put a clock tower on top." He shook his head. "Gettin' to be so a man won't have need of his Illinois watch no more."

"Since when did you learn to tell time?" the deputy said.

The driver sighed, shook his head, and whispered something Daniel could not hear.

By then, Oajuicauojué and the other women were walking back to the wagon to fetch the blankets.

So the women sat on blankets; the men stood in the shade of a live oak; and the colonel talked to the mayor and an old man in the uniform of a Long Knives leader. Billy Kyne talked to a man in a porkpie hat that Daniel guessed, from the way the man kept scribbling in his pad, to be a newspaper reporter.

Eventually, men and women, keeping a tight grip on the hands of their little ones, found enough courage to walk across the streets and onto the lawn where the courthouse stood, the taibos talked, and The People, and the lone Kiowa, sat on blankets or stood in silence.

"It is not as bad as Fort Worth," Ecahcueré said as the parade of staring, silent people filed past.

"Because there are not as many taibos here as they were in the last place," Twice Bent Nose said.

"What are they saying, Ma?" a redheaded boy in denim pants asked.

"Don't you listen to none of that heathen tongue, Ralph." The prim woman gripped the kid's hand like one would a lance.

When the throng of gawkers died, Daniel noticed Red Buffalo sitting, his back against the tree, his head down, lips moving silently. He slipped past the Kiowa and Ben Buffalo Bone and stood next to the Kwahadi holy man.

"Is something wrong?" Daniel whispered.

Red Buffalo did not look up or open his eyes, but he stopped his prayer, whisper, whatever he had been doing.

"We should not be here," he said.

Daniel knelt. "Is there something wrong with this town?" It couldn't be the taibos who had just passed. The People heard that kind of talk whenever they were near most Texans.

"This . . ." The old man's eyes opened. ". . . place I do not know."

"Albany," Daniel said. "It is a new town. Newer than Fort Worth or Dallas."

"It lies in the country that once belonged to The People," Red Buffalo Bone said.

Ecahcueré had come over, too. "Most of the land claimed now by Tejanos once belonged to The People," he said.

"All of the land claimed by Tejanos was The People's land," Ben Buffalo Bone corrected.

Twice Bent Nose shook his head. "This is where Tonkawas lived."

"Tonkawas." Ecahcueré spat. "They would eat those they killed. They were cowards. When we began killing them all, for they deserved to die—flesh-eaters—they hid with the Long Knives."

"No," Red Buffalo said. "This town smells not of Tonkawas. It smells of death."

Daniel filled his lungs, then slowly exhaled. He saw the eyes staring at him. Even Red Buffalo looked up. They knew that a Nermernuh who had lived in the taibo world, who still, as a longtime member of the tribal police, lived in that world, would know of such things.

"This town," he said, "from what I have heard and from what I have read, is not yet twenty years old. The Long Knives soldier-fort—called Griffin—was that way." He motioned toward the northeast. "On the river . . ." and he gave the name The People called what the Tejanos knew as the Clear Fork of the Brazos. He waited.

"I remember that place." Red Buffalo's head bobbed. "That is where the hide hunters gathered. After they had slaughtered cuhtz."

"This is that place?" Ben Buffalo Bone shouted.

"No," Daniel said. "That place was what the Pale Eyes called The Flat. This place was more for cattle." He pointed again northeast. "The Flat. The hide hunters. Fort Griffin. That was there." He gestured toward the depot. "The Fire Wagon did not come here till after all The People had left the war trails."

"This is still our country," Ben Buffalo Bone said. "My father took the scalps of two Tonkawas near here."

Daniel pressed his lips together. Argument was futile.

"No," Red Buffalo said. "This has nothing to do with the tai-bos. Or the hide men. Or the longhorn cattle. It has to do with us. Those of us who are here. There is something cold in my blood and bones. I feel we are in danger. My nose smells . . . the stench of death."

But at that moment, Colonel Titus Wheeler walked up, Billy Kyne and two men holding the black boxes that took the likenesses of men, women, mountains, and animals, and said,

"Dan'l, we're gonna have us a hell of a good time here. The mayor is gonna let us put up a tent on the courthouse grounds. Yes, sir, we'll be right in the heart of Albany. Course, the show will be smaller than Fort Worth, but what the hell, Albany ain't Fort Worth. We're gonna have us a hell of a show. Not as many folks to perform. Not nigh as many bluecoats. So, Dan'l, right here, right about where we all is standing, by grab, this is gonna be where we show these Texans what the Comanch is all about."

The courthouse dwarfed the tent when they opened the following afternoon. Apiatan pointed that out. "The saloon on that corner comes close to dwarfing the tent," Daniel joked.

Although a cattle town like Fort Worth, Albany had no "Cowboy Band," but the exhibition opened with "The Yellow Rose of Texas," sung by a twelve-year-old girl. "The Star-Spangled Banner" came next, but the colonel must have decided to cut the Stephen Foster song, and no music accompanied Colonel Titus Wheeler's grand entrance, but he rode with enthusiasm, waving at the Spartan crowd just as if he were performing before thousands, instead of, maybe, a hundred.

Veterans from Fort Griffin rode out next, led by the Ancient Bluecoat Daniel had seen at the gathering the previous day. Confederate veterans followed, and many in the crowd sang "Dixie."

The stagecoach—which the colonel apparently owned as it traveled in the train with the tent and stands and saddles and tack and flags and such—followed, with the specially selected passengers. This time, Rabid Wolf Jones rode next to the driver of the stagecoach. He was drunk, but he did not fall off the *taibo* wagon.

There were no vaqueros in Albany, but three leathery, mean-looking men wearing dingy buckskins and carrying big rifles—one of which had a brass telescopic sight affixed to the barrel—

rode out in their place.

"And here," Ivy Inman yelled into the horn that carried his voice into the stands, "are Shackelford County's true heroes."

A tall, red-mustached man in a flat-brimmed straw hat had yelled through that big horn in Fort Worth, but he had quit, and now the manager had to do the job. Corporal Canton told Daniel that the man had quit over his salary.

"Not enough money, I guess," Canton said.

Billy Kyne sniggered. "No money," he said.

Inman kept yelling into the horn. "The men that really ended the savage Indian wars in the Great State of Texas. Who almost wiped the buffalo out of existence and in so doing drove the savage redskins to the reservations north of the Red River. Here, ladies and gentlemen, are the buffalo hunters!"

Ben Buffalo Bone spat, turned in his saddle, and began translating to The People and the Kiowa who did not understand the taibo language.

"And now, here are the men these hide hunters, and our cowboys, and our gallant soldiers from Fort Richardson tamed!"

"Fort Griffin, you stupid son of a bitch!" someone in the crowd yelled.

"All right, Daniel," Kyne said. "You're up next. Give them a show."

"The most fierce red devils ever to ride the ranges," Inman yelled. "The Comanches, their chief, their medicine man, their warriors and their squaws!"

"We make fools of ourselves for the Pale Eyes," Ben Buffalo Bone said when they were back at yet another siding where the Texas Central had put the colonel's special cars. "For what?"

He held up a plate of beans, biscuits, and thinly sliced steak. "To eat what Tejanos eat?"

"They promise us taibo money," Kwasinaboo said.

"Have you seen any money?" Ben Buffalo Bone shook his head. "And they made us ride behind the butchers who starved us, who killed the buffalo for nothing more than the hides. The People used everything that buffalo gave us. Now there is no buffalo to eat, just . . ." He emptied the food on his plate into the trash can.

Daniel had no response.

"We are here," Red Buffalo said. "We are here till they send us back."

"Why?" Ben Buffalo Bone demanded.

"Because we said we would go." Red Buffalo's face hardened, and Ben Buffalo Bone stared at his moccasins. "We are not Pale Eyes, my son, and we certainly are not Tejanos," the holy man said, somewhat softer though intensity fueled his eyes. "We are The People. What we say, we do."

And that is what they did in the not-as-big tent on the grounds of the county courthouse in Albany, Texas. Another show on Friday, two on Saturday, with the biggest crowd, of maybe one hundred and fifty, on Saturday's early performance.

On Sunday, when they expected to rest at the siding, the colonel and Billy Kyne rode up and asked for six volunteers, three men, three of the prettiest women, to stay on the courthouse ground and sing songs and dance after the churches let out.

"It might get the folks more excited," Titus Wheeler explained. "It might help us with the rest of our run here, get more people inside. Hell, I could've played to a bigger crowd at Harold's Barber Shop yesterday afternoon. And . . . we've got these."

Billy Kyne stepped on his cigarette, and removed a purse hanging from his shoulder. He opened it, reached inside, and pulled out some beads, of various colors, which he let fall back into the container.

"Y'all can sell 'em," the colonel said gleefully. "Maybe string some necklaces or such. If your women feels like it. We'll tell them these is genuine Comanch trade beads."

He was met with silence.

"Y'all get to keep all the money," Wheeler pleaded. "I ain't gonna make a dime on this. Fact is, I bought these beads the other day at a trading post. I'm gonna lose money. But it sure would help the rest of our run here."

"Maybe," Billy Kyne whispered, and grabbed the string that held his tobacco.

He started making his cigarette, when Ben Buffalo Bone said, in English, "Yes, I will sit on the lawn, and my sister will string your beads."

All eyes fell upon the fierce Kotsoteka.

"It will take us into the clean air," he said. "And at least I might see the money that has been promised The People."

So Ben Buffalo Bone and Oajuicauojué, Twice Bent Nose and his wife, and the two Penatekas, Tuhuupi and the fine singer, Ecahcueré, left with the pouch of beads, the colonel, and Billy Kyne.

They did not say much when they returned that afternoon, but Daniel noticed the beads in the pouch did not look much lower.

On Monday, the show resumed. On Tuesday, they had a bigger crowd, and on Wednesday morning, Oajuicauojué came to Daniel as he saddled his horse.

"I do not feel well," she whispered. Daniel dropped his hackamore. He saw the fear in her eyes. He touched her forehead. His heart raced.

"How long have you felt feverish?" he asked.

She shrugged. "The day we sold beads, or tried to sell beads, my back hurt so much I wanted to cry," she said.

"Why did you go?"

"My brother said I must go," she said.

He felt the blood racing to his head, and his fists clenched, and he imagined himself beating Oajuicauojué's brother's brains out.

Somehow, he pushed back the temper. He tried to keep his voice calm. "You are warm. Your back hurts. Is there more?"

That's when she collapsed. He caught her, and carried her away from the stock car. The Kiowa and Twice Bent Nose saw what had happened, and left their horses, catching up with Daniel as he carried Oajuicauojué into the parlor car. He laid the feverish woman on the closest couch.

Her eyes opened.

"You will be all right," Daniel told her.

She tried to smile.

"Is there more I need to know?" Daniel asked.

"I just feel weak, tired, worthless." Her eyes closed. "And my head hurts from the inside."

"You will be all right," he repeated. He stood, and looked at Apiatan and Twice Bent Nose.

"He Whose Arrows Fly Straight Into The Hearts Of His Enemies." Oajuicauojué spoke his Nermernuh name in a dream-like voice. "There is more."

Daniel knelt beside her again, took her right hand in his own, and waited till her eyes opened.

"Tuhuupi," Oajuicauojué whispered, "does not feel well, either."

CHAPTER SEVENTEEN

They waited outside on the siding, The People and the Kiowa near the parlor car; Black Yellow Stripes sitting on an overturned box by himself; Billy Kyne, Ivy Inman, and the colonel farther away, debating with the Albany marshal, the mayor who had been so welcoming a few days earlier, and the old Long Knives leader. Even farther away, armed guards wearing the tin stars kept the newspaper reporters and other citizens of Albany away. The scene reminded Daniel of their brief stay in El Reno.

How long ago had that been?

It did not matter.

Daniel had left the siding and found the colonel enjoying his breakfast at the fancy hotel on the square. He had been lucky. He doubted if the hotel would have let him inside, but the colonel was eating at a table near the window. When Daniel tapped on the glass, the colonel, Kyne, and, unfortunately, the mayor had walked outside. Daniel had hoped to inform the colonel in private, but Titus Wheeler had been drinking rye with his coffee, and said, "Speak your mind, Dan'l. My coffee's gettin' cold."

Daniel's eyes studied the faces of the reporter and the mayor, and so he spoke in the language of The People. "Oajuicauojué," he said softly, "and Tuhuupi are sick."

It seemed like a good plan to Daniel, but the colonel roared out in English: "What the devil do you mean by sick?"

"They have fevers. They are fatigued," he said in English.

"Reckon they ate some bad grub?" The colonel might have been pleading to his God. He smiled at the mayor, and wet his lips when he turned back to Daniel. His head bobbed. "That's what you're tellin' me, ain't it, Dan'l." He laughed. "Well, that's why we have more than two injun squaws. We'll keep the show goin'. Yes, sir. That's what . . . it is . . . ain't it . . . Dan'l?"

He spoke again in his own language. "It could be The Rotting Face."

Titus Wheeler had to grip the ornately carved column for support. He seemed unable to catch his breath.

"Titus," the mayor said hopefully.

The colonel looked around, his face flushed. "Billy, Ivy, where the hell is Toby? Toby Canton? The corporal who works at the Fort Sill hospital?" He managed to choke out those words, and he found a silk handkerchief in his morning suit and mopped his face.

"I haven't seen Canton since last night," Inman said. "Must be sleeping off a drunk in his hotel room."

"Find him."

He coughed, cursed, and looked at the mayor. "You got a doctor in this town?"

"Of course," the mayor said.

"Get him."

"What is it, Titus?" Ivy Inman hurried over.

"Get the damned doc!" Wheeler roared. "Those two squaws . . ." He turned to face his breakfast companions, and lowered his voice to a whisper. "It could be—the smallpox."

Well, Daniel thought now, they could not have kept this a secret forever, and it would not have been right not to let the taibos know. The doctor had arrived shortly after Wheeler and Daniel returned to the siding, with Kyne ordered to let the crew members know what was going on, and to wire the "investors," and the mayor running off to the town marshal's office.

151

By now, Daniel figured, word had spread across Shackelford County, maybe all the way to Dallas, and up to Fort Sill. Still, he did not see many people in the town, and he had not seen any crowds when he had gone to find the colonel. And the doctor had not come out of the car to give his verdict.

As soon as that thought reached Daniel, the door opened, and the doctor stepped off the railroad car.

He was an old man, with blue eyes underneath the gold-wire spectacles that must have cut into his nose and ears, and long, flowing whiskers that stretched down his cheeks and past his jaw. *Dundrearies* he had heard these growths called. He wore a blue and white bandana over his mouth and nose, but now he pulled it down with his left hand and breathed in and out deeply. His right hand held the black bag.

The old man pushed back his white jacket, and found a circular tin in his vest pocket. He stopped long enough to unscrew the lid, reach inside, and pinch the brown tobacco flakes and stick them in his lower gum. After the tin was closed and returned to its hiding place, he glanced at Daniel and the others, wet his lips with his tongue, and turned to walk toward the taibos.

"Why does he not tell us anything?" Ben Buffalo Bone roared. "That is my sister."

Oajuicauojué's brother was right. The People should be the first to know. The two sick women inside the railroad car were Nermernuh.

"I will hear what he has to tell the Pale Eyes," Daniel said, and he walked slowly behind the tired old *natsu* taibo.

The town marshal stepped in front of the others, and put his right hand on the butt of his revolver. "Colonel," he said, but kept his eyes trained on Daniel, "tell your buck there to stop, or I stop him permanently."

"Dan'l," Wheeler said, "don't come no farther."

152

Daniel stopped, but he said, "The sick women are of The People. We deserve to know how they are mending." Mending was what he hoped the old man would say.

"Just stay where you are."

"Well, Isaiah," the mayor said. "How bad is it?"

The old man turned and spit. He wiped his mouth with the back of his hand and said, "The women are sick. Running fevers of one hundred and three, one hundred and four."

"It's smallpox," shouted a man in the back.

The doctor sighed. "It might be. It very likely is. But we ought to wait. If red spots start breaking out in a day or two, I'll know for sure."

"The dirty red savages brought the smallpox to us!" someone shouted.

One of the reporters ran out of the crowd, likely headed to his newspaper or maybe the telegraph office.

Billy Kyne broke the silence with a calm question. "What do you think? Smallpox? Influenza? What?"

"I do not deal with thoughts," the old man said. "I deal with science. The red spots will tell us in a day or two."

"We already know what it is," said one of the armed deputies. "LeRoy Younger's in his shanty and his face is covered with red spots."

A murmur began and grew into a roiling hatred.

"I have not heard of that drunken sot being sick," the doctor said.

"Well, he is!" someone yelled.

"I bet those redskins give it to Younger," another voice rang out.

"Maybe," Daniel said, "this LeRoy Younger gave my friends The Rotting Face."

"Shut up, you red bastard!"

"Marshal," the mayor pleaded.

153

"Dear God," Titus Wheeler said, then blasphemed his God.

"Listen," the doctor said, "I will visit LeRoy Younger. I should have been told if he had smallpox. How long has he been sick?"

No one answered.

"Could he have gotten it from these injuns?" a reporter asked.

"I don't know." The doctor spit again. "I don't even know for sure that that worthless drunk has smallpox. And for the last time, I am a man of medicine, not speculation."

"Give us some facts," a reporter demanded.

So the doctor sighed. "From my own experience, treating smallpox, from the medical journals I have read, a person can be infected with smallpox for maybe a week—"

"These redskins and this stupid Wild West show have been here more than a week," the loudmouthed deputy interrupted.

"Maybe a little more than two weeks," the doctor continued. "Then the signs begin. Fever. Back pain that can be intense. But those symptoms are also associated with influenza. When the red spots appear, then we know it's smallpox. Those become blisters, the blisters burst, pus flows out, then the wounds scab over, resulting in scars."

Daniel rubbed his own scarred face. He could feel the scars, but his were small. The holy man had been good to Daniel all those years ago. He prayed Red Buffalo and this taibo doctor could keep Oajuicauojué beautiful. No, she would always be beautiful in Daniel's eyes.

"If," the doctor said, "they live that long."

"Kill the redskins now," someone shouted. "That's the best thing to do."

"And burn that damned train!"

"Marshal," the colonel pleaded. "Mayor."

"Listen to me, damn your idiotic souls!"

The doctor's shout silenced the crowd. "We are lucky. So far. We have two possible cases here. Two Indian women. We have all the Indians right here. If they brought the smallpox here, we can contain it. By containing them. And once I check on Le-Roy, we can keep him from other people."

He stopped. Rabid Wolf Jones was running, on foot. He looked even sober. No, Daniel realized as the man stopped near the crowd, and tried to catch his breath. The old scout looked scared.

"What?" Billy Kyne demanded.

"It's that . . . Yankee corporal," Rabid Wolf Jones managed. "He's in his room in the hotel. Sicker than a dog. Burnin' up with fever."

"Jesus God help us all," someone whispered.

The doctor with the long side whiskers cleared his throat. "I'll check on the corporal now." He wiped his brow. "The best thing, the safest thing, you people can do is go home, stay put, stay away from other people. What we do know about smallpox is that it spreads from contact. Breath. Touch. Possibly even clothes and such. And we can prevent it. With inoculations."

"Hell. That means putting that sickness in our own bodies."

"That's like committin' suicide!"

"It saves lives." The doctor spit again.

"Doctor," the colonel said. "We can keep my Indians here. On the train. Away from the rest of the town. Till this sickness goes away. Hell, they've hardly had any contact—"

"They've had enough contact with far too many good folks here the past week and a half," the marshal said. "Mayor, I say we run these scoundrels out of town."

"You can't do that," the mayor said. "Nobody's leaving Albany. We don't want this to turn into Daingerfield. Put guards at every road, Marshal. From now on, nobody comes into Albany, and nobody leaves Albany."

"Gentlemen," the doctor said. "I need to send a telegraph immediately to the state health officer in Austin." He turned to

155

Daniel. "I'll be back, son. Thank you for all you have done."

"What can I do now?" Daniel asked.

"You've had the pox, haven't you?"

Daniel nodded.

"You should be immune. You can look after the two girls till I return. If you see red spots, let me know immediately."

Daniel nodded.

"These Comanch will stay right here," the mayor said.

"No," the marshal interrupted. "This is too hard to guard." He pointed to the scrub on the other side of the tracks. "An injun, especially a Comanche buck, they could get into that wilderness and vanish. Next thing you know, we got smallpox all over the county, halfway across the state. They ain't staying here."

"How 'bout Owens's livery?" one of the deputies suggested. "It's been empty since he died last year. Far enough from the square and most of the folks in town. Easy enough to guard. Let's put 'em all in the livery."

"I like that idea," the marshal said.

"Wait a minute," the colonel said. "Some of these injuns of mine have already had smallpox. They can't spread—"

"We don't know that for certain," the marshal said.

"Doctor, tell them—"

"I said we don't know that for certain," the marshal said, and the colonel stared at the revolver, and wet his lips.

"How about the two sick squaws?" someone asked.

"They go with the others," the marshal said.

The doctor hooked the tobacco out of his mouth with a finger, wiped his lips, and said, "If it's all right with you, Marshal, I'm going to the telegraph office. Then to see LeRoy Younger. Then this Corporal Canton."

"Get Canton out of my hotel!" a voice bellowed.

"Virgil!" the colonel called, and the Black White Man, still sitting on the crate, looked up. He had not spoken during the entire exchange, but Daniel had noticed that Black White Men were like The People in the eyes of taibos. They were not seen, until taibos decided they were worth looking at, out of fear, or out of hatred, or both.

"Get our stuff out of the cars, anything that doesn't belong to our injuns. Get—"

"Nothing leaves those cars except them two sick squaws," the town marshal said.

"He's right, Titus," Billy Kyne said in a calm voice. "Clothes, blankets, anything those Comanches have touched . . . that could carry the smallpox to the public here."

"Damn."

"And that's another thing," the lawman said. "That darky. He goes in with the injuns. In Ned Olsen's old livery."

Black Yellow Stripes rose, his face turning hard, eyes blazing.

But they softened a moment later when the Ancient Bluecoat stepped out in front of Titus Wheeler and stared at the Black White Man.

"Corporal?" the old soldier said in a hoarse whisper. "Corporal Pry? Is that really you?"

The dark-skinned man came to attention, and snapped a salute. "Yes, sir, Colonel. Corporal Virgil Pry, reportin' for duty, sir." He smiled, but that did not last.

"Pry, boy," the marshal said, "if you got any gear on that train, get it off and fall in. You'll be bunkin' with the Comanches now. In the livery."

"Wait," the colonel said. "Virg, you've had the pox, ain't you?" He turned toward the marshal and the mayor. "See, if Virg has had the pox, he can't get it no more, and . . ."

"I don't rightly give a damn," the marshal said. "If it was up to me, you'd be bunkin' with them bastards, too, Colonel

157

Wheeler." But the lawman turned and stared at Black Yellow Stripes.

"But have you had the pox, boy?"

"No, sir," the dark man answered, softly, and stared at his worn boots.

"But, Virgil—" the Ancient Bluecoat said.

But the lawman interrupted the old man. "Then do like I said, boy. Get your possibles and fall in line with the others."

Being Kotsotekas, Ben Buffalo Bone and Kwasinaboo carried Oajuicauojué on a blanket from the siding to the crumbling livery stable just a block from the square. Ecahcueré, singing a healing song, carried Tuhuupi, assisted by Apiatan, the Kiowa. Red Buffalo led the convoy, rattling his gourd and singing his own song of healing. The others—Daniel; the two Nokonis, Tamasual and Ebicuyonit; and Twice Bent Nose and his wife, Huuhwiya—followed.

Daniel did not like this at all. It felt like the taibo funerals he had seen. Only Oajuicauojué was not dead. Nor was Tuhuupi.

Black Yellow Stripes brought up the rear, followed by the armed deputies of the town marshal. And newspaper reporters. Those could not all be from Albany, Daniel realized. But another Texas Central train had arrived, bringing in writers from other towns, and two Texas Rangers. It would be the last train to arrive in Albany. And it would not leave until The Rotting Face was no more in this taibo city.

The livery owned by this Mr. Olsen was not much, but it was big. They laid Oajuicauojué in one stall in the middle of the barn, Tuhuupi across from her. Those who had been sick with The Rotting Face stayed in the stalls closest to the two women; those who bore no telling signs of The Rotting Face closer to the big door. Black Yellow Stripes had the stall closest to the door. And he was the only one allowed to keep his firearm.

Because, Daniel figured, a Black White Man was closer to being a taibo than one of The People.

But these taibos were not good at searching The People for firearms, perhaps because they did not get close to those they were escorting to this place for taibo horses, this place that they were now turning into a prison for men and women, sick and healthy, with red skin. And one with black skin. Daniel kept his old Remington. Ben Buffalo Bone sneaked in his small Smith & Wesson that he had taken from a Chickasaw whiskey runner.

Red Buffalo said that the stalls at the back of the barn must remain empty. For now.

"Why?" the Kiowa asked.

"Those places will be taken," Red Buffalo said with his tongue and his hands, "by those among us who will soon travel to The Land Beyond The Sun."

Apiatan looked as though the Kwahadi holy man was speaking about him.

CHAPTER EIGHTEEN

Oajuicauojué felt warmer, but her eyes opened as soon as Daniel removed his hand from her forehead. When she tried to swallow, but couldn't, Daniel found the bucket of water that some of Albany's citizens, those belonging to the Presbyterian tribe, had brought, along with ladles made from gourds, to help "the oppressed."

Hatred did not flow through the blood of all taibos. Others had brought cold biscuits and greasy bacon.

"Get away from my sister."

Daniel glanced at Ben Buffalo Bone. *Just as understanding does not flow through the blood of all The People.* Ignoring the Kotsoteka, he turned back to the sick woman, lifted her head, and let her drink.

When Daniel turned to refill the ladle, Oajuicauojué's oldest brother kicked Daniel's wrist. The ladle flew against the heavy wooden walls of the stall, but did not break, and Daniel, shaking his hand, rose.

"Stop." Oajuicauojué's voice barely reached the two men's ears.

They stared at each other, then Daniel knelt again.

"She is my concern, not yours!" Ben Buffalo Bone yelled.

"Oajuicauojué," Daniel whispered, and wiped the perspiration off her forehead. Her eyes remained closed. He called her name again, adding, "my love."

Behind him, Ben Buffalo Bone spoke a taibo curse, but

Daniel kept his attention on the sick woman.

Her eyes opened just a slit.

"How long have you felt sick?" he asked.

When she tried to speak, but couldn't, Daniel slid over to the ladle, retrieved it, gave Ben Buffalo Bone a look that told him not to say, not to do one thing, and he let the water fill the deep spoon, and brought it again to Oajuicauojué's lips.

She drank.

"How long?" Daniel asked.

"Two days," she whispered. "Three." The last word he knew only from reading her lips.

He let her drink again, just a small swallow, and he found the rag by her left ear. He poured the remaining water onto it, squeezed it slightly, and laid the damp rag on her head.

"You are doing well," he told her. "You are strong. Red Buffalo brings you good medicine. You rest." His voice began to crack and he felt the strange wetness in his eyes. "There is too much for you and I to see, to do."

He did not turn around until he had dammed the tears, until he felt his breathing as close to normal.

Ben Buffalo Bone glared. "What does it matter how many days she has felt sick? You drain her strength making her talk."

He thought about not answering. But that might cause more trouble between Ben Buffalo Bone and himself, and enough trouble had entered this home for horses. He thought of his own home, the cabin Ben Buffalo Bone's father had once made into stables for his best ponies. He wished he were there now.

After dropping the ladle in the bucket, he looked into Ben Buffalo Bone's cold eyes. "Do you remember when your father's father had The Rotting Face?"

"No. Remembering bad things rots one's heart."

Daniel thought of the irony of those words coming from that mouth.

"We left our homes more than a moon ago," Daniel said in the tongue of The People. "Even the Pale Eyes doctor with the hair on his cheeks that should be braided and wrapped in otter skins and the one at the soldier-fort near our home have said that the sickness that brings The Rotting Face does not begin till ten, maybe fourteen days after the illness is in our bodies. Only then can The Rotting Face spread from one person to another."

Ben Buffalo Bone just stared, lips flattened, eyes burning.

"If what they say is true, then we could not have brought The Rotting Face with us. If the Yamparikas had spread the sickness to us, Oajuicauojué and Tuhuupi would have become sick when we were in the town called for a soldier-fort that is no longer there."

"What does it matter where my sister got The Rotting Face?"

"The Pale Eyes believe we brought this sickness to them." Daniel shook his head. "They brought it to us."

Ben Buffalo Bone's laugh was mirthless. "He Whose Arrows Fly Straight Into The Hearts Of His Enemies, you are a fool. Of course, Pale Eyes brought The Rotting Face to us. Before our fathers' fathers were born. They have killed more of us with their diseases and their whiskey than they could ever kill us with their guns and long knives."

"Come!" a voice shouted from near the front of the livery.

Daniel and Ben Buffalo Bone turned and hurried away, leaving Tuhuupi and Oajuicauojué, struggling to fill their lungs with ragged breaths, in their respective stalls.

The Tin Star man called "Deputy" with the sawed-off shotgun in his hands and two revolvers in his belt turned around when the door creaked open.

"Easy does it, boys," the taibo said, and the thumb on his left hand nuzzled the hammers of the big gun.

Kwasinaboo had seen the bright light of the fire through the cracks in the wall of the livery. Now the men stared through the open doorway. Deputy seemed to realize these prisoners did not mean to escape, but were as curious as Deputy was. But he did not look back at the orange sky in the blackness of night.

The smell of the smoke told Daniel what burned was not just wood. It stank of taibo things. Whatever it was, it burned hot, and what burned had to be big. But it was not the stone courthouse. Daniel could see its outline against the light from the flames. Nor was it any of the buildings on the square. Part of those were outlined, too, and this fire burned farther away.

Then, Daniel understood, and a sigh escaped his breath.

Twice Bent Nose did, as well. "It is," he said, "the Houses On Wheels of the Fire Wagon that brought us here."

The next morning, the door to the livery opened and a new deputy, younger and fatter than the one the night before but still armed with two revolvers and that deadly shotgun, stepped back. "I need the one called Killstraight," he said.

Twice Bent Nose found Daniel in the stall with Oajuicauojué. Across the path of boards, dirt and hay, Red Buffalo sang his song of healing and waved his rattle over Tuhuupi. After hearing the summons, Daniel frowned.

"Huuhwiya will look after Oajuicauojué," Twice Bent Nose said, "until Red Buffalo uses his healing powers on Oajuicauojué."

Daniel just stared at the sick woman before him.

"He Whose Arrows Fly Straight Into The Hearts Of His Enemies," Twice Bent Nose said. "There is nothing you can do for her right now. And the Pale Eyes are not patient men."

The deputy with the shotgun walked Daniel across the street to the gruff taibo marshal, who removed the cigar from his mouth and said, "Your boss wants to see you."

He noticed the CLOSED signs on the doors of many of the businesses. Few horses were tethered to the hitch rails. A handful of people lounged on the benches in the lawn in front of the courthouse, but even that tall building appeared practically empty. No chatter emerged from the saloon, but it was early morning, and even Tejanos had to sleep. A handful of men gathered in front of the barbershop, but not for haircuts, Daniel understood. Leaning against the striped poll was Colonel Titus Wheeler.

"Sheriff," the big man said.

"Marshal," the lawman corrected. "The sheriff is busy spreading word throughout the county about the smallpox you brought here."

"I beg to differ, sir," the colonel said, straightening into the ramrod position he could hold for a few minutes only. "The surgeon at Fort Sill gave each and every one of us a clean bill of health. This disease cannot be blamed on us. But I am blaming this town for the arson of the rolling stock loaned to me by myriad investors."

Daniel realized that the colonel was not talking to the marshal, but to the newspapermen. Those are the ones who had gathered this morning to hear his interview, though no one was asking questions at the moment. Men and one woman scribbled words on paper with fast-moving pencils. Even Billy Kyne, leaning against a column that supported the barbershop's awning, occasionally wrote a word or two in the pad he held.

"Your train, sir," the lawman said, "was burned to protect this city, this county, and this state. We've had enough smallpox already, Colonel. And you cannot deny that those squaws was sick."

"But," the colonel said, "we have not yet determined it is smallpox."

"It is," Daniel said. His heart sank at his words.

Every eye on that boardwalk stared at him.

"Red spots appeared last night on the face of Blackjack Oak," he said, using the taibo translation for the Penateka woman's name. "And this morning on the forehead of the sister of Ben Buffalo Bone."

Pencils scratched at a frenetic pace.

The colonel dropped and kneeled, his head bowed, his breath ragged. One of the newspapermen shoved the pencil over an earlobe, the pad into a coat pocket, and raced off in the direction of the telegraph office, but he stopped when a buggy turned the corner. Then he ran toward the mule-driven phaeton. So did a few other reporters when they realized that the driver was the doctor with the long whiskers on his cheeks.

"Them squaws' faces are blistered all to hell," one of the men shouted. "What's the next stage?"

The doctor did not answer, but he stopped the buggy in front of the barbershop. "Is that true, Orville?"

The marshal shrugged. "The Comanch here just told us. Two women. The sick ones. Ain't that right, buck?"

"It is," Daniel said, "The Rotting Face."

"How many again," the doctor said, "of those in the barn who haven't had smallpox?"

"Of my people," Daniel said, "just four. The Kiowa. Ben Buffalo Bone. Ebicuyonit. And Ecahcueré."

"How do you say that last two in English, pardner?" a reporter asked.

"Roadrunner and Woodpecker."

A few of the men laughed, but still wrote the words on their papers.

"Keep them away from the two infected girls," the doctor said. He reached for the whip, but stopped at the next question, this one asked by the woman.

"How is LeRoy Younger doing?"

The hand tightened against the whip's handle, and the old man's eyes closed as though he had prayed this question would not be asked. But it had been. And he knew he had to answer. At least, that's how it seemed to Daniel.

"LeRoy Younger," the doctor said, "died this morning." He swallowed, paused for maybe half a minute, and then continued.

"Clarabelle Hopkins is sick with the smallpox, too. And her boy, Carter. I'm on my way to see Murdock Harker. The Army boy from Sill, Canton, is in my office. His face and back are practically all blisters now."

How are they, Doctor? . . . Does the kid have the pox, too? . . . Where does this Clarabelle live? . . . Is Harker sick with the smallpox? . . . How hard was Younger's death? . . . How many of these people attended Colonel Wheeler's show? . . . How much longer do you think those squaws have to live? . . . What's the chances of the damnyankee dying?

More questions blurred together. The doctor did not answer. He whipped the mule with a fury, and two of the reporters, standing in the street, had to jump out of the mule and the phaeton's path.

But as soon as the buggy and the doctor had turned down a side street, with only two of the reporters running after the old man, another rider trotted up.

"Howdy, Dan'l," the dust-coated man on the lathered horse said. "You don't look sick to me."

Daniel blinked, shook his head, and looked again. It was Homer Blomstrom, civilian scout out of Fort Sill.

The reporters studied the man briefly, then surrounded Titus Wheeler, calling out his name, pounding him with questions in a rush so that no one could understand what was being asked.

"Wait a damned minute." The town marshal studied Blomstrom for a moment, waved his finger, and said, "I'll speak to you in a minute, stranger." He whirled to the colonel, looked at the crowd, and said, "Where's that manager of yours? And the drunken sot you call a famous Rabid-something Army scout?"

Wheeler's shoulders sagged. "They . . . deserted me. Lit out last night."

A string of curses left the marshal's throat. "Damn it all to hell. This town's under quarantine. Telegraph Austin." Daniel didn't know to whom that order was directed. "Nobody comes in here. Nobody leaves. Send another wire to Fort Worth, Jacksboro, hell, send it to Austin, too. Say that scout and that damned loudmouth who works for Wheeler need to be arrested and detained. Get their names from that piece of shit who brought Comanches and smallpox to Albany."

He took a few steps, stopped, and pointed again at the Fort Sill scout. "And you don't leave here, mister. You don't leave here at all."

Blomstrom's eyes were bloodshot, but that likely came from a hard ride in a dusty country. His voice sounded tired, not drunk. And now he grinned and pointed at the big hat, about all of the colonel that could be seen behind the mass of reporters.

"Is that that col'nel feller who wrote all them yarns about you, Dan'l? . . . You know, that Colonel Titan Wheeler?"

One reporter had not followed the colonel. He stepped closer to the horseman and Daniel.

"Who's your pal, partner?" Billy Kyne asked.

The scout turned, studied Kyne, chuckled, and spit tobacco juice into the street. "Folks call me Homer," he said, and held out his hand. "Homer Blomstrom. I scout for the bluebellies up at Fort Sill."

Kyne shook, and did not flinch at Blomstrom's grip.

"Name's Kyne," the newspaperman and the colonel's press man said.

Daniel interrupted the introductions. "How are my people? How is Quanah? What is The Rotting Face like among the Yamparikas?" He stopped himself. He sounded like one of those newspapermen.

"Hell, pard." Blomstrom turned to Daniel. "I don't know exactly. Oh, you mean the pox. Well, I been ridin' hard a spell, so things might could've changed. Quanah was fine, last I heard. The pox seems to be contained to just the Yamparikas. But, hell, that can change like a prairie fire with the wind."

He looked around the town square. "Hell, this place is deader than a graveyard."

"What brought you here?" Billy Kyne said.

"Hell." The scout laughed. "That smallpox might be just with that one band, but I ain't one to risk my perty face. I lit a shuck for here. Me? I ain't gettin' no smallpox." He kept looking around the square, wetting his lips.

"Mister," Billy Kyne said, "you should've come to another town."

CHAPTER NINETEEN

He woke up, sleeping on the hay without covers, and rolled over, letting his eyes adjust to the dim lanterns hanging on the posts. The taibos had insisted that the livery stable remain lit during the night. "Perhaps," Kwasinaboo had said, "they hope a lantern will break, and we will all burn."

At least, the taibos agreed to let them turn the lanterns down during the night.

He saw dust motes, and particles of hay, descending in the dim light. Now he sat up, listening. Footsteps. Daniel followed the sound. A moment later, Ben Buffalo Bone descended the ladder, jumping the last two feet, landing softly, and looking around. The lantern hanging on the post near Daniel's stall likely spoiled his eyesight. Daniel only made him out through the slats in the stall, and the lantern on the wall near the ladder.

Ben Buffalo Bone rose, and crept toward the stalls where the sick, including his sister, lay. Over his shoulder was a canvas sack that rattled slightly as he disappeared deeper into the livery.

Daniel laid back down now, hands cradling his head, and remembered.

"Wake up, boy."

He tries to cement his eyelids. Not another, he prays. The wooden ruler slaps his bare feet, but he dares not cry out.

"Wake up, boy," the taibo witch says. "Or I slit your throat and I find another red-skinned gravedigger and I bury you with this girl."

This time, the ruler pounds his nose.

He gasps, covers his nose with both hands, and cries out, "Yee! Tʉtsanʉnu̠ʔitʉ!"

"Ohhh." Miss Brunot laughs. The ruler raps his knuckles. " 'No,' the Comanche warrior says. 'Stop.' " She draws out the last word, as Daniel's eyes open. She stares at him, laughs again. Her breath stinks of whiskey. And she says:

"Pʉhkai!"

Stop crying, *she had just told him. But she spoke in the language of The People.*

"That's right, Danny, my favorite gravedigger. I understand every damned word you say. I know exactly what you call me. I can understand what the Sioux say, too. And enough Cheyenne to get by in some parleys. Now get up, boy. There's an Arapaho to bury."

She raises the ruler, but Daniel cringes, and sits up suddenly. His chest heaves.

The Carlisle witch smiles. "Don't worry, Daniel. This one isn't contagious. The bitch hanged herself last night. Get up. Now, boy. Put your shoes on. No need for a coat. It's a right pleasant evening. The shovel's waiting. It's time to dig another grave."

He did not know how long he stared at the planks above him. He did not sleep. When the traces of a wagon jingled its harmony to the clomping of oxen's hooves, he sat up, found the stall with the slop buckets, the ones the taibos had yet to empty or allow their prisoners to empty, and urinated. He started to wipe his hands on a dingy towel, but remembered the Albany doctor saying that The Rotting Face could be spread through clothing, bedding, things of that nature. "It just takes, we think, a little longer to be transmitted that way," he had told the newspapermen and the one newspaperwoman. He wiped his hands on his pants legs, and walked quietly until he reached Oajuicauojué's stall.

Ben Buffalo Bone stood behind the stalls where his sister and Tuhuupi lay. But someone was inside Oajuicauojué's stall.

Daniel walked past Ben Buffalo Bone and stared at Red Buffalo, who covered the sores on Oajuicauojué's with something from a jar—and other jars were tossed about in the hay.

PETROLEUM JELLY
CARBONATED

Most of the other jars were of the same brand, but Daniel also spotted Ron's Reliable Work Cakes, Doctor Becker's Prime Nerve Tonic, Camphor Cold Cream, Liver Pills, Female Pills, Witch Hazel Toilet Cream, Whale Oil, and Schmidt's Herb Tea-Regulator for all Disorders.

The holy man turned, nodded at Daniel, and resumed applying a mixture of the carbonated petroleum jelly and whale oil to Oajuicauojué's face. Then he picked up a tiny bell and rang it six times over both of her cheeks, six times over her forehead, and then he turned her over gently, pulled down the dress, and began applying the salve to the more numerous blisters on her shoulders and upper arms.

He sang as he worked.

> The bell is your magic
> It is your name
> It cures you
> The taibo medicine cures you
> You will live
> You will live
> You will live
> The bell is your magic
> It is your name
> It cures you

Daniel just stood there, watching, as the morning light began sneaking through the cracks of the outer wall.

When Red Buffalo had finished, he screwed on the lids, and wiped his hands on his pants legs.

"Help me to my feet, my son," the Kwahadi said.

"I will," Ben Buffalo Bone said.

"No." Red Buffalo's voice was firm. "You have not had The Rotting Face. You will stay away from your sister."

The Kotsoteka glared, but let Daniel pass.

When all three stood in the aisle, Red Buffalo put his hand on the left shoulder of Oajuicauojué's brother. "You did fine work, my son. I thank you, and your sister will thank you."

"I do not like putting Pale Eyes medicine on my sister."

Ben Buffalo Bone's face remained hard, but the holy man grinned. "You wear the shirt of a Pale Eye," he said. "You have a short gun of a Pale Eye." He laughed. "The horse you ride you probably stole from a Pale Eye." His eyes moved to Daniel. "There is much The People can learn from the Pale Eyes. Including how to stop The Rotting Face."

Red Buffalo's head bobbed. "When The Rotting Face first struck The People, I was not even born. The first time I saw it, I had seen ten winters. I have seen it many times since. Too many to count. The holy man of my village fought it with song and rattle. I do that still, though it is just to honor the holy man who taught me, guided me, helped me on my journey. But songs and rattles, do they work? I do not know. It is like the songs The Jesus People sing. The prayers the Pale Eyes offer to their Jesus, or their Jesus's Mother. Does their Jesus listen? Does their God answer them? Maybe. If their God feels generous. If you ask a Pale Eye, he might tell you that The People are not known for generosity. But he is wrong."

He looked back at Ben Buffalo Bone. "And we have been wrong, too."

The old man turned again, smiled at the sleeping woman in the stall, and then asked Daniel, "When you had The Rotting Face, He Whose Arrows Fly Straight Into The Hearts Of His Enemies, what did the holy man in your village do to cure you?"

Daniel shook his head. "I can only answer what my mother and my father told me. And what I think I remember. But I was crazy. I was a boy. I do not remember much." He nodded, remembering. "He sang and danced and called upon the spirits. The holy man . . ." He would not say the name of the great man, though he remembered it well, would never forget it, because that great man had gone years ago on the road to The Land Beyond The Sun. "He turned the evil that had invaded my body into a stone. He took the stone away. He buried it deep beneath a stone. And I lived. He was a good holy man. He taught me much. He saved my life." He rubbed his cheeks. "I was blessed, though I do not know why. My face is not as bad as others." His head shook, then hung down. "But my left shoulder runs thick with pocks and scars."

Red Buffalo remained quiet for just a minute. "Do you believe the stone the holy man showed your parents and buried was the cause of The Rotting Face?"

Daniel realized he was biting his lower lip. No one had ever asked him such a question, and to ask him in front of Ben Buffalo Bone made the blood rush through Daniel's body. He felt light-headed, but when he raised his eyes and saw the gentle face, the loving eyes of the holy man, a calmness overcame him. And he answered.

"No."

"You are not of The People," Ben Buffalo Bone said. "You lived too long with the Pale Eyes, and your mother—"

"Enough." Red Buffalo turned toward the Kotsoteka. "I will not tell you again. Your anger, your mouth bring trouble to The People. You did me a kind service last night. I thank you for that. Your sister will thank you, too. But you will be quiet now and hear me. He Whose Arrows Fly Straight Into The Hearts Of His Enemies is right."

He laughed, and shook his head. "I have never turned anything into a pebble, except a larger stone, and then it became many pebbles." The laugh faded, as did the gentleness in his eyes, and his head shook again.

"We tried sweating out the sickness. Into the sweat lodge, we would send those with The Rotting Face. Then they would dive into a cold stream. That did not stop The Rotting Face. It likely helped send many to The Land Beyond The Sun. But The People are smart. We have always been smart. Smart at stealing horses. Of driving away our enemies. Until Bad Hand killed our ponies. And forced Quanah to take us to the soldier-fort and surrender to the Long Knives."

"You Kwahadis were not stuck behind the walls as we were," Ben Buffalo Bone whispered.

"No, we were not. And we were allowed to keep some of our ponies. But that was the decision of Bad Hand. And that is not of which I speak."

He drew in a breath, let it out, and continued.

"We learned that the way to kill off The Rotting Face is isolation." He nodded again. "The Tejanos were right in putting us here. And that is why we have put the sick here, away from those who have not yet shown the signs of The Rotting Face." He turned and stared hard at Ben Buffalo Bone. "And that is why you are not allowed near your sister. You have not had The Rotting Face. You should pray that you never have The Rotting Face. You are a handsome man. A powerful man among the Kotsotekas. You did a brave thing for me last night. You must be even braver for your sister—and the rest of your family."

A taibo shouted outside the barn, somewhere farther away. A horse trotted past. The day was beginning in Albany.

"We talk too loud," Red Buffalo said. "Come, let your sister sleep. I will be back later to apply more of the Pale Eyes medicine."

"What are the other bottles and jars for?" Daniel whispered.

Red Buffalo smiled. "I sent this brave Kotsoteka for petroleum oil and whale oil. I have been using those for years. I showed the bottles I brought with me to him. He does not read Pale Eyes' marks well, but he is smart and brave. I do not know what the other medicines are. Perhaps you can read them and tell us. Maybe they are good medicines, too."

Daniel felt slighted. "You could have sent me," he told the holy man. "I read, write, and speak the tongue better . . ."

Daniel's voice trailed off. He was jealous. And suddenly he remembered that scene he had recalled earlier. He read, wrote, and spoke the taibo tongue because of what he had learned in Carlisle. But he had paid a huge sum for that education, those long years. The taibo witch would haunt him till he traveled to The Land Beyond The Sun.

"No," Red Buffalo said. "I could not have sent you, my son. The Pale Eyes would have caught you."

Delight filled Ben Buffalo Bone's eyes, but there was nothing Daniel could do. The Kwahadi holy man was right, so Daniel changed the subject.

"What of Tuhuupi?" he asked. "Have you applied the medicine to her . . . ?"

The face of Red Buffalo Bone stopped him, and he knew what the holy man was going to tell him before the words left his mouth.

"My son, the Penateka child is making her journey to The Land Beyond The Sun."

He knew he would have to open the big door, tell whoever was guarding the prisoners that one of them had died. How would the Tejanos react? Would they let the Penateka girl be buried? Would they leave her to rot with the rest of them? Or would that be the catalyst that led them to douse the outer walls of the livery stable with coal oil and set it ablaze?

They passed the stall where Apiatan lay still asleep, then arrived where the others had gathered, eating what little food they still had. In the stall nearest the door, Black Yellow Stripes carved tobacco with a pocketknife.

Daniel sighed and started for the door, but stopped at the sudden pounding.

A moment later, the door opened just enough to allow light, and—not the deputy or one of the hired guards with the two pistols and the shotgun—but the town marshal. He held his own revolver in his right hand, and the hammer had been eared back to full cock.

"Killstraight," the lawman said. "Get out here. Hands where I can see them. Pronto."

The brightness of the sun, although it remained still early morning, caused Daniel to shield his eyes. He hoped the town marshal could still see his hands. Squinting, he lowered his arms, keeping them well away from his sides, and saw three deputies, Billy Kyne, and Titus Wheeler. The colonel still wore a nightshirt, loosely stuffed into his britches. The suspenders hung at his boots, which were on the wrong feet.

The newspaperman who was now a press man finished rolling a cigarette, and stuck it in his mouth, lighted it, and struck a calm pose. His boss's face was not calm, but for once, the big man was not talking.

"All right." The town marshal's right hand still held the revolver, but his left gripped an old canvas sack. "Roland, lead the way."

"Jesus Christ." Billy Kyne tossed his cigarette away.

Between a cobbler's store and a gun shop, they had entered an alley that led to the town square. Daniel could see the fancy hotel where the colonel and Billy Kyne had been staying since they had arrived in Shackelford County. The big courthouse looked abandoned again.

Then he made himself look at the dead man.

"Check out the knife, injun," the marshal said. "But watch how you hold it. Roland, if you so much as think he's gonna use that blade on one of us, blow the son of a bitch's head off."

The barrel of a shotgun pressed against Daniel's back, and he stepped closer to the corpse. Most of the blood had dried, but there was a lot of blood. Kneeling, he reached over and studied the knife. Dark stains remained on the handle, and even the blade.

"It's an injun knife." The marshal's voice was icy. "Ain't it?"

The handle was rectangular, bone ivory, the end topped with pounded nickel. The blade, maybe eight inches from handle to end, was steel, the top coming down at a straight angle, the bottom curving to a spear-like point. It might have been from a tai-bo's Bowie knife, then stuck onto the bone handle. It had to be old, though, from the wear of both bone and steel. Forty years? Fifty?

"The sheath," the lawman said. "That definitely didn't belong to any white man."

That was old, too, and it lay by the corpse's scalped head. The sheath was beaded, blue, green, yellow, black, white, and gold trade beads—of much better quality than what Colonel Wheeler had given the women to make necklaces for taibos on the courthouse grounds. The fringe at the bottom and along both sides had been decorated with tiny tin cones.

"Well." The marshal's impatience grew.

"The knife and the sheath," Daniel said, "are Southern Cheyenne."

"Horseshit," said one of the deputies. "It's Comanch."

Daniel turned his head toward the marshal.

"It is Southern Cheyenne," he repeated.

The marshal had holstered his revolver. Now he reached into the sack, and pulled out a small, paperbound book that was also stained with blood. He flipped it and it sailed end over end, but landed at the dead man's feet.

Despite the blackened blood, Daniel could see enough of the cover to recognize it.

Prince of the Prairie; or, the Demon of the Dakota Prairie, by Colonel Titus Wheeler.

He looked away from the penny dreadful and at the butchered body of Homer Blomstrom, whose eyes fastened on Daniel, but saw nothing—at least, not on this side of The Land Beyond The Sun.

CHAPTER TWENTY

They leaned against the hitch rail in front of the gun shop, or sat on the bench in front of the cobbler's store, or stood in front of the walls of the two buildings, smoking cigarettes, or staring at their feet.

No one spoke until the Albany doctor with the long side whiskers came out of the alley, wiping his bloody hands with a towel. Then he reached into the pocket of his duster, and withdrew the bloody topknot, which he tossed at the lawman's feet.

"That was in the trash box." The doctor made a casual gesture toward the far end of the alley. "Reckon your intelligent deputies didn't think to look there."

"What else can you tell me, Isaiah?" the lawman said. "Without your smart-aleck comments."

The doctor went back to cleansing his hands, but he would need much soap and much hot water and a lot of time to do a thorough job.

"The old boy—" He stopped suddenly, and found the colonel. "What was his name again?"

Titus Wheeler looked surprised, and he turned for help from Billy Kyne, but the reporter shrugged. "He said it, but damned if I remember it."

"Homer Blomstrom," Daniel answered. "He scouted for the Army at Fort Sill."

"So you admit to knowing what's left of that damnyankee."

The marshal tapped the ash off his cigarette on the post in front of the hitch rail.

"I knew him," Daniel said. "You know I knew him."

The marshal pulled on his cigarette and exhaled, never taking his eyes off Daniel. "It's a long, hard ride from Fort Sill. His horse was quite worn out when he showed up yesterday."

Daniel had nothing to add to that.

"You talked to him," the lawman said. He looked again at Kyne. "You, too." When neither offered any more thoughts, the marshal turned back to the doctor. "Well?"

"He was killed sometime last night, Orville, maybe early this morning. Not much of a sign of a struggle, so my guess is that he was stabbed in the back. That was just for starters. That likely would have killed him, but whoever did this wanted to make a statement, an example, or just hated the poor bastard enough to keep right on stabbing. I stopped counting after forty-two. That doesn't include the deep cut across his throat. Or the . . ." He stopped, swallowed, and looked at the scalp on the boardwalk.

"Pick that up, Roland," the lawman said. "And put it back in this sack." He tossed the grain sack onto the planks.

"It wasn't robbery," the marshal said. "Found a purse with a good chunk of his payday, I warrant. Why'd he come down here, Killstraight? Why'd he bring that dime novel with your name on it?"

"I do not know. He did not say."

The cigarette flipped end over end into the street. "Well, I've got a dead man who knew you, who came all the way down from Fort Sill. Who talked to you. And who got cut into ribbons and had his topknot took off . . . with a Comanche knife."

"Southern Cheyenne," Daniel said.

"Says you."

"Says anyone who has seen the beadwork of *Sarii Tuhka?*,"

Daniel said. "None does it better."

"It's Cheyenne, all right." The colonel stepped forward.

"Well, where were you last night, Colonel?" The lawman frowned.

"Drinkin'. A lot. And then sleepin' it off, till I got roused by your damned deputy, Mister Roland. And I bet anyone walking on the top floor of your fine hotel heard me. Ask Roland."

The deputy cut off his chuckle. "Like a freight train, Boss."

"How about you, Killstraight?" the marshal asked. "Where were you last night?"

"In a stall in the livery stable you have put us in."

"See anybody leave last night? Any Comanch, I mean? Or the darky? That Kiowa buck?"

He could answer honestly. "I saw no one leave."

"Figured that's what you'd say." He sighed. "It's still an injun knife," the lawman said to no one in particular, "and we got plenty of injuns to pin this on."

"Open your eyes, Marshal." Billy Kyne sounded disgusted. "An Indian wouldn't leave a knife like that, or a finely beaded sheath. Those were left for one purpose. To make you imbeciles blame these Indians for this grisly crime. And those Indians you keep wanting to blame for this, they were locked in that rundown livery. How the hell do you think they got out without being spotted?"

The lawman's smile unsteadied those arguing with him. "That's easy, Mister Inkslinger. Roland found Benji Chandler with his head practically cracked open in front of the barn door when Roland went to relieve him this morning." He looked at the doctor. "By the way, Doc, how is Benji faring now?"

"Concussion," the doctor said. "He'll live. But his head is going to hurt for quite some time. Once the laudanum wears off."

Billy Kyne looked stunned. He went back to focusing on his smoking.

"Maybe," the lawman said, and his eyes found Daniel again. "Maybe a smart injun figured that leaving a Cheyenne knife and the fancy sheath behind would make us think it weren't no damned Comanch who killed this old boy. And from what I hear, you, Mister Killstraight, being educated in all our ways at that damnyankee school in Pennsylvania, maybe you scalped that Mister Blomstrom, too. How do you argue that, Killstraight?"

Daniel had had enough. "None of my people," he said, "took that taibo's scalp. That was taken by someone who doesn't know how to take a scalp."

He regretted those words immediately. If the lawman was smart, he might suggest that Daniel, being educated at Carlisle, might have never taken a scalp himself. And then a thought made Daniel shiver.

Ben Buffalo Bone had never scalped an enemy, either.

The Tejanos decided to let Daniel return to the livery. "Maybe the pox will kill them all," one of the deputies said. And that reminded Daniel.

"It has killed one of us already," he whispered.

The doctor sighed. "Which one?" he asked, although he likely knew none of the names of those in the livery, and knew Daniel only by the name he had been given at Carlisle.

"The Penateka girl," he said. "She wore the buckskin dress." He motioned with his hands. "To her knees. With paintings of buffalo on the bottoms, and porcupine plumes on the top." He smiled. "She was very proud of that dress. Her mother helped her make it. Her earrings sang when she danced. She loved to dance."

Billy Kyne now found his pencil and his pad. "What was her name?"

Daniel paused. "You would have called her Blackjack Oak.

182

She was as strong as the trunk of that tree, though not strong enough." He stared at the boardwalk. *Breathe in, breathe out, look up,* he told himself, then made himself obey his orders. His eyes found the lawman.

"We should bury her," he said.

"Stick her in the back of the stables," the lawman said. "Ain't none of you bucks or bitches coming out of that livery till this plague is past us."

"Orville, for the love of God," the doctor started, but he realized the hopelessness of arguing.

"And," the marshal continued, "till I have the man who murdered that damnyankee scout."

The doctor shook his head, then said, "The Comanche girl isn't the only one who died last night. Corporal Canton is dead."

"He was a good man, Canton," Billy Kyne said as he walked beside Daniel, two armed deputies behind him.

"A brave man," Daniel said. "He came with us even when he had never had The Rotting Face. He should have stayed with the Long Knives."

"Probably wishes he had, now."

They walked.

"I'm sorry, Killstraight. That was a callous thing to say."

They reached the edge of the old livery. "Daniel," Kyne whispered when Daniel reached the opened door.

He turned.

"Did you see anyone leave here last night?" He smiled without humor. "I'm asking as a newspaperman."

"I saw no one leave." He turned back toward the door.

"How about return?"

This time, Daniel, holding his head down, did not answer.

When the door closed behind him, Daniel looked up to find

The People waiting for him, their faces concerned. Not for him, he realized.

"What has happened?" he asked in a whisper.

"The Kiowa," Twice Bent Nose said. "The Rotting Face has struck him."

Two deputies let Daniel out again the next morning, and those two deputies remained behind while a third escorted him to the square.

Daniel tried to picture the tent where they had performed the amusement, the smiling faces, and the frightened faces of the taibo men, women, and children. The women of The People making necklaces out of the cheap beads the colonel had given them. And reading that novel, penned by Billy Kyne but under Titus Wheeler's name, for *Gerald P. Shumaker, Publisher, 13 Rose Avenue, New York,* by the fire in front of the cabin the taibos had built for Ben Buffalo Bone's father, and Ben Buffalo Bone, then one of his longest and best friends, telling Daniel it was to be his home. Ben Buffalo Bone could have driven Daniel away. Maybe he should have.

He saw the newspapermen and the one newspaperwoman waiting, and knew why he had been summoned. What he did not understand was why the colonel was screaming at Billy Kyne.

But as he and the deputy crossed the empty street toward the courthouse lawn, he soon found out.

"You can read, can't you, Kyne?" The colonel waved a newspaper in front of the smoking press agent. "You can read. That!" He pointed a finger. "That's your name, ain't it?"

Kyne snatched the flapping paper from Wheeler's left hand, and looked down the page.

"It says," the colonel snapped, " 'as reported from the scene by Wm. Which means William, to my understanding. Kyne.

W-m Kyne. For the *New-York Tribune.*"

The colonel turned away, trying to catch his breath, then pulling off his big hat—he wore no yellow wig this morning—and slapping it against the closest tree.

Kyne spit out his cigarette, wadded up the paper, and pitched it onto the grass. "K-*I*-n-e? I bet the bastards at the *Dallas Herald* did that on purpose. Hell, I wrote for that paper years back. K-i-n-e. Chickenshit tramp printer. It had better be. The *New-York Tribune* best not have misspelled my name. Or they'll rue the day."

"You admit it. You admit it. You wrote about my show . . . being . . . ruined. You . . . you're a turncoat."

Kyne kicked the paper he had discarded. "I wrote about an outbreak of smallpox that had struck Comanches appearing in the glorious Wild West extravaganza headlined by the legendary Colonel Titus Wheeler. It's publicity, old man. Your name was in the *New-York Tribune*. I am your press man."

"You were my press man, you back-stabbing bastard." The colonel stormed away, heading for the hotel, where the saloon, Daniel figured, would be open despite the early hour.

Kyne grinned while he found the makings.

"All right," the deputy behind Daniel said when they reached the edge of the grass. "The marshal says you got five minutes. Then I got to get this buck back with the others."

The questions came at him so fast he couldn't understand any of them. When they paused, some holding pencils to paper, others just listening, the woman asked, "Any new smallpox outbreaks at Ned Olsen's Occidental Hotel?"

Some of the men chuckled. Daniel did not catch the joke, but he understood the question.

"The Kiowa," he said. "Apiatan. He has a fever."

"How 'bout the girl."

"She improves." He prayed that remained true.

"How bad has the pox butchered her face?"

"Jesus, Darrin," one reporter asked. "That's a hell of a question."

"It's what men, women, kids, and dogs want to read in Chicago, Brad."

More laughter.

Daniel did not, would not, answer that question.

Billy Kyne walked over, pulled out his notebook, and said, "How are you holding up, Daniel?"

A shrug became his answer.

"It must be a strain," the woman said.

That was no question, so he felt no need to say anything.

"Stoic Indian," the woman said, smiling. "Just like everyone says they are."

Billy Kyne had heard enough and walked away.

Daniel wished they would let him leave, too, but he stayed there, listening to questions, some of which he answered with a few words, some he ignored. Mercifully, the deputy brought an end, and nudged Daniel. The men and women hurled more questions as Daniel and the deputy crossed the street, then went through the alley where Homer Blomstrom had been cut to pieces, and emerged on the other side.

Billy Kyne joined them there, surprising Daniel, but not the deputy.

"Be quick, Kyne," the Tejano said. "Or it's both of our asses."

"Anything you need, Killstraight?" Kyne asked.

"I feel fine," Daniel said. "Do you need anything?"

Kyne laughed. "What could I need?"

"A job?"

He laughed harder. "Wheeler has fired me before, and he always hires me back. He'll realize that that little note that I sent to the *Trib* will help him more than it'll hurt him. Makes him out to be the victim. That might—might, mind you—make his investors somewhat sympathetic. And now we've got a murder. That scout did us a favor. That'll keep this story going for a while."

Daniel stopped. The shotgun of the deputy pressed between Daniel's shoulder blades. "Keep movin', injun."

But Daniel did not budge. "You once said you needed a story . . ." He paused, trying to picture and remember the details. "A massacre . . . a tornado . . ." His head bobbed. "Yes. You said that might get you away from the colonel . . ."

"Now hold on, partner."

But Daniel finished. "Get you hired by a . . ." He smiled, remembering Kyne's exact words. ". . . *a job with a first-rate newspaper.*"

Kyne backed away. "I had nothing to do with Blomstrom's death. You know that." The reporter's eyes glanced at the deputy, then went straight to Daniel. "Don't joke with me." He tried to smile, but it would not hold. "Honest, Kill- . . . Honest, Daniel. I'm here to help you."

"I think you help yourself," Daniel said. "At the expense of The People."

He walked away. The deputy followed. Neither looked back at the colonel's press man who stood alone on an empty street.

CHAPTER TWENTY-ONE

He woke to a quietness he had never experienced, and for a moment, he feared The Rotting Face had sneaked like a Pawnee into the livery stable–now prison. And had killed everyone but him.

Twice Bent Nose's snores removed that stupid thought, and Daniel shook his head at his own silliness, trying to forget the fright he had not felt since those horrible nights at Carlisle when the witch would come to his room and tell him there was another young Indian to bury. He rose, drawn toward the morning light creeping through the outer wall's cracks. Crouching, leaning closer, he looked at the big empty.

He remembered how alive these streets had been when they had arrived here on the Fire Wagon. Albany was a small town, really, by the standards of most taibos, but it seemed huge to most of The People. Giant, loud, filled with ugly people, but some good horses.

Something moved. Daniel held his breath.

He had seen deer before. He had hunted them, killed them, eaten their raw hearts, used their skins, their horns, their meat. Never, however, had he seen a deer in the middle of a Tejano town.

The big buck stopped, turned, and seemed to look directly into Daniel's eyes.

In the woods, it would not have seemed surreal. But here, Daniel held his beath. The deer remained frozen, standing in the street between Cannon's Hardware—Shackelford County's Finest, and Fuhrman's Music Store—Selling Chickering, Steinway and Hale Pianos * Smith-American and New England Organs * Violins, Cellos, Guitars, Strings * Accordions, Organettes, Harps of All Kinds * Sheet Music and Music-Books * Nothing But Standard Goods Sold.

His power had never come from a deer, but from the marsh hawk, which had long brought strength to Daniel's father. But now Daniel remembered a conversation with Quanah some two or three years earlier. "Your spirit animal is good, strong," Quanah had told him. "But your strength also resides in the fact that you, as I, are from two worlds. Mine by birth. Yours by force. My mother was a taibo. You lived in the taibo world. Thus, we understand the taibos more than any of The People."

"I have another world," Daniel remembered telling Quanah. "My mother was Mescalero."

And Quanah had laughed aloud. Even reached over and slapped Daniel's shoulder. "A good world to have," he had said. "One of my wives is Mescalero."

The deer seemed frozen, its ears and eyes alert. The antlers were perfect, eight points, evenly balanced. He could almost feel the softness of the animal's coat. He studied the inner sides of the buck's legs, their paleness contrasting with the dark coat on the deer's sides. Anyplace else, and Daniel would have been thinking how many a buck like this could feed.

But he thought nothing. He listened. And before the buck turned and ran away, away from the empty city streets, back to the surrounding forests, it spoke to Daniel.

"This," the deer told him, "is the day you are free."

Billy Kyne was not at the courthouse lawn when Daniel again had to walk to tell the inkslingers what had happened in the livery stable, that the Kiowa had died. That Ecahcueré and

Ebicuyonit were sick with The Rotting Face. That Red Buffalo felt his powers as a holy man were lost. Daniel wondered if he remained in Albany. Or had he fled.

No, Kyne could not leave Albany. No one could leave Albany. The roads were guarded by armed men.

When the newspapermen and the one newspaperwoman finished their string of questions no one could understand, Daniel remembered the buck. He remembered what the animal had whispered to him. *Freedom?* Daniel thought he must have been drunk on Choctaw beer. There was no freedom. But the questions had stopped, and reporters never ran out of questions.

So Daniel tested the freedom the buck had promised him—though he could not explain where this thought came from—with a question of his own.

"Where do you get your newspapers? No one is allowed in Albany. The train has not come here in days."

They stared as if he were a mute who had just spoken.

The deputy behind him began an explanation.

"Train stops a mile out of town. Ever' afternoon 'round three. There's a sidin' there, and a shed. No people. But the train boys is allowed to unload any items in the express car, and the mail, that's bound, I mean, for Albany. Most of the freight stays in the shed. Tommy tells me it's pret' near packed to the rafters already, so I reckon we'll be coverin' the next load the Texas Central brings with a tarp. And prayin' there don't come no turd float."

"The newspapers?" Daniel asked.

"Well, them we bring in. We's as starved for news as y'all is at gettin' some." He coughed. "Now, don't y'all put none of this in your writin's. Don't want my head in no noose."

The reporters laughed.

The man Daniel recalled saying something about Chicago

readers held out a paper. "Here's *The Daily Inter Ocean.* What I write for. This one's a week old, but here Doc DeWolf says, and I quote, 'The loathsome disease of smallpox cannot be stamped out or checked until every soul is vaccinated.' "

The Albany editor snatched the paper from his hand.

"I said," *The Daily Inter Ocean* correspondent said, "there isn't anything about Albany or Texas in that edition."

Daniel smiled, and asked: "Does the *Inter Ocean* say anything about The Rotting Face being spread by blankets . . . or newspapers?"

The Albany man dropped the newspaper and stepped back, wiping his hands on the sides of his britches, and blaspheming his God, his peers, and Comanches in general.

Billy Kyne had returned with his colleagues the next day. But he asked no questions, and never looked directly at Daniel, even though half of the reporters had gone to the square's far corner, where a man wearing a torn duster, well-patched britches, and a misshapen hat kept screaming and waving his arms. Every now and then he spoke clearly and loud enough to be understood across the square.

"It's the remedy, I tell you . . . Cures smallpox clean as church glass . . . Yeah, yellow fever. Cholera, too . . . Grippe ain't no match for it . . . So cheap, it's practically free . . . Because my paps, he was a physician. No, not some faker, he got his studyin' done in Baltimore . . . Sure, he's a Yank, but I wore this hat and these britches fightin' the blue . . . It cures. It cures. It cures . . . Putrefaction. That's what's killin' us all. Putrefaction . . . That ain't just what my pa says, it's been writ up in all the journals. London, too. Switzerland even . . . Putrefaction. The putrefaction of our innards . . . Salt. That's all you need . . . I done tol' y'all, salt! . . . Don't smile, stop laughin', just take salt . . . Two teaspoons in glass of water . . .

No, just three times a day . . . It's gospel, folks. Salt . . . My pa saved hundreds of lives . . . Stopped a yellow fever plague with it down in Red River Parish . . . Nursed the good folk in Nacogdoches through a cholera scare . . . Well, add some vinegar to it. Makes the salt water more palatable . . . Honest as a day is long . . . Efficacy done been tested, time and time ag'in . . . Efficacy. Need me to spell it for you . . . Don't look at me like I'm some dumb shit. I studied doctorin', too . . . Give it up. War cured me of doctorin' . . . Keep doin' it for a week, maybe two . . . Don't need no vaccination, nothin', just salted water with a bit of vinegar . . . No, the vinegar ain't required, it's jus' that some folks can't drink salt water . . . Makes 'em sick, I reckon. Like you ain't supposed to guzzle down ocean water . . . Just remember, folks, this conversation. And it's salt. . . . Preserver of life. Proved time after time."

The man started walking away, toward the saloon. The reporters began heading back toward Daniel and the others.

Suddenly, the reporters stopped. Daniel turned. He heard the noise, strange but familiar. *Hooves.* Hooves with iron shoes. A horse was trotting from the east, and the guards outside of town were not due in until the change was made at noon.

When the figure rounded the corner, all of the reporters raced toward the horseman. So did the guard assigned to Daniel.

Daniel stood straight. A door banged open from the courthouse, and the town marshal raced down the steps. He must have heard, then seen, the rider from an office window. Even the lawman rushed past as though Daniel were invisible.

I should stay here, Daniel told himself. *If I walk away, even back to the livery, they might think I am escaping, and they will kill me.*

Daniel turned his head. The man who had praised salt water as the cure for practically all diseases had disappeared, so he looked again to the rider.

He was a tall man, dark-skinned. He wore a linen duster. A tall silk hat. The horse was a bay, a good horse, sixteen hands. The saddle was the kind a *taibo* might sit upon, but the horseman. He was . . . Indian.

Daniel started walking. He increased his pace.

The rider pulled the bay to a stop, and pulled off his hat. His hair was blacker than a night without the moon.

Reporters started their questions, but stopped when Albany's marshal swore savagely, then thrust out his arm, extended his pointer finger, and screamed: "How the hell did you get into town, buster?"

"I rode in." Hugh Gunter smiled. "Howdy, Daniel."

Several reporters turned back to Daniel. The marshal yelled, "I asked you a question. How did you get past my guards?"

"I rode in." Hugh Gunter did not look away from Daniel. "And I didn't see any guards."

The sheriff fired off a string of curses, then ordered the deputy named Roland to ride out and send the deputy who was supposed to be guarding the east road into Albany back to town to be flayed and, possibly, jailed.

"Been a long time, Daniel." Hugh Gunter smiled.

"It has," Daniel said.

"Are you Comanche?" the woman reporter asked.

"Ma'am, I am insulted. I am too tall, too educated, too handsome to be mistaken for a Comanche. But if I were Comanche, I would like to be just like that fine, outstanding young man over yonder." He put his hat back on and straightened in the saddle. "I am Cherokee."

He spoke the truth. Daniel had met Hugh Gunter, a member of the U.S. Indian Police, when he first returned from Carlisle all those years ago. Hugh Gunter had become a valued friend. He had saved Daniel's hide more than once. He had helped teach Daniel what one needed to know to survive as an Indian policeman in what was then known as Indian Territory.

But Daniel did not know what in the hell the old Cherokee was doing in Albany, Texas.

Which was the next question the marshal asked.

"Well, sir," Gunter answered easily, "I heard Daniel—we've been friends for a while, even if he's a savage and I'm one of y'all's civilized Indians. So, when I read in a Muskogee newspaper . . . Muskogee newspaper. That makes me laugh. Like any Creek, civilized or not, can read. Be that as it may, when I read that some Comanches, including the new hero of some dime novels by some gent named Wheeler, were appearing in a bunch of exhibitions in northern Texas, I had to see this for myself."

"Don't you know this city is in quarantine?" the *Inter Ocean* man shouted. "Don't you know there's smallpox here?"

"Well, I didn't know that till I rode into Dallas." Gunter found a handkerchief in his vest pocket and started wiping his face. "It's been a right hot trip," he said. "Can't a body get a drink of water in this town?"

"You came?" The marshal was thunderstruck. "Knowing there's smallpox here?" Before Gunter could answer, the woman reporter fired off: "You've had the smallpox already. Right? That's why you rode here."

"Not exactly," Hugh Gunter said. "And it deeply offends me." He returned his handkerchief. "That a woman as lovely as you could mistake this handsome face for one that has been pitted by the pocks and scars left by that horrible malady."

"Then why did you come?" the Albany editor demanded.

"I've been vaccinated."

"Listen, lady and gents." Again, Hugh Gunter wiped his face, but smiled when the Jacksboro reporter brought him a glass of sarsaparilla from the saloon. He paused long enough to drink about half of the glass. "My people, the Cherokees, back before that son of a bitch—apologies for my truthful, if profane, language, ladies and Christians—Jackson kicked us out of our homes, we suffered through smallpox like every other human being. Human being is a general description, and not entirely accurate, naturally, depending on the humans."

He finished his drink, wiped his lip, and appeared to be enjoying the attention.

Pencils scratched paper. More people had risked emerging from their hotel rooms. Even Colonel Wheeler stood under a tree, sipping on a glass that likely did not hold sarsaparilla. He was talking to, of all people, Billy Kyne.

"In my father's childhood," Hugh Gunter continued, "*Ahtawhhungnah* was supposed to stop the smallpox. That was the Smallpox Dance. Later, my ancestors separated the sick. They burned the homes of the infected. They blamed the disease on anything." He shook his head and let out a slight chuckle. "One holy man said this was punishment for fornicating in cornfields." He looked again at the woman reporter. "Apologies again, ma'am."

"None needed," she said. "I've done it in less interesting places."

The silence held for half a minute.

"Another . . ." Hugh Gunter stopped, cleared his throat. He shook his head, grinned again at what the lady had said, then found his voice. "Another said that animals created the disease, to protect the animals from human beings."

Some of the reporters had stopped writing down Hugh Gunter's words. They seemed hypnotized.

"And early in this century, when my father was a young boy, my people got wise. The Great Spirit, my ancestors were told, had blessed a white man, across the great water—that would be the Atlantic Ocean, my white friends—to cure all people of all lands of all races of this horrible malady that struck without knowledge or care of one's skin color."

"You mean . . . you . . . Indians . . . started getting inoculations?" the Albany newspaperman asked.

"Yes."

The conversation stopped when Roland The Deputy rode back into town with the deputy who had been guarding the eastern road into town. Daniel could understand why this taibo had not seen Hugh Gunter ride into town. Benji Chandler's head was heavily bandaged, and Daniel recalled the name. Young Benji Chandler had been knocked out while guarding the front door to the barn on the night Homer Blomstrom was murdered. But the town marshal seemed interested only in lambasting the unfortunate deputy.

"You were talking about Cherokees getting vaccinated," the *Inter Ocean* man reminded Gunter.

"Yes, I was."

"You're telling us," said the *Inter Ocean* man, "that you got yourself stuck with that stuff?"

"Yes. Of course."

"You must be a damned fool," said the saloon owner, who had left his establishment because all of his customers had come to the lawn. "Sticking smallpox into your own body?"

Hugh Gunter leaned his head back and laughed heartily.

"Not smallpox, my good man," he said when he stopped chuckling. "Cowpox. Not as nasty. Missionaries told us what to do. When one became sick with cowpox, my ancestors drew the pus from the ill, passed it to the healthy. There would be breakouts here and there. And still are. But not as bad." He sighed. "Had we been smarter. Had the Great Spirit blessed us with this knowledge sooner, perhaps the number of my people would be doubled now. Even higher. But who am I to question the Great Spirit?"

"He's right."

Heads turned to find Albany's doctor with the long side whiskers standing on the sidewalk. He smiled at Gunter, nodded his appreciation, and said, "I've ordered vaccine points, lances, and antiseptic sponges from the health office in Austin. It's the best preventative known. And I don't know what the damned holdup is."

The deputy with the aching head, said, "Doc, I think that stuff arrived two days ago."

And now poor Benji Chandler, with the thick white bandages wrapped around his head, was battered with the old doctor's verbal wrath.

"*Two* days ago? *Two* days ago? I might not have been able to save Clarabelle Hopkins or Murdock Harker. Certainly not Corporal Canton. And Robert Hopkins's son will live, maybe, no thanks to you. And the rest of the Harkers might pull through, though I'm not confident the little boy will make it. But do you realize—*two* damned days? *Two damned days.* This is a smallpox outbreak, Chandler. It's not the son-of-bitching grippe or a headache. You're young, but you're not stupid. My God! Is there anyone here with a lick of sense other than a Cherokee, a Comanche, and me?"

Hugh Gunter removed his hat when he entered Olsen's livery stable. Ben Buffalo Bone recognized him, but only Twice Bent Nose walked over and made a friendly, formal greeting.

The town doctor had sent the Cherokee to the livery with one vaccination. The old man had told Daniel that the dose was good only for those who had not been infected. The fate of Oajuicauojué and the others sick with The Rotting Face was up to a higher power. Or perhaps, he did not want to risk the few medicines he had received from Austin on sick Indians. He had his own race to protect.

Hugh Gunter explained what was wanted of Ben Buffalo Bone.

"There is a danger," the Cherokee said, "that the smallpox is being formed already in your body. I do not know. We were told, though, when I accepted the lance point years ago, that anyone, even an infant, who has been exposed should be inoculated."

"Inoculated?" Ben Buffalo Bone asked.

"I stick the lance into your body. I plunge the cowpox into you."

"And that . . . ?"

"It is a little lance. Not a Comanche lance."

The joke did not make anyone smile other than its teller.

Gunter's tone turned serious. "If your Great Spirit is kind, it means you should never suffer as those who have gone before you."

The Kotsoteka straightened. "I am as brave as any of The People who have gone before me."

"If you are brave," Red Buffalo said from the corner. "You will do this for The People."

"Can you give it to my sister?" Ben Buffalo Bone asked.

Gunter shook his head. "Not now. It is too late for her. But she mends, I am told."

"And the others?" Ben Buffalo Bone's voice cracked.

"No. You are the last. They gave me only once lance point, one vaccine."

"Could I die?"

Hugh Gunter grinned. "You all will die, my friend. It is only a question of when.

"But I," Hugh Gunter said, "plan to live forever."

Ben Buffalo Bone dropped to his knees, and held out his arm. A moment later, the Cherokee opened the bottle, dipped the two-pronged needle into the solution. Hugh Gunter spoke as he worked. "I'll stab you with this little lance about fifteen times, putting just a bit of the stuff in you. Not deep, but your upper arm will be sore for a day. You shouldn't bleed too much. If it takes, you'll feel a bump where I've jabbed you. Don't worry. Do not scratch. It'll itch. And you might feel poorly for a couple of days. The bump will turn into a blister. It'll drain, dry up, form a scar. But you're Comanche. You like scars. This'll just be a little one. Scab should be gone in three weeks. You ready?"

It was over in minutes. The Cherokee slapped the antiseptic sponge over the puncture points, and dropped the items into an empty Arbuckles can.

CHAPTER TWENTY-TWO

"How . . . many?"

Her voice startled Daniel. He had hardly heard Oajuicauojué speak for weeks, just moan, and when she had talked, the words made no sense for she always sang out in delirium. Even now, Daniel wasn't certain what she had said for her voice was raw, too hoarse to understand.

Daniel stopped washing her face. He pulled away the wet rag and stared into her eyes, clear for the first time since forever, but how tired she looked.

She tried wetting her lips with her tongue, and Daniel tossed aside the rag, and slid over to the bucket of drinking water. He found the gourd ladle, filled it with water, and carefully slid back to Oajuicauojué, where he lifted her head with his free hand, and let her drink.

"Slowly," he whispered.

Her breath remained ragged, but when she had finished drinking, he lowered her head, felt her forehead, and returned to the bucket. She drank that ladle empty, too, but when Daniel started for more water, she shook her head.

"How many?" she said again, clearer this time, though still weak.

How many what? Scabs? Oajuicauojué had been lucky. Her face had not been spared, though only the left side had been brutalized, but pus-filled pustules covered her back and down both arms to the elbows. Maybe Red Buffalo had found magic in the taibo medicines Ben Buffalo Bone had stolen, in the petroleum jelly and the whale oil he had spread over the woman's blisters. Or maybe Red Buffalo's song had been heard.

Daniel set the ladle on the blanket.

"How many have gone to The Land Beyond The Sun?" Oajuicauojué asked.

Daniel frowned. "Do not think of that now. You must get well."

"How many?"

"Three," Daniel said. He saw the fear in her eyes. "Your brother lives." Daniel tried to smile. "Ben Buffalo Bone did a brave thing. He let himself be given the vaccination."

Tears welled in Oajuicauojué's eyes. "It did not make him sick?"

Daniel shook his head. He answered in English. "How could taibo medicine make your brother ill? Ben Buffalo Bone is indestructible."

He hoped to see her smile, but the lips remained flat. "The medicine works." She used The People's tongue.

"Red Buffalo says it was his magic that worked."

"You do not believe that."

Daniel made himself smile. "I would never doubt the magic of a Kwahadi holy man."

She wet her lips again, swallowed, and asked: "Who?"

"It is not good to think of such things," Daniel told her.

"*Who?*"

Daniel frowned. "The Kiowa," he began. He could never say their names aloud. Apiatan. Tuhuupi. Ecahcueré.

She turned away and cried.

"Your fever is breaking," Daniel told her when she looked back at him. "You will be well soon."

She started to reach for her face, but Daniel intercepted her hand. His head shook. "Do not scratch. Do not touch."

201

"Am I ugly?"

Daniel shook his head. "Oajuicauojué could never be ugly."

She sniffed. "I am sad."

"We are all sad."

"I am ugly."

"No." He leaned over her and whispered. "You are the most beautiful woman of The People. You will always be the most beautiful woman of The People." And he realized she was even prettier than her dead sister, who Daniel had also loved.

He heard footsteps behind him, and rose, turning to see Ben Buffalo Bone coming from the other side of the barn. The Kotoseka's face was hard, but when he saw his sister awake, he rushed to her, sliding to his knees and yelling, "My sister. My sister." He grabbed her hand, brought it to his lips, and sighed. "I thought I might lose you."

Oajuicauojué cried again.

"How is she?" Ben Buffalo Bone looked at Daniel.

"The fever is falling. She drank water." Daniel turned to her. "Are you hungry?"

She stopped her tears and said, "Maybe . . . a little."

Daniel studied the Kotsoteka. "How do you feel?"

"I am fine." He stared at his sister. "Did he tell you?"

"Yes. You are brave. But you are always brave."

"Come." Ben Buffalo Bone stood. "A Pale Eyes woman with the heart of The People brought a big bucket of soup. My brother, He Whose Arrows Fly Straight Into The Hearts Of His Enemies, and I will bring you some."

Daniel looked up, understanding. He breathed in deeply, exhaled, and turned back to Oajuicauojué. Smiling, he whispered, "We will be back in a few minutes." But Oajuicauojué had fallen asleep.

Suddenly, Daniel realized Ben Buffalo Bone had called him "my brother," words Daniel had not heard from him in years.

Perhaps that was a choice, a lie, for the sake of his sister.

Ben Buffalo Bone stood, without speaking and took his wolf-like steps, and Daniel followed him. They did not walk to the front of the barn, where the healthy rested and ate and slept and lived the lives of the prisoners the taibos had made them. They walked to the back, and Daniel whispered to himself.

Four.

The Nokoni dancer called Roadrunner had joined the others in The Land Beyond The Sun.

"At least," Ben Buffalo Bone whispered, "his face will not be scarred when he joins our ancestors."

The fever had killed Ebicuyonit, as The Rotting Face often did. Taken him away even before his face blistered.

Daniel heard the voice of the taibo witch at Carlisle. *Bury him deep.*

Then he heard his own voice: "I will tell Tin Star that we have one more to bury."

Ben Buffalo Bone looked away from the face of Ebicuyonit and stared hard at Daniel. "He is the last that we will bury."

It was not a question, but Daniel answered him. "Your sister heals. The fever fades. She should live."

"She *will* live." Ben Buffalo Bone rose. "I will tell Tin Star. Can you bring our Nokoni brother to the big door?"

Daniel nodded. "He was always tiny. This blanket weighs more than . . ."

He had seen the blanket more times than he could count, but only now did he really see it.

"This," he said in English, "blanket. Son of a bitch. This *blanket.*"

Ben Buffalo Bone looked hard at Daniel, but his eyes soon dropped and focused on the blanket.

It was simple in its design, wool with six black stripes, six white stripes, and one large black stripe in the center. Daniel fingered the texture, woven so tightly it could hold off rain. Soft and shining, maybe five by six feet with tassels on the corners. No one among The People could weave such a blanket as this. This was the work of the Diné. This was what the Diné called a "chief's blanket."

A long moment passed before Ben Buffalo Bone gasped in recognition.

"I know this blanket. It belongs to—"

"The brother of White Wolf," Daniel said. Cut Up Into Pieces carried that blanket with him everywhere, even though White Wolf was regarded as the chief, not his brother.

"Tsihpoma," Ben Buffalo Bone whispered. "Yes. This is the blanket of Tsihpoma."

Tsihpoma was Yamparika. And The Rotting Face had begun in White Wolf's Yamparika camp.

"I do not understand." Ben Buffalo Bone held up one end of the blanket, staring at it, then flinging the corner away not in fear, but disgust.

Daniel rose. "I understand."

They carried the body of the Nokoni dancer on the chief's blanket, past Ben Buffalo Bone's still-sleeping sister, past the silent, staring faces of Red Buffalo, Tamasual, Kwasinaboo, and Twice Bent Nose and his wife. Twice Bent Nose started to stand, but Daniel shook his head.

They stopped at the first stall, and laid the body and the blanket at the feet of Black Yellow Stripes.

The snoring man jerked awake, reaching for his revolver until he recognized the two men standing in front of the stall. The Black White Man glanced at the body for just a moment before fastening his hard glare on Daniel.

"I ain't your slave, boy. I don't bury no stinkin' Comanch."

"No," Daniel said. "You just kill them."

The black eyes glared. "Smallpox killed this one, boy. Just like it killed them other three." He pointed his head toward the wall. "And who knows how many God-fearin' men, women, and kids out yonder."

"You brought The Rotting Face to us." Daniel pointed. "On this."

Black Yellow Stripes snorted out a laugh. "You are loco. Smallpox ain't spread that way."

"Yes, it is. So says the newspapers. So says Hugh Gunter, my friend the Cherokee. So says Colonel Titus Wheeler. So says the taibo doctor here in Albany. So said the taibos at Carlisle. And so said the doctor-major from Fort Sill."

"And just why would I want to kill you injuns?"

"You will tell us," Ben Buffalo Bone demanded.

"I ain't tellin' you a damned thing." He turned away. "I get put in here with you red . . . you Comanch. If that blanket's carryin' the pox, get it the hell away from me. Because I ain't had that smallpox, and they stuck me in here with you just because I'm a colored man and—"

"You had The Rotting Face," Daniel said. "That is why you did not run away."

"I ain't never had—"

"We will cut off your beard," Ben Buffalo Bone said, "and see if The Rotting Face scarred your face as it has done my sister's."

"You ain't comin' close to my whiskers with one of your scalpin' knives." He sat up straighter, and looked again at the holstered revolver on the bale of hay near him.

"That first night after we left Fort Sill," Daniel said. "You rode off late that night, around midnight, I'd say."

"To cover our back trail," Black Yellow Stripes said.

Daniel's head shook. "No." He stared at the blanket, trying

not to notice the body of the dead Nokoni. "To bring this back."

"I must be a hell of a horseman."

"You rode with the Long Knives," Ben Buffalo Bone reminded him.

"If I wanted to bring a blanket with smallpox, why didn't I fetch it to begin with?"

That was a question Daniel had not figured out, but he would not let that deter him. He looked at the man's gun belt, and saw the tintype of the young woman of color next to it.

"Where is your woman?" Daniel asked.

Black Yellow Stripes turned as if he heard a rattlesnake, snatched the tintype, and shoved it underneath his blanket. "You scalpin' fiends don't get to look at her. Never again. You—"

That's when Daniel guessed.

"Your woman was killed." He spoke the sentence somewhere between statement and question, calmly, testing the taibo words. But as soon as he had finished, he recognized the truth in the former soldier's eyes. "Killed by . . . Indians."

"Butchered!" Black Yellow Stripes sprang to his feet. "Butchered. Scalped, you red devils. Scalped by Comanches. Hell, for all I know, scalped and killed by you two bastards."

"So that is why you brought The Rotting Face to us." Stoic, even calm, Daniel also felt a million years old at that moment.

Ben Buffalo Bone reached for his revolver, but Daniel shook his head. "No, my brother," he told his friend. "We will let the taibo law handle this."

"Hell." The Black White Man laughed without mirth. "Like I could get a fair trial with that mob. Like any colored man could get a fair trial in Texas. Anywhere in this hate-filled country."

"The taibos will let him go," Ben Buffalo Bone protested in English. "He is a Black White Man."

"No, damn you." The man named Virgil Pry roared. "I'm a *Black* man. There ain't no *white* to me. Haven't you figured it out that a man of my skin don't get no better treatment than you savage bucks and bitches get?"

He laughed, then, shook his head, and said, "You stupid sons of bitches."

Surprisingly, Daniel remained calm. Even a bigger shock was that Ben Buffalo Bone made no other attempt to kill Black Yellow Stripes.

"When was your wife killed?" Daniel asked.

The man glared. Daniel wasn't certain he would answer. But the man, his eyes brimming with hatred, said, "The eleventh of September, eighteen and seventy-three." He let out a mirthless laugh. "A raiding moon, the scouts all said. You sons of bitches. I'd quit Uncle Sam's Army. Married her. Got us a little hay farm. Went to The Flat for supplies. Come back . . ."

His breathing intensified. His eyes turned wet, but those dark eyes brimmed with more hatred than Daniel had seen in years. "I re-upped, got my stripes back, and spent the next years hoping to get into a good battle with you sons of bitches. But then, ol' Quanah turned hisself in at Sill, and the injun wars was over, at least in northern Texas."

Daniel thought about when the Black White Man had said his wife had been killed in a raid. "Nineteen years ago," Daniel said.

"Feels like nineteen hundred to me, you sons of bitches."

"You," Ben Buffalo Bone said, "are the son of a bitch. Nineteen summers ago, my sister was not yet born. Nor was the Kiowa you killed with The Rotting Face. He came into this world even later than my sister."

Daniel thought about the dead man that had laid in the stall. He had seen only sixteen winters, and would see no more. And Tuhuupi? Ecahcueré? "The one behind me was not born either." His voice sounded sad, but Daniel kept talking. "The one who sang so loud, who now sings with his ancestors, and the Penateka woman—they were babies when the raiders killed your woman."

"Like my baby boy who never got to draw a breath." Black Yellow Stripes spoke in a hoarse whisper. "The baby you butchers cut out of the womb."

"I remember no songs about this raid." Ben Buffalo Bone glanced at Daniel, who shook his head.

"I do not, either. It could have been from another camp. It could have been Kiowas. The People were all angry in those times. The killing of cuhtz. The Rotting Face. Those were days of anger. Of hatred."

"And we would have been too young . . ." Ben Buffalo Bone sounded suddenly tired. "They would not have let us ride on a raid."

"My wife and my unborn kid got killed. By injuns. That's all that mattered to me." The man spat. His eyes reminded Daniel of a rabid wolf.

"And the scout?" Daniel said. "You murdered him, too."

"Homer Blomstrom was an idiot," the cornered animal confessed. "He must have picked up the sign back in the territory, but he thought that blowhard Wheeler was behind it all. Talked to me about what he had found. Tracks mostly. And some injuns was cryin' over a damned missing chief's blanket. Asked me to help him out. Figured to split whatever he could get blackmailing Wheeler, the damned fool. Blomstrom cold-cocked the guard, came into the barn. Told me his plan. So I followed him. We got into the alley, and I cut him good with that knife.

"The knife you bucks left after you butchered my family."

Daniel let out a tired sigh. "The knife was of a Southern Cheyenne."

"Don't play me for a fool. You bucks traded with each other before I ever set foot in your country."

"You thought," Daniel said, "killing the scout as savagely as you did, the taibos would blame it on us, which they did. You thought they would rise up, kill us all."

"Maybe." Black Yellow Stripes laughed again. "I had to shut that loudmouthed son of a bitch up, though. And that's . . . *that's* what those white bastards'll hang me for, you dirty red butchers. Not for killin' redskins. But for cutting that idiot scout to pieces."

"And the doctor-soldier from the soldier-fort," Ben Buffalo Bone said. "Canton. You killed him, too."

"Son of a bitch should have deserted."

"There are three taibos, I think, from town who are dead, too," Ben Buffalo Bone reminded him. "Is that right, Brother?"

Daniel did not try to count the dead outside this livery. He had seen enough death here.

"I don't think I had nothin' to do with them fools," Black Yellow Stripes said. "They gots the smallpox from some other place. It's everywhere this year." He pointed at the papers scattered about the stall. "Read for yourself."

"Let me kill him, Brother," Ben Buffalo Bone pleaded.

"No," Daniel said. "We need him to tell the taibos exactly what he has done. Or they might blame us for his death, too."

Corporal Virgil Pry laughed. "Hell's fire, I might get my vengeance after all. And, hell, like Sergeant Greene always said, 'Die game.' "

His right hand grabbed the butt of the revolver, but by the time he got it out of the holster he was dead. Ben Buffalo Bone shot him in the head, sending him against the wood. He shot him again. And again. He pulled the trigger, cocked the hammer, pulled the trigger—until the hammer clicked on an empty chamber, and even then he still cocked and pulled, cocked and pulled. He did not quit until a Tin Star ran into the barn, his own gun drawn, and almost swallowed the tobacco in his cheek.

209

"God A'mighty!" the Tin Star yelled, lowering his Colt and staring at the bloody body in the stall. "Why'd you gun down the ol' colored boy?"

CHAPTER TWENTY-THREE

The taibo judge, the town marshal, Ancient Bluecoat from the long-abandoned soldier-fort called Griffin, Billy Kyne, and Colonel Titus Wheeler stared after Daniel finished his account. Daniel studied their eyes and waited.

Colonel Titus Wheeler spoke first. "That don't make a damned bit of sense to me. My boy Virg—"

"His wife was killed by Indians." The white-haired bluecoat sighed. "Late summer back in 'seventy-three. The Tenth had just been transferred here." The Ancient Bluecoat shook his head. "We never found the Indians responsible. Not that we searched very hard, the woman being a Negro."

"You remember after all those years?" The judge sounded skeptical. The colonel just held his mouth open, for once at a loss for words. Billy Kyne held his pencil over his notebook but had not written anything down.

The taibo lawman took advantage. "We're taking the word of these bucks? That dead darky's one thing, but there are dead white folks from Albany, Judge. Dead of smallpox. Brought to us by these red butchers. Plus that scout from Sill that was gutted like a fish. And that corporal from Sill who died in Isaiah's office. I don't believe one word that's been said here." The words came out in a flash, and when the marshal had to catch his breath, the Ancient Bluecoat spoke.

"I believe everything Killstraight has told us." His eyes started to glisten, and his voice fell to a whisper. "She was with child."

A long silence followed. "You don't need to hear the rest. No, Judge. I don't think I'll ever forget that, even if she were colored." He spit into the cuspidor, found his cane, and pushed himself out of the chair. "He was a fine soldier, Virgil Pry," he whispered. "Once."

An eternity later, the door closed behind him.

"Mister Kyne," the judge said later. "I would appreciate it if you would forget you are a newspaperman. We'll make up a story about Corporal Pry's death."

"I'm not a newspaperman, Your Honor." Billy Kyne stuck the pencil over his ear and closed the notebook. "I'm a press man for Colonel Wheeler."

The lawman opened his mouth, but closed it when the judge stared at him. "It's over, Orville. Let it be. The Indian Wars are over. At least here in Texas. Maybe Virgil Pry is the last casualty. But let's have some peace for once. We still have a smallpox outbreak to fight."

The lawman flattened his lips, wet them, then whispered, "And how do we explain Blomstrom's murder?"

"LeRoy Younger's dead of smallpox. That's no great loss to Albany or Texas or the human race. LeRoy Younger killed the Fort Sill scout in a drunken rage. God delivered his justice."

Daniel kept quiet. LeRoy Younger died before Homer Blomstrom arrived in Albany. But Tejanos were stupid. And Daniel doubted if anyone would pay much attention to days, just deaths. Taibos, he had learned, liked tidy endings.

The judge looked at Colonel Wheeler, who had sunk back in his chair, his face still, colorless.

"Colonel. As soon as your sick Comanche girl is well enough to travel, you'll do me the honor of loading your Indians on the first available train. Orville, consider that a verbal writ."

The lawman just stared at his boots, but he whispered, "It'll be done, Judge."

"Colonel," the judge said. "I hope you have better success in Waco and Austin than you did here. For the sake of the good citizens of Waco and Austin."

"San Antonio," Billy Kyne corrected. "And Austin." He let out a humorless laugh. "They're all safe, Your Honor. They canceled our appearances as soon as they learned of the outbreak."

"I'm busted," Colonel Titus Wheeler said in a whisper. "Ruint. Hell's fire. We woulda had a mighty fine run . . ."

A gallon of whiskey, Daniel figured, must have revitalized Colonel Titus Wheeler's plans.

The wig had returned, and he wore the heavily beaded buckskins and enormous hat. Eyes bright, cheeks rosy, and the voice boisterous.

"Dan'l!" The colonel slapped Daniel's back and put that arm around his shoulder. "Son, this show, this season, well, it . . . it was a . . . a . . . algorithm."

"Anomaly," whispered Billy Kyne, rolling his eyes.

"But we'll be back next year, bigger and better, with no murderous, scheming, vindictive bastards thwarting our presentations."

Sometimes, whiskey was not a bad thing. For a man like Colonel Titus Wheeler at least. It made the taibo funny. If only whiskey could do that for The People, but that never happened. Whiskey made The People miserable. All of The People. Even those, like Daniel, who did not drink the bad medicine.

They stood at the Texas Central depot where a Baldwin locomotive hissed and belched smoke and steam. It was a small train, an express car, three passenger cars, and the caboose. Daniel spotted more than a half dozen taibos in big hats, two wearing small badges pinned onto their vests. Badges he had seen before. Texas Rangers. And the horses of The People were with the Rangers and the other men. He knew that none of The People would be taking the train back to Oklahoma Territory. The colonel was just taking his time before bringing up that matter.

A glance at Twice Bent Nose and Ben Buffalo Bone made Daniel interrupt Titus Wheeler's speech.

"My friends wonder why those Pale Eyes have our horses," Daniel said.

Colonel Titus Wheeler stopped talking. He pulled a cigar from his vest pocket and handed it to Daniel.

"Well, Dan'l, it's like this." The colonel tried to grin. "That's a fine cigar. Havana. Good smoke. Mighty fine."

Wheeler shot Billy Kyne a nervous look. The colonel pulled the cigar away from Daniel, and returned it to a pocket.

The newspaperman, apparently back on the colonel's payroll, took over.

"The two men with the badges are Texas Rangers," Kyne said. "They are to escort you to the Red River, where soldiers from Fort Sill will guide you back to your agency. The other members of the . . ." Now the newspaperman struggled for the right word.

"Posse," Titus Wheeler said.

"Escort party," Kyne said, though Daniel—and likely Billy Kyne—knew *posse* fit better.

"They be volunteers from Albany," Wheeler said. "It's a hundred and twenty or a hundred and thirty miles, thereabouts. You're all well-mounted. That Ranger sergeant, Josiah Pierce, says four days and you all will be home."

Daniel smiled. "We could be home sooner than that without the escort."

"Well, Dan'l," the colonel said. "Truth is, the Texas Central don't want y'all on their train."

"That was not what I meant," Daniel said.

Billy Kyne grinned. "I know." He sighed and shrugged.

"I will tell my sister and the others," Ben Buffalo Bone said. He glared at Kyne and the colonel, spit on the ground toward the escort party, and walked to the boardwalk where the survivors waited.

The colonel stepped forward, reached into a pocket of his coat, and withdrew a rawhide pouch. "Here's some money, Dan'l. When . . . if . . . I get paid what them sponsors promised me, I'll wire the rest to that Mister McLeish."

Coins rattled as Titus Wheeler put the brittle pouch in Daniel's left hand. Daniel remembered the pouch. It had belonged to Black Yellow Stripes. The pouch was not heavy, and the music the coins made did not sound like a symphony. A few dollars, Daniel guessed, or perhaps mere pennies. But he would not embarrass the colonel by opening the pouch now.

Colonel Titus Wheeler smiled when Daniel stuck the pouch in his grip.

"I'll send the rest of the money later, Dan'l. You know I'm good for it."

"Thank you, Colonel," Daniel said. He still had the two double eagles Titus Wheeler had paid him. When they were home, he would trade the coins for paper money, and divide that among those who had traveled with this "amusement," and the families of those whose bodies were buried in Albany in unmarked graves in what the taibos called a potter's field.

The colonel responded in the language of The People. "It is not enough for all that you have done for me, Friend. *I was born upon the prairie, where the wind blew free, and there was nothing to break the light of the sun. I was born where there were no enclosures, and where everything drew a free breath.*"

Daniel remembered the words, though he had never heard them spoken by the great leader of The People, Ten Bears, at the Medicine Lodge treaty talks.

215

"It cannot be that way again," he told the colonel.

Titus Wheeler nodded. "And," he said, moving to English. "That's a damned shame."

He held out his hand, which Daniel accepted.

Colonel Titus Wheeler pulled a watch from his pocket, nodded, returned the timepiece and looked at Billy Kyne. "Train leaves in forty-two minutes. I'll be havin' some breakfast." He waved at Twice Bent Nose and the rest of his Comanche talent and walked, not toward the café, but the closest saloon.

He stopped, though, in the middle of the street, whirled around, and cupped his hands over his mouth.

"I know you think I ain't nothin' but a skinflint. And you're thinkin' is dead-on." Then he switched to The People's language. "But you'll find a stallion in the stall behind you. And a bill of sale from me to you, legal-like, tacked to the inside gate. Don't run him to death the first time out, my friend."

Laughing, he spun around and disappeared into the saloon.

Billy Kyne asked, "Do you need anything, partner?"

Shaking his head, Daniel watched the colonel disappear. He glanced at the escort party before looking at the journalist. "Do you think we will make it to the agency alive?"

"Killstraight . . ." Kyne started, but Daniel's grin stopped him. Kyne's head shook. "And everyone says Indians don't have a sense of humor."

Daniel held out his hand. "You have been a friend, Billy Kyne. You are welcome in my lodge any time."

"I think I owe my career to you, Daniel. Stories I wrote about you for newspapers got me where I am today." He sighed. "Well, maybe not the shit I've been cranking out lately but . . . the stories I wrote from here to the *New-York Trib.*"

"I am not responsible for those stories. The People did not bring The Rotting Face here."

"I know," Kyne said in a hoarse whisper.

"You will return to what you do best," Daniel told him, trying to sound like a man who was not angry, and sounding, he knew, like a man who was trying to disguise his anger.

"Maybe," Billy Kyne said. "And you?"

Daniel shrugged. "I am still here."

They looked at each other. The Ranger sergeant grunted and spit tobacco juice into the dirt.

Daniel held out his hand, which Kyne accepted. The newspaperman pulled his pencil from above his ear, found his notepad, and walked to the Ranger. "Billy Kyne, Sergeant. I'm writing for the *New-York Tribune,* I hope. Wonder if you could spare a few minutes for an interview about your mission. Your name's Josiah, right? Pierce? Is that with an i-e or an e-a? . . ."

The journey to the Red River turned out to be uneventful. The taibos did not murder anyone; they barely spoke to those they had to escort out of Texas. Perhaps they still feared The Rotting Face. It did not really matter. Early in the afternoon of the fourth day, they reached the river, which was low—by the Red's standards—and easily forded.

One of the volunteers called out, "I thought soldiers was supposed to meet 'em here." He sounded worried.

The far bank remained empty except for the cottonwoods and other trees and brush.

"What'd you expect from a Yankee?" the Texas Ranger who was not Josiah Pierce said.

Daniel was the last to cross, but before he left the soil of the Texans—once land belonging to The People—he dismounted his new stallion and found the valise he had tied behind the saddle. He opened the grip, and found the old pouch that had once belonged to Black Yellow Stripes.

The Texas Ranger named Pierce stared at him. The volunteers from Albany waited without much patience. Until Daniel dumped the coins from the pouch into the palm of his left hand, though a few spilled out and landed in the damp ground between his moccasins. Nine men, counting the two Rangers. Twelve coins, most of them Morgan dollars, but not all. Two were Liberty Head nickels. One was an Indian Head penny minted just in 1890, and one was an 1876 Liberty Head $2.50 piece.

After dropping the money back into the rough pouch, Daniel stooped to pick up the coins he had dropped into the dirt. An 1850 three-cent piece, a French coin worth fifty centimes, 1887; two half-dollars, one American, another Canadian; and a Morgan dollar. These he also began dropping into the pouch. The dollar coin stopped him. He stared at it, started to put it in with the others, then looked at it closer, and shoved it into his left moccasin.

After tightening the cord on the pouch, Daniel rose and walked to the Texas Ranger sergeant. He held the leather toward the blue-eyed, mustached man.

The Ranger said nothing, and made no movement for Black Yellow Stripes's pouch.

After clearing his throat, Daniel said, "I am told the men from Albany volunteered. This is not much, but it is all we have. It is for you, as the Pale Eye in charge, to divide with these men. We appreciate you escorting us to our home."

Josiah Pierce shifted the tobacco he was chewing into the other cheek. He studied Daniel for a moment, before his partner grunted something unintelligible.

"It is not much money," Daniel said again.

"It'll spend, Sarge," Josiah Pierce's partner said. "Take it."

A gloved hand left the horn of the saddle and took the pouch.

"All right," the Ranger said, nodding his appreciation.

"What about the Yankees?" the worried Albany man cried out again.

"My job was to deliver these Comanches to the territory," Pierce said. "As soon as this one crosses, my job is done. If you want to escort 'em to Fort Sill, be my guest. My jurisdiction ends on this side of the river." He spit juice.

The worried man's lips moved no longer, and he stared at his horse's neck.

"Good luck," Daniel said.

The sergeant nodded. "Same to you."

Daniel mounted the fine blood bay, kicked its sides, and let the stallion plunge into the water. By the time he was in Oklahoma Territory and turned around as his horse shook off the water, the two Texas Rangers and the posse were loping south.

"We are near the village of the Yamparikas," Oajuicauojué said. "Where The Rotting Face began."

"I know," her brother said.

"Let us go home," Twice Bent Nose said, and his horse showed that it was ready to run. So did Daniel's gelding, the horse Twice Bent Nose pulled behind him. "And now that we have no Pale Eyes to slow us down, let us ride like The People."

The survivors rode north. Daniel's new stallion wanted to run after them, but he let it twist and fight the hackamore for a moment while he looked eastward toward the camp of White Wolf. Daniel whispered the words of Ben Buffalo Bone's sister.

"Where The Rotting Face began."

Hoofbeats thundered, and Daniel looked up to see Twice Bent Nose jerking his horse to a sliding stop, Daniel's gelding snorting and twisting against the rope Twice Bent Nose held. "Is your horse lame, Brother?" his friend called out.

Daniel shook his head.

"Then why do you just sit there and look silly? When Ben Buffalo Bone thinks he has the fastest horse among The People?"

Daniel made himself smile. He kicked his stallion's sides and felt the wind blowing his hair.

CHAPTER TWENTY-FOUR

Daniel awakened to the sound of Ben Buffalo Bone's bay colt urinating in the neighboring stall.

Staring at the ceiling, keeping his hands under his braids, he thought, not as a taibo might, but as Nermernuh.

When the piebald's bladder finally emptied, Daniel sat up and found the Remington revolver in the holster hung over a peg. Usually, he pulled his battered black hat over his head next. That was his routine. This time, he checked the loads in the .44 caliber, slid it back into the holster. Then he found his hat, stood, and buckled on the belt.

He heard the sound of an unshod pony outside, and Daniel went to the stall that held the fine blood bay stallion Colonel Titus Wheeler had presented him in Albany, Texas, a few days before. Colonel Titus Wheeler's Authentic Wild West Exhibition had closed early, but the robust man bragged that he would return, bigger, better, and bolder the following year, once the outbreaks of smallpox had died down.

Daniel went to another stall, and here he grained his older horse, the gelding, and made sure it had plenty of water, too.

After pulling on his vest, he glanced at the badge pinned to a pocket. For the first time in a long memory, he untied the scarf around his neck and polished the piece of tin. The stallion stamped its forefeet, and Daniel slid into the stall, rubbed the horse down, rubbed its neck, and let it eat the apple core he had saved from last night. He slipped on the hackamore, then

221

found blanket and saddle. In a few minutes, he led the stallion through the opening that once had a door.

Ben Buffalo Bone sat in his saddle, a well-used bow braced against his thigh. Shirtless, he wore a breastplate, the tin badge pinned in the center between the small white bones. His hat was gone, too, replaced by a scalp lock where his hair parted in the middle, two turkey feathers and four buzzard feathers hanging down. He wore buckskin pants, fringed from the calves to the ankles, and plain moccasins. He carried no revolver, no carbine, just a quiver with a handful of arrows on his back, and a short-bladed knife sheathed on his left side.

Ben Buffalo Bone asked, "Are you ready to ride?"

Daniel swung and mounted the stallion, which stutter stepped, excited at the prospect of a morning run. "It is a good day to ride," Daniel said.

"Among The People," Ben Buffalo Bone said, "any day is a good day to ride."

He tugged on his hackamore, and kicked the black horse into a lope. Daniel's new stallion followed with an eagerness.

They saw no one on the trail through the Wichitas, just a few deer that bolted when the loping horses startled them. When they reached Fort Sill, they paid no attention to the staring Long Knives they passed. The Pale Eyes focused on Ben Buffalo Bone, not Daniel. Ben Buffalo Bone looked like a warrior of The People. Daniel looked like what he was, a Metal Shirt, a reservation Comanche.

They reined up in front of the agency. Daniel stared, frowned, and moved his horse closer to the door, which was closed. He leaned in his saddle and looked through one of the windows, but could make out nothing inside. Then he eased his horse toward the side, and looked at the path that led to Agent Athol McLeish's house. No sign of movement came from there, either.

Frowning, Daniel turned the stallion back to Ben Buffalo

Bone, and shook his head.

"What is this day called among the Pale Eyes?" Ben Buffalo Bone asked in The People's tongue.

"Wednesday," Daniel guessed. "I think."

Oajuicauojué's oldest brother nodded. "Good. I thought it might be their holy day."

"I do not think so," Daniel said. "But he could have been called away. To Washington City. Another agency." He looked toward the fort. "Or with the Long Knives."

"That," Ben Buffalo Bone said in English, "would be bad. I wish to speak to him."

When their horses cooled down, they eased them to the trough in front of the hitch rail. They let them drink their fill, but neither man drank.

"We will wait," Daniel said.

They remained in the saddles. A dog barked somewhere. A raven flew overhead, *cawing* three times.

Taibos liked to say that Indians of any tribe had the patience of an oyster. Daniel knew little about oysters, and would never eat one, but he did not feel patient. He felt as restless as his new stallion. His heart raced. He ground his teeth.

And at some point, shod hooves sang against stone and gravel, and Ben Buffalo Bone looked up, Daniel twisted in the saddle, and a gray mule carrying Agent Ugly Mouth rounded the curve. The agent smoked a cigar, and pulled up short when he saw Ben Buffalo Bone. But once he recognized Daniel, he smiled.

"Daniel," he said, kicking the mule several times before it inched the remaining distance to the hitch rail. "And Ben. By thunder, lad, you look real splendid in that outfit. Is that what you wore when you were riding around those arenas in Texas with that damned fool Wheeler?"

He spit the cigar into the trough, awkwardly dismounted, and tethered the ugly animal.

"What brings you boys to the agency? Things are quiet. And it isn't payday."

"We wish to speak to you," Daniel said. "About the murderer of our friends."

The man stared for a moment, pulled off his hat, wiped his forehead, and said, "Oh." He wet his lips with his tongue. "Well, I don't know if there's any reward coming to you. I'll have to check with Harry at the fort, and send some wires to Albany and Austin, check with my bosses in Washington City. Pry was a darky, too, and prices on darkies aren't what they are for white outlaws. But I'll be mighty proud to pay you something extra come next payday."

He smiled.

Ben Buffalo Bone said: "We will talk to you."

The agent ran his right hand over his chin. "Sure," he said a moment later. "I was just settling some matters at the fort. Come on in, boys. There might be some coffee left on the stove. Probably cold, though."

Ben Buffalo Bone stepped off his horse.

"We will talk," he said.

McLeish opened a window, left the front door open to cause a draft, and lighted a lantern on the wall for extra light. After motioning at the chairs and bench, he moved behind his big desk, took off his hat, tossed it atop a bookcase, and sank into his big leather chair.

"Coffee's on the stove." He waved. "Help yourselves. But, like I said, it's likely cold."

They passed the stove and stood on either side of the front of the agent's desk.

"That's a nice bow you got there, Ben," the agent said. "Kill any big bucks lately?"

Bucks. Daniel remembered the eight-pointer he had seen in the empty streets of Albany, Texas. Suddenly, he felt as calm as he had on that morning.

"What can you tell us about the man who brought The Rotting Face to The People?" Daniel asked. "The Black White Man."

The man shook his head. "I can't tell you hardly anything, boys. I didn't know Pry. He was employed by Titus Wheeler. You'd have to ask that drunken reprobate what he knows. I'm just your agent."

"Before he worked for Wheeler," Daniel said, "he served at the soldier-fort."

McLeish nodded. "So I heard. Yeah. I remember now. He was a corporal, I think. But the agency isn't connected with the United States Army. The man you need to talk to is down at Fort Sill. Get the sergeant major. Or I'll write you a note to give to . . ."

"We talk to you," Ben Buffalo Bone said.

The man's eyes hardened. "Boys, I've said this once, and I'll say it one final time. I don't know a damned thing about that colored boy. He didn't work for me. I didn't know him at all. You boys savvy that?"

Daniel said, "When we left here to go to El Reno, the Black White Man rode with us."

"Right." McLeish nodded. "He was Wheeler's driver. Wheeler had hired him in El Reno. That's the report I read."

"That first night we camped," Daniel said. "He took the lieutenant's horse. The best horse among the Long Knives. I thought he was running away, fearing we carried The Rotting Face. He said he rode to keep watch on our back trail."

McLeish kept nodding, following along.

"But that is not what he did."

"I know that, Daniel." McLeish opened a drawer, withdrew a

folded newspaper, and slapped it on the desk. "That's what's in the *Oklahoma Democrat*. From what I've been hearing. That's what has been printed in every newspaper from the Atlantic to Pacific. And that story might even wind up in England or Spain." He tapped the paper with his forefinger. "Corporal Pry—former Corporal Pry, I should say—rode back to the Yamparika camp. He got that blanket. Rode back to your camp. Gave that blanket, which carried the pox, to one of your women. And that's what spread the pox, The Rotting Face as you call it." His head shook. "What a dastardly act. I know it's wrong for any Christian to think this way, but I sincerely hope Pry burns in hell."

"You," Ben Buffalo Bone said, "are no Christian."

The agent's face reddened and he stared hard at Oajuicauojué's oldest brother.

"How far is it to White Wolf's camp near the Big Pasture?" Daniel asked.

McLeish's glare turned into confusion. He whipped back toward Daniel. "What?"

Daniel repeated the question.

Confused, Agent Ugly Mouth shook his head. "Oh, I wouldn't know. Twenty miles, maybe."

"Maybe thirty," Daniel said. "Probably forty."

Ben Buffalo Bone spit on the floor.

McLeish glared at the Kotsoteka. "I suppose you think I'm not a Christian for lying to you two policemen. Well, I'm not lying. But I don't get down to see White Wolf often," McLeish said. "And I haven't been agent here all that long. And I still hope that murdering darky burns in the hottest pit in hell."

"We rode maybe ten miles that first day," Daniel said.

"I don't see where you boys are headed," McLeish said. His face flushed. He glanced at the drawer that held his pills.

"Ten miles here," Daniel said casually. "Forty miles to the

226

Yamparika village. Forty miles back. Plus ten more. One hundred miles. And the Black White Man was back at our camp before the lieutenant had crawled out of his covers for breakfast."

"I don't think it's forty miles there. I said twenty."

Daniel shrugged. "Then twenty plus twenty plus another twenty. Sixty miles." He smiled. "They taught math real well at Carlisle. *When I wasn't being forced at night to bury the children who died there. Children my age. Or younger.*" His head shook, slowed his breathing, let his fingers come out of fists on both hands. "I have ridden one hundred miles in a day, on my best horse, but I am Nermernuh. But a hundred miles, or even sixty, in six hours? I don't think any man, Black or *taibo*, could do that. Not even one of The People, on the best horse we have."

"You bucks try my patient. If you want to keep your jobs on the tribal police, you'll—"

"You will listen," Ben Buffalo Bone said in a steeled voice, "to what my brother says. Then we will listen to you."

"I'll be damned if I will." The man came to his feet, pressed both hands against the desktop. "What the hell are you suggesting?"

Daniel reached inside his coat pocket, found the coin, and tossed it to the agent. It landed on the folded newspaper.

McLeish stared at it. "It's a dollar. A Morgan dollar. What of it?"

"It is a dollar taken off the body of the Black White Man my brother here killed." He would not speak Virgil Pry's name aloud. "The colonel gave us a pouch of money when we left Albany. This coin was in that pouch."

"What of it?"

"It is one of the dollars you paid me that day," Daniel said. *"Remember?"*

The man breathed hard. His face whitened, but he managed

227

to laugh. "You can't tell one Morgan dollar from another. They're all minted the same."

"But this one has marks on it. Marks like teeth. I remember questioning it when I saw it, wondering if it was worth less because of its faults. And then you reminded me that I had to pay the agency a dollar for the badge I lost."

Athol McLeish sank into his chair. Now his face flushed, and he pounded the newspaper with a closed fist.

"How dare you accuse me of having anything to do with that darky's scheme. Virgil Pry was insane. Driven insane because you Comanches butchered his wife on one of your deplorable, blood and savage raids. I can't fault him for wanting to kill you, but he did it the wrong way. What he did could have killed many innocent men, women, and children."

"Like you did."

McLeish paled again, and he looked into the cold black eyes of Ben Buffalo Bone, who had spoken the last sentence.

"Now," the agent said after a minute. "Let's be reasonable here. Talk things over. I assure you." He reached up and jerked off the paper collar, then loosened the top two buttons on his white shirt. "It's hot in here. I'm . . . ." He opened another drawer, and found his bottle that carried the white pills he took whenever he got too excited.

"You paid the Black White Man," Ben Buffalo Bone said. "You paid him to kill us."

"He did it cheap," Daniel added. "Because, as you have said, he had reason to want us dead."

The man's hands shook so hard he could not get the top off the bottle. "Because . . . No . . . I had nothing . . . Why would I want any . . . of you . . . dead?"

"Not any of us," Daniel said. "You gave a list of names to the colonel. Names of The People who resisted settling for the price you say our country is worth. Quanah would not let you do that. He picked his own people. And you had no choice. Your plan did not work in one way. It did not kill The People you wished dead. But it killed The People. And taibos. As you said ... men ... women ... and children ... even a Long Knife from the soldier-fort."

The top came off and white pills scattered across the floor.

"That's a damned lie," Athol McLeish said. He picked up a coffee cup, found a pill, realized that the cup was empty, and flung it across the room. "I had nothing . . ."

"The dollar," Daniel said, "says otherwise."

A breeze cleaned out some of the fear, and part of the stink, in the agency.

"You're wrong. Damned wrong. But even if you were right, I'll tell you one thing," McLeish said, his voice quivering, and his breath ragged. "You'll never . . . prove that . . . in a . . . white man's . . . court."

"You are not being tried by a taibo court," Daniel told him. "You are being tried by The People."

The pill in the agent's fingers slipped, and he stood up, ripped his shirt farther open, panting, eyes now wide. "You can't . . ." It came out as more gasp than whisper.

"When the Black White Man returned the next morning to our camp," Daniel said, "he made the music. The chimes. I remembered thinking it was the sound the spurs make. But the Black White Man served with the Long Knives. His spurs do not make that music. It was the money you paid him. That was the sound I heard."

The wind moaned. The clock on the wall ticked loudly. But the only sound the two tribal policemen heard was the wheezing of the white-face agent before them. Daniel waited another long while, but McLeish did not seem to be able to say anything.

"What does not make sense," Daniel said, "is why you wanted to kill us. When you thought you would choose who went with the colonel, that I could understand. You wanted the supporters of Quanah to go with the colonel. But Quanah would not allow that. So why did you want to kill a young Kiowa? A Penateka whose singing voice impressed even the Baptist holy man who tries to save our souls? And a beautiful Penateka girl who decided to follow your Jesus? A young Nokoni dancer? Why?"

The taibo just stood there until Ben Buffalo Bone drew an arrow from his quiver.

"Wait!" McLeish cried out. "This was . . . all . . . Pry's doing. Yes, we . . . thought about . . . trying to, not kill . . . certainly not murder . . . just . . . but . . . you're . . . right . . ." He could hardly speak one word without gasping, and now his eyes were wild like a rabid wolf's, and his face turning whiter and whiter.

"I . . . told . . . Pry . . . no . . . it's . . . over . . . said . . . no . . . but . . . he . . . would . . . wouldn't . . . listen . . . I . . . I . . . I . . ."

Ben Buffalo Bone pulled his bow around.

"I'll give you anything!" McLeish got that sentence out in a quick breath. "What . . . is it . . . anything . . . what . . . do you . . . want?"

"What I want," Ben Buffalo Bone said, "is to be able to speak the names of those buried in the country of the Tejanos. I want my sister not to have holes in her face, down her upper arms, on her back. Holes that you gave her. I want to avenge the deaths that you brought to my friends. The death of the Long Knives two stripes who had the courage to come with us, to try to protect us from The Rotting Face that carried him to The Land Beyond The Sun. Deaths that you brought to taibos like you that you never even met."

"You . . . can't . . . do . . . this." McLeish reached for the bottle, but Ben Buffalo Bone swiped it with his bow, sending it to the wall behind the stove.

"Please," the agent screamed, his eyes wild. He started for

the bottle that rolled on the warped floor. Then he dropped behind the desk.

Daniel pulled his revolver and ran to the left. Ben Buffalo Bone nocked an arrow and leaped on the desk.

Both stopped and stared at Athol McLeish.

His eyes looked up at the ceiling, but saw nothing. One hand pressed above the heart that must have exploded inside his chest.

Ben Buffalo Bone leaped down, his legs straddling the dead taibo. He whipped his bow across the dead man's legs.

"I claim first coup," Ben Buffalo Bone said.

Daniel kicked McLeish's nearest shoe. "I claim second coup."

They looked at the dead man. The wind did not die down. The clock kept ticking.

Ben Buffalo Bone drew in a deep breath, and eventually exhaled. "Coup on a coward like this is not worth taking." He returned the arrow to the quiver, laid the bow on the desk, and started to draw his knife, then shoved it into the sheath. "Nor is his scalp."

The clock still ticked. The agent's eyes still stared up at nothing.

"He is not even worth spitting on," Ben Buffalo Bone said.

Daniel nodded. "It is true."

Ben Buffalo Bone found his bow. He stared at Daniel. Tears welled in the Kotsoteka's eyes, and his lips trembled. Daniel did not understand this reaction at all. Since explaining to Ben Buffalo Bone the previous evening what he thought had happened, Daniel knew they would kill Athol McLeish. So did Ben Buffalo Bone. Taibo justice be damned. They had ridden here on a vengeance raid, the way The People would have done before The Rotting Face decimated their numbers, before they understood that they could keep killing and killing but no matter how many The People killed, more taibos would replace them. The taibos were like flies.

They had ridden out that morning thinking of the days before Palo Duro Canyon, before Quanah had been forced to travel from the Llano Estacado to surrender to the Long Knives at Fort Sill in the year the taibos called 1875. Ben Buffalo Bone and Daniel came here to kill the murderer of their friends. Daniel felt no remorse whatsoever.

Finally, Ben Buffalo Bone spoke. "I have missed our friendship, Brother."

Daniel must have gasped. He had longed to hear that, and now he spoke words he never thought he would have a chance to say. "As have I." He felt the wetness on his cheeks.

They stared at one another until the clock chimed.

When the noise ended, Ben Buffalo Bone nodded.

"I do not agree with everything Quanah says," he said. "But I will listen. We will listen. As soon as this scourge, this Rotting Face, has passed."

"I will listen, too. And Quanah, he always listens."

Ben Buffalo Bone suddenly looked down at the dead taibo. Probably to hide the tears coming down his cheeks. Daniel did not bother to hide his tears.

"His mouth is open," Ben Buffalo Bone said. "I wonder if he speaks to his god."

"I doubt," Daniel said, "if his god hears anything he says."

They walked to the door. Daniel opened it, looked outside, but saw only the mule and two fine horses of The People. They walked out into the sun, and stepped up onto their mounts, backed the horses up, turned them around, and rode down the path.

Past the fort, to the trail that led through the Wichita Mountains. They kept the horses at a walk at first.

"I dreamed last night of my father," Ben Buffalo Bone said.

Daniel waited.

"Your father was in my dream, too."

Now Daniel turned and looked. Ben Buffalo Bone stared ahead, holding bow in one hand, hackamore in another.

"I listened to my father. I listened to your father. For I knew the wisdom, and the bravery, that flowed in their blood." He kept looking ahead. "Your father said that no one races a faster horse than a Kwahadi."

They covered another twenty yards.

"And my father told him, 'No one races a faster horse than a Kotsoteka.' "

Now Ben Buffalo Bone turned, a smile bigger than any Daniel had seen in years, and slapped his horse's rear with the bow.

The movement startled the new stallion Daniel rode, and Ben Buffalo Bone had covered fifty yards before Daniel could kick the stallion, and chase after him.

Daniel could not see because of the tears and the dust. But he laughed like he had as a child, before Carlisle, and then he released a guttural cry. Leaning forward, he kicked and grinned, the wind slapping his face. His battered black hat flew off, but Daniel did not care. That was a cheap taibo hat, old and stinking of sweat and dust.

Daniel was one of The People.

Letting the stallion run his own race, Daniel suddenly laughed. How he looked forward to seeing Ben Buffalo Bone's face when Daniel passed him.

EPILOGUE

August 1901

He had ridden over with Twice Bent Nose to watch the show, but Daniel's old friend quickly grew bored and rode back home to see his new grandbaby.

Holding the hackamore to his new bay colt, Daniel sat on a stump on the low hillside and hoped his brain could comprehend the chaos below. He also prayed that he could remember all the details to tell his family when he returned to the Wichita Mountains.

Where nothing had been yesterday, now a white city of tents sprang up not far from Fort Sill. Men, and quite a few women, raced around, like ants whose mound had been kicked by a Nermernuh boy, or a taibo boy, a Kiowa boy, any boy of any color, of any nation. Daniel remembered doing that many times when he was a youth in the caprock of the Texas Panhandle or here in what was now Oklahoma Territory.

Yet it was not just the sights. The noise reminded Daniel of those times he heard the bands practicing in cities like Fort Worth, or Fort Smith, or even during Colonel Titus Wheeler's carnivals that he called "not theater, but authentic Wild West exhibitions." Or his "amusement." On this day, a man pawed at a banjo, accompanied by a Seminole woman playing a mouth organ, but no one danced. And no one, so far, had tossed coins into the coffee can in front of the musicians. The banjo player was a Black White Man. No, Daniel thought, remembering

234

Corporal Virgil Pry. A *Black* man.

Most of the music lacked any harmony. Saws buzzing. Ball pein and clawhammers striking nails. Shovels and pickaxes cutting into the earth. Sledgehammers pounding stakes or posts. Wheelbarrows dumping bricks. From the frenetic work he witnessed, these tents would be replaced soon, perhaps as early as tomorrow, with picket houses, sod houses, even a frame building. Two masons laid bricks on mortar they shoveled as if they were in a race with the carpenters. The masons would lose. Wooden houses would open first, but the brick buildings, Daniel had learned, likely would last longer.

Daniel wasn't the only observer. He turned to find two men at the foot of the hill.

A taibo in a pale suit and straw hat stood talking to another man, coatless, with his sleeves rolled to his elbows, and his cap pushed back. That man steadied one of those big black boxes that sat on a tripod. *Kobe Nabu?* As The People called those cameras. *One of these days, I shall pay for a likeness taken of me, and Oajuicauojué, and our children.* A few among The People, mostly the old ones, argued that the black box stole one's shadow—if not one's soul—but Quanah had been photographed many times, and Daniel still saw Quanah's shadow. If the old man's soul was gone, it had not changed the man who still led The People.

The man in the pale suit turned and looked up the hill. He must have seen Daniel, for he pointed, speaking to the man working the black box, but that taibo waved his hand behind his back, then stuck his body underneath a dark sheet attached to the camera.

The man in the pale suit began walking up the hill toward Daniel, whose bay horse snorted, stamped its feet, wanting to run. Daniel whispered a song in his native tongue, trying to soothe the young horse, though Daniel's voice had never been adequate in singing. The bay shook its head, but Daniel's hold on the hackamore remained firm, and after a few more fruitless tugs, the horse quit its protest, and decided to graze.

Halfway up the hill, the taibo stopped, removed his hat, and wiped his face with a white handkerchief he pulled out of a vest pocket. The man was bald, but something about him seemed familiar. He was also fat. Huffing, he found the will to continue the climb, though this was hardly more than an anthill compared to the Wichita Mountains where Daniel lived.

Years had passed since Daniel had even thought of the agent who had been responsible for the scars on Oajuicauojué's face, though hardly noticed now, and the deaths of three of The People and a young Kiowa. Now Daniel wondered if this bald taibo would feel his heart burst the way the vile agent's had, and die with his hand over his chest and his eyes open.

The taibo reached the top, and fought for his breath. But this man seemed to recover after he sucked much air in and out of his lungs. Still the man sweated, but his face was flushed, not pale as the agent's had before he had died. Even though six feet separated the Pale Eyes from Daniel, the smoke was heavy on the man's breath and his clothes. Yet he still pulled out one of those pre-rolled cigarettes, stuck it in his mouth, found a match, and lighted the end.

"Some show, eh?" the man said after taking several puffs. The sentence came out as a gasp.

Smoking a pipe was one thing. But how anyone found pleasure in one of those tiny papers, Daniel could not fathom. He did not answer.

Maybe Twice Bent Nose was right. That there was magic to those cigarettes. Because after several drags on the smoking paper, the man seemed to recover.

"I'm with the *New York-Tribune*," he said.

True, the sentence came out as though the taibo was catching his breath, but the heaving stopped, and his lungs began working without stress. The voice, Daniel realized, was also familiar. He stared at the man.

The fat taibo found his notepad in one coat pocket and pulled a pencil from the top of his ear. "Covering the land run . . ." He laughed without humor and shook his head. "Land run, hell. *Auction.*"

There was something familiar in that voice.

"You're Comanche, aren't you?"

Daniel just looked, and listened.

"I was hoping you could talk to me about what it's like. Savvy English?"

Daniel smiled. The face had changed. The man had gained weight. Much weight. Even more than Daniel. The taibo had lost most of his hair. But he was still what he had always been. A newspaperman. A reporter.

"You," Daniel said in English, "are Billy Kyne."

The cigarette fell out of the man's mouth. He blinked. "I'll be damned," he whispered. "Daniel? Daniel Killstraight."

He remembered the cigarette. Daniel thought he would crush it out with the toe of his city shoes, but the man picked it up and stuck it back in his mouth. After another drag and exhale, he swallowed and said, "You are . . . aren't you?" He laughed. "Hell, you have to be. No other Indian here knows me from Adam's tomcat."

"It has been a long time," Daniel said. He rose, keeping the hackamore tight in his left hand, but extending his right.

"Gosh," Billy Kyne said, shaking Daniel's hand warmly. "Long time's right." He laughed, stuck the cigarette in his mouth, and whipped off his hat. "I got scalped, you see. Pretty damned quick. The hair was thinning, but I wasn't bald last time I saw you."

"You weren't with the *New York-Tribune,* either," Daniel said.

"Or were you?"

"Oh, yeah. Well, Titus Wheeler was a hell of a guy, but he had not one ounce of sense when it came to running a business. I thought the *Trib* would hire me after that . . . Well, you remember. But the editors just thanked me then. Said to stay in touch. And Wheeler paid money, sometimes. Anyway, finally I got sick and tired of working for next to nothing but for plenty of promises, so I left him in Milwaukee the year after we were down in Texas with you. Got a job with the *Daily Reporter*. Worked my way to New York City. Now, finally, at the *Trib*. Pay's regular, and, despite what you might hear of New York, nobody shoots at me."

Daniel nodded, but a gunshot sounded in the white city, and Daniel and Kyne looked at the fight. The gun, a rifle, had been fired in the air by an old taibo woman. Probably to stop the two men from pounding each other, but they kept right on rolling around in the dirt, hitting whenever they could. A few taibos gathered to watch, but most went right on building their city.

"Fistfight's not news," Billy Kyne said. "Now if someone gets killed, I'll have to go down this hill."

Daniel nodded.

"That's something, though, isn't it?" Billy Kyne said. "Hours ago there was nothing there. Now it's the beginning of a new town. A new city. Lawton, Oklahoma." He laughed. "John Paul and I"—He stopped to point at the man with the camera—"We counted twenty-seven saloons already. Johnny's from New York, too. Has a studio upstairs of me. Twenty-seven, and I'm betting there will be fifty before it's all done." He laughed again. "One of the watering holes is called The Carrie Nation. That's something now. That's hilarious." He looked back at Daniel. "Carrie," he said. "Carrie Nation. She's . . ."

"We have heard of Carrie Nation," Daniel told him.

Billy Kyne nodded, and turned back to watch the tent city grow.

The bay pawed the sand.

Below, the photographer began disassembling his camera. He looked at the tent city, but Billy Kyne cupped his hands over his mouth and yelled: "It's just two guys having a go at fisticuffs, Johnny. Fight'll be over before you get there with your camera." He caught another glance of the fight. "Hell, it's practically over now."

The old woman had started swinging the rifle down on the hindquarters of one of the fighting men.

"Did you get your allotment?" Billy Kyne asked, looking back at Daniel.

"I did." He pointed. "In the Wichita Mountains. Not many Pale Eyes saw the value in such a place. So I am happy. My neighbors are all Nermernuh."

"Did you ever marry that girl?"

Daniel smiled. "Yes. We are very happy. We have a son. And a daughter. Oajuicauojué says our daughter looks like her older sister. The son, I think, is lucky. He does not look like me."

Billy Kyne looked down again and saw the cameraman walking up the hill.

"Titus Wheeler," Kyne said, and slowly turned around. "He died. I guess you knew that."

"I did not know." Daniel felt sad for that flamboyant man with such big dreams.

"Yeah. Probably too much work and too much booze and never slowing down, never trying to make an honest buck. Somewhere in Ohio—can't recall the name of the city—I just read about it on the Associated Press wire. In his sleep, though. Two years back. Just missed seeing the dawn of this new century. He never caught up with Buffalo Bill, that's for sure."

"Do you miss writing his books for him?"

"Nah." Kyne laughed hard, and this time he dropped what little remained of his cigarette and crushed it into the dirt. "That wasn't even what I'd call writing. What was that? Ten years ago? Twelve?"

Daniel tilted his head. "When Titus Wheeler died?"

"No, no." Kyne looked at the progress his photographer was making. "When . . . you know all that . . . the killings . . . the smallpox."

The Rotting Face was something else that Daniel had not thought about in years. "It was not as long as twelve." Daniel thought. His son was only seven years old. "I do not think ten, either."

"Who's your redskin friend, William?" the photographer asked. Unlike Billy Kyne, this man was neither panting nor sweating. "All right if I take his photograph? Hey, Buck, don't fret. It won't steal your soul."

"John Paul," Billy Kyne said. "Just get a shot of the tent city from up here. And keep your loud mouth shut. You won't swallow flies that way. And you might live to get back down that hill, with your hair still on your head. This ain't your normal Indian, you see. This here's a Comanche."

The newspaperman turned back to Daniel, shrugging, muttering a silent apology, and finally, winking.

Daniel could not hide his smile.

Billy Kyne walked to Daniel, smiled at the horse, then drew in a deep breath, holding it for a long time before letting it out and breathing in again.

"Well, I guess I ought to ask you what you're thinking, Daniel. This isn't for one of Wheeler's penny dreadfuls. It's for a good newspaper. One of the best in the city, the country, and the world. You're a Comanche. And this is what looks to be the last of the great land runs—even if this wasn't really a run, just a lottery, like they call it."

Daniel pointed to the south. "There is the Big Pasture just north of the Red River," he said. He tried to remember how many acres that was. Half a million, he wanted to guess, but even he had trouble knowing exactly what an acre was, and he owned one hundred and sixty.

"Maybe they'll open that up," Kyne said. "But it won't be anything like this. And this wasn't anything like the other runs. When was the last one? 'Ninety-five? And it was so puny. The *Trib* wouldn't have sent me here, except they knew I had been with some Comanches with Wheeler's Wild West, and I knew the country and all, having worked in Dallas, Wichita, Waco, Ellsworth, Fort Smith, and Cincinnati—which is west to anyone living on that side of the Hudson River."

Daniel stared at the white city. The fight was over, unless the old woman decided to hit her man with the rifle again.

"I tried to get Quanah, but he wasn't talking today. About all I have is from the folks who got lucky, got their lottery number called, and a few from those who didn't and were drinking away their sorrows at The Carrie Nation." He laughed. "You know what the saloonkeepers are calling what they're selling to those unlucky souls?"

"Bottled Compensation." Daniel kept staring at what was becoming, in a matter of hours, the city of Lawton.

He looked at the surprised Billy Kyne. "It is what whiskey runners called it when they sold it to my people," Daniel explained. "When taibos were stealing our cattle, our ponies." He shrugged. "Our land."

"Is that a quote for the *Trib*?"

Daniel shook his head. He held out his right hand. "It is good to see you again, Billy Kyne. But I must leave now. I have seen enough of Lawton. I want to see my family. Good luck to you. Good luck with your newspaper story. Quanah, he might talk to you . . . tomorrow."

241

He swung easily into his saddle, and let the bay gallop down the far side of the hill, but when he reached bottom, Daniel pulled the stallion to a stop, and looked uphill. Turning the stallion, he loped back, reining the young horse to stop a few yards from the newspaperman and John Paul, Billy Kyne's photographer friend.

John Paul stood just a few feet behind Kyne, staring, his face turning white as though he thought he might become the last taibo to be scalped by a warrior of The People.

Daniel dismissed him and grinned at Kyne. "Here," he said, trying to keep control of the horse that wanted so much to run. "Here is what you can tell those who buy your *Tribune*. Here is what I say. I am still here." He held his head high. "*We* are still here. This is our home, our land."

Three times, he pounded his chest with his free hand. "We, The People, will always be here."

Then he turned the bay around, and let it race down the hill. He galloped west, following the sun as it lowered its bright ball toward the tops of the Wichita Mountains.

"Son of a bitch," the photographer whispered. "That buck can ride like the best jockey at Morris Park."

"Damn right," Billy Kyne said, and started searching for his flask. "That boy, that *man*, is Comanche. To the bone. No matter how much we tried to make him think he wasn't, that he shouldn't be, that we tried harder than hell to beat out of him. Killstraight has always been Comanche. And, God love him, he always will be."

He found his pencil, turned to a clean page in his pad, and smiled as he wrote, underlining each word.

John Paul asked: "You reckon they'll print that in the *Trib*?"

"I don't rightly give a damn if they do or don't." Kyne passed the flask to the photographer. "I'm hanging it on my wall."

Billy Kyne stared at what he had written. He didn't even notice John Paul offering him the last of the rye in his flask.

<u>I am still here</u>
<u>We are still here . . .</u>
<u>We, The People, will always be here</u>

AUTHOR'S NOTE

Some readers might be tempted to read the COVID-19 pandemic into this novel. That was never my attention. The seed was planted in 2004, when I was interviewing my Comanche friend, Nocona Burgess, for a magazine article. "They didn't beat us on the battlefield," Nocona said. "They beat us with smallpox."

I also wanted to end this series on a positive note. I've been chided by some friends that in most of my novels, the hero doesn't wind up with the girl. Daniel Killstraight was always going to get this girl. I knew that, after I sent in my draft of *Killstraight* (2008) and my then-agent, the late Jon Tuska, told me: "You are going to turn this into a series."

It didn't sound like a question.

So when I mapped out a game plan for a series, this was the ending.

The name Killstraight is not actually Comanche, but common among the Northern Plains Nations. I liked the name, though, and remembered John Jakes telling me about considering the power of the letter "K" when he began his best-selling Kent Family Chronicles in the 1970s. I had bounced around the idea of a Northern Plains character, but then I met Nocona Burgess and his brother, Quanah—both descendants of Comanche leader Quanah Parker—at the Santa Fe Indian Market.

That led to a magazine assignment on the two artists, which

led to myriad interviews with Nocona or Quanah or their father for other magazine articles. And I remembered another quote from Nocona: "I think that's why [Comanches] fought so hard. They were so devoted to the family."

Nocona also told me that Comanches are generally fun-loving people, "but we can be aggressive to a fault."

I wanted to depict Comanches as real people. In most Western fiction and countless Western films, Comanches have been depicted as ruthless savages, more monsters than men, and seldom depicted as anything other than one-dimensional. My friend Lucia St. Clair Robson's inspiring *Ride the Wind* is one notable exception—and one of the best Western novels ever written.

I don't know if I succeeded, but I tried. If I could go back in time, I would have changed Killstraight's name to something authentically Nermernuh. But we can't go back in time. The late Tony Hillerman once told me that he had similar reservations about his creation of Joe Leaphorn, the Navajo tribal policeman of his long-running mystery series, now continued by his daughter Anne. Leaphorn isn't Diné.

Nocona Burgess has always been generous with his time, helping me understand Comanche customs, always agreeing to proofread my drafts and correct anything I got wrong. One of the highlights of my literary career came when Nocona asked me to write an original short story for a catalog of one of his Santa Fe Indian Market exhibits. Before I read that story at the gallery opening in front of a crowd of largely Native Americans and art lovers, I said, "I'm not Comanche." That got a lot of laughs, which calmed my nerves. The applause after reading the story was even a bigger reward than the Spur Award finalist honor that "Comanche Camp at Dawn" received in 2017. The story remains a personal favorite.

In addition to Nocona, I should point out other key sources.

First and foremost was *United States-Comanche Relations: The Reservation Years* by William T. Hagan (University of Oklahoma Press, 1990).

Other main sources regarding the Comanches included *Carbine and Lance: The Story of Old Fort Sill* by Colonel W.S. Nye (University of Oklahoma Press, twelfth printing, 1988); *Quanah: The Eagle of the Comanches* by Zoe A. Tilghman (Harlow Publishing Corporation, 1938); *The Last Comanche Chief: The Life and Times of Quanah Parker* by Bill Neeley (John Wiley and Sons, 1995); *Comanches: The Destruction of a People* by T.R. Fehrenbach (Da Capo Press, 1994); *The Comanches: Lords of the South Plains* by Ernest Wallace and E. Adamson Hoebel (University of Oklahoma Press, ninth printing, 1986); and *The Comanches: A History, 1706–1875* by Thomas W. Kavanagh (Bison Books, 1999).

S.C. Gwynne's *Empire of the Summer Moon: Quanah Parker and the Rise and Fall of the Comanches, the Most Powerful Indian Tribe in American History* (2010), shortlisted for the Pulitzer Prize, was helpful, and it was S.C., who I also interviewed for a magazine article when his book first came out, who directed me to check out Quanah Parker's Star House in Cache, Oklahoma, which I did in the early 2000s.

For Comanche language, I relied on *Comanche Dictionary and Grammar, Second Edition* by Lila Wistrand-Robinson and James Armagost (SIL International, 2012) and *Comanche Vocabulary: Trilingual Edition*, compiled by Manuel García Rejón and translated and edited by Daniel J. Gelo (University of Texas Press, 1995).

For smallpox, I turned to *The Greatest Killer: Smallpox in History* by Donald R. Hopkins (The University of Chicago Press, 1983, 2002); *Cherokee Medicine, Colonial Germs: An Indigenous Nation's Fight against Smallpox, 1518–1824* by Paul Kelton (University of Oklahoma Press, 2015); *Rotting Face: Smallpox and the American Indian* by R.G. Robertson (Caxton Press, 2001); and *American Contagions: Epidemics and the Law from Smallpox to COVID-19* by John Fabian Witt (Yale University Press, 2020).

I also logged on to Newspapers.com and NewspaperArchives .com, studying several newspaper accounts from the 1890s regarding smallpox outbreaks. The salt "remedy" is based on an article first published in the *Pittsburgh Dispatch* and reprinted in several newspapers across the nation; I used one from the *El Paso Times.* The story about the outbreak among Japanese railroad workers in Idaho was also found in the *El Paso Times.* Other outbreak stories were pulled from the *Austin* (Texas) *Weekly Statesman; Austin American-Statesman; Evening Statesman* in Marshall, Texas; (Emporia, Kansas) *Weekly Republican;* Fort Worth (Texas) *Daily Gazette; Galveston* (Texas) *Daily News; St. Louis Globe-Democrat; San Saba County* (Texas) *News; Spokane* (Washington) *Chronicle;* and *Tacoma* (Washington) *Daily Ledger.* Likewise, viewings of two El Reno, Oklahoma, newspapers—the *Oklahoma Democrat* and *Canadian County Courier*—helped in describing that territorial railroad town of the early 1890s.

Other sources include *Shackelford County Sketches* by Don H. Biggers (The Clear Fork Press, 1974) and websites of the Oklahoma Historical Society and Texas State Historical Association.

I should also offer a shout of thanks to the staffs at Frontier Texas!, a museum in Abilene; Fort Griffin State Historic Site near Albany, Texas; Palo Canyon State Park near Canyon, Texas; Caprock Canyon State Park near Quitaque, Texas; Panhandle Plains Historical Museum in Canyon, Texas; Fort Sill Museum on the still-active Army post in Lawton, Oklahoma; Comanche National Museum and Cultural Center, also in Lawton; Chisholm Trail Heritage Center in Lawton, Oklahoma; Cache (Oklahoma) Trading Post; Quartz Mountain State Park near

Lone Wolf, Oklahoma; and Wichita Mountains Wildlife Refuge near Indiahoma, Oklahoma.

And finally a big thanks to the people of the friendly Texas towns of Abilene, Albany, Amarillo, Canyon, Fort Worth, Turkey, and Quitaque; and Oklahoma towns of Cache, Duncan, and Lawton, who made my research that much more enjoyable.

Johnny D. Boggs
Santa Fe, New Mexico
November 2021

ABOUT THE AUTHOR

Nine-time Spur Award winner **Johnny D. Boggs** is the recipient of Western Writers of America's 2020 Owen Wister Award for Lifetime Contributions to Western Literature.

The employees of Five Star Publishing hope you have enjoyed this book.

Our Five Star novels explore little-known chapters from America's history, stories told from unique perspectives that will entertain a broad range of readers.

Other Five Star books are available at your local library, bookstore, all major book distributors, and directly from Five Star/Gale.

Connect with Five Star Publishing

Website:
gale.com/five-star

Facebook:
facebook.com/FiveStarCengage

Twitter:
twitter.com/FiveStarCengage

Email:
FiveStar@cengage.com

For information about titles and placing orders:
(800) 223-1244
gale.orders@cengage.com

To share your comments, write to us:
Five Star Publishing
Attn: Publisher
10 Water St., Suite 310
Waterville, ME 04901